# Extended Bridge

## *Passionate Beats trilogy, book 2*

## Arell Rivers

## EXTENDED BRIDGE

Book 2 in the **Passionate Beats** trilogy in the Untamed Coaster series

ARELL RIVERS

Copyright ©2025 Tarnished Halo Publishing LLC
Published by Tarnished Halo Publishing LLC
2025 Edition

ISBN (digital): 979-8-9869346-5-5

ISBN (print): 979-8-9869346-6-2

### Arell's Team

Editing:

Plot Coach Theresa Leigh, The FairyPlot-Mother

Developmental Editor Trenda Lundin, It's Your Story Content Editing

Editor Nancy Smay, Evident Ink

Proofreading: Roxanne Bluin

Cover design: Dar Albert, Wicked Smart Designs

# Dedication

*For Gwyn Novak.*
*Thank you, thank you very much!*

## Torn Between Two Tracks: Can Love Conquer Fear?

Bennett Hardy. Rock god. Heartbreaker. The world's most wanted man. And he's looking at me like I'm his one and only.

Branded "Black Widow" in the media due to the death of my boyfriend, the band's keyboardist, fear is a constant beat underneath my skin. Fear of reliving the nightmares of my past, fear of getting my heart shattered again. Mom says I need a change, a clean break. My bestie whispers, "Let him love you." But can I trust him? Can I trust myself?

Suddenly, I'm drowning in the intoxicating chaos of Untamed Coaster's world. One hug was the line I drew when I agreed to return. Strictly professional. But Bennett...he sees the scars I hide and ignites a passion I swore was dead. He's not alone, because I see the abandoned little boy he once was. One unbridled night, and I'm lost in a love that feels too good to be true.

Then, the world explodes. A devious attack. A devastating interview. A desperate call. Just like that, I'm running again, torn between the man who owns my soul and the ones who desperately need my help.

Now I can't help but wonder if I gave up my only chance at something real.

# Chapter One

T he *Gossip*'s headline mocks my every move—**Black Widow Prepares to Strike Again**

There's the awful term again. Black Widow. When the press first called me that, I was too shocked at the ugly name to do anything more than bury my head in the proverbial sand. They've kept at it, and now I feel like most of my time in therapy following Darren's death was for naught. I have no control. Guilt is more crushing than ever.

All the air in my body lodges in my throat.

Without a backward glance, I toss on my shirt and sprint out of the bedroom I had commandeered. Seize my purse. Speed down the mansion's stairs. Grab my keys from the table in the entry foyer. While I race to my SUV, I click open the front door and slide in, dumping my bag on the passenger seat and pressing the button for the car to start. My foot hits the accelerator a second later.

Secluded Rest, the rental house of Bennett Hardy, the lead singer of Untamed Coaster, finally appears in the rearview mirror. I take my first long breath since Courtney's text arrived. And pound the steering wheel.

I thought I'd escaped the vitriol from Darren's family years ago, only to be plunked right back to the time when he died. I repeat the mantra from my psychotherapist: I'm not responsible for Darren getting addicted or for his death. The only things I take blame for are falling for him—and enjoying his playful pranks—and over-the-top lifestyle. So unlike my own.

I swipe the tears flowing down my cheeks. Before I get caught up in memories of the first man who changed my life, I need to regroup. Talking with the person at the center of the current shitstorm—the second such man—won't help either.

Bennett.

At the mere thought of the sexy lead singer who I shared a shower with not even thirty minutes ago, my body freezes. Before boarding the helicopter to return to Aroostook, his manager whispered into my ear, "I like how B is with you. You two make a great couple. Don't break his heart."

But who's going to protect mine?

I wave at the security guard manning the entrance to Bennett's gated community and head out, where a gaggle of reporters lie in wait. For me. I stomp on the gas and take off at a fast clip, the majority of them hot on my tail.

If I want some space, I can't go to a public place. My house is off-limits, as are those of my friends' and Ma's. The clinics come to mind. They'll be safe. Reporters aren't legally able to enter private areas. Given the time of day, I pray there aren't too many patients to interrupt.

With squealing tires, I take the final turn into the private driveway leading to my first At Your Service PT location. Parking behind the building, I exhale over the steering wheel. How can this be my life again?

My phone rings and my bestie's name appears on the screen. Trying to regulate my breathing, I say, "I'm in the parking lot."

"Great. Come on up and we'll talk about this."

Court's a good egg. We met in physical therapy school and hit it off immediately. We worked together in a couple of clinics, and now she's my right hand—in charge of my flagship location. I run all major decisions by her. What is she going to say about this mess?

Checking the rooftops for telephoto lenses like Bennett taught me, I scurry to the back door, and ignoring the elevator, take the stairs up. I need to expend energy. When I cross the threshold, Court stands with her arms open. I fling myself into them.

The tears I'd hoped I banished return double time. Court pats my back. "Come on, honey. Let's go to the office." She leads us into her corner office with windows facing the waiting room. After directing me to her couch, she closes the blinds.

A tissue waves before my eyes. "Where would you like to begin?"

I blow my nose. "I don't know." Tears continue to fall.

"I'm so sorry this is happening again. I thought once it blew over with Darren's family, we'd seen the end of it."

"It doesn't seem like his mother or sister got the memo." I drop a used tissue on the floor and pluck a new one.

"They want you away from UC. The least they could've done is wish that awful Lissa woman disappeared as well."

At the name of Bennett's high school ex-girlfriend, I gulp more air. "Bennett and Lissa dated in high school. She dumped him for his best friend, who was a year older and offered to take her to the senior prom. They never looked back to see the wreckage they left in their wake."

"I wondered what the true story was there. The article made it seem like you were Camilla in Charles and Diana's marriage."

I scrunch up my face. "No way. *Lissa* came to our table during dinner and caused a scene. Frankly, Bennett didn't talk about her too much afterwards. He really is over her, although the scars linger." Namely, he doesn't call anyone "friend." Plus, he hasn't had a girl-friend since her—but he did tell me he loves me.

"What a bitch."

I laugh for the first time following my escape from the mansion. "She's something, for sure. All plastic surgery and hair extensions."

Court raises her left eyebrow. "I bet a size zero as well?"

"Don't you know it." The reality of what's happening hits me. "What am I going to do?"

"I think you need to come out strong to the reporters. Tell your side of the story."

"Which is what? Darren was prescribed pain meds, abused them without my knowledge, and overdosed? Been there, done that, bought the T-shirt."

Her shoulders lower. "You're right. I was there, I remember. If they didn't believe you then, how will they believe you now?"

My entire torso droops. A moment later, I sit up straight. "It's different because I'm a different woman. I have two physical therapy clinics, just got a bank loan to open a third, and can use the money I'm getting from treating Bennett for a fourth. I'm respected in the community. Our services are highly regarded."

"All that is true, but I feel we need something extra." She pauses. "What about Bennett?"

My response is swift. "What about him?"

"Well." Her gaze bounces around the room. "Are you hooking up with him? Going to join him on tour like the article said?"

"Courtney! You know therapists can't cross the line with our patients." Although I did. Several times. Barely an hour ago. My lady parts tingle.

"I know, I know. Just saying, I wouldn't blame you. That man is fine. With a capital F." She nudges my shoulder.

And capital I, N, and E as well. I resist the urge to nudge her back. I'm not about to reveal my shameful breach of ethics, so I choose the other truth. "Bennett wants me to join the tour as his physical therapist. We met with his doctor yesterday"—was it only twenty-four hours ago?—"who prescribed continued PT until he's fully healed." When it all went down, I had shared with her all about his grade three groin pull and my misdiagnosis as a grade two, and Court knows about our PT work together.

"How's he coming along?"

"His muscle pull is healing. Between you and me and the doctor who saw him yesterday, we believe it will be at least three more months of PT before he's fully recovered. The doctor and I agreed not to tell Bennett this, though. Honestly, if he keeps on reinjuring it, it'll take longer."

"What's delaying his progress?"

"Oh, the usual. Making too fast of a movement." My lips purse. "Usually caused by reporters following him like bloodhounds."

"Sounds as if he needs you with him on tour. Do you think he'll be okay onstage?"

She's hit on my main fear. With injuries like his, recovery can take longer if they're not babied. There's no telling what crazy thing he'll do while performing that could set him back weeks, if not months.

"Honestly, I'm unsure. He's reckless." I use Darren's descriptor of him, even though the man I've gotten to spend time with is anything but. More like broken. I shake my head. "After all, he caused the groin pull by executing a crazy jump during their performance following the premiere of *Untamed Coaster Unleashed.*"

"I finally got to see the movie, by the way. I liked how you were portrayed."

I offer her my first real smile since leaving Bennett's place. "Thanks. Quinn Walker, the director, has a gentle hand. To me, it showcased everyone as they really are, but with an undercurrent of quiet positivity." I shrug. "Maybe that's how they are nowadays. More introspective."

Although I say this, I'm not sure. The only time I've interacted with all of them since Darren's funeral was when I diagnosed Bennett backstage. When I was with their keyboardist, the band was hyper-focused on making it to the next level. He was the prankster, although their drummer took a close second with his huge personality.

"Perhaps they've grown up."

Things might have changed for them—they certainly have for me. "Haven't we all?"

In the time since Darren's death, I've had to do a lot of that. Moving houses, starting my business. Going to intensive psychotherapy at Ma's urging. As she put it, "I didn't take you when my mother died, and you need to resolve these issues to move on." As usual, she was right. There wasn't any time for frivolities like concerts or even movie theaters during my recent past. My singular focus has been building my business. Despite my doubts as to whether Darren and I would've lasted long term, considering how different we were, I still want to open ten clinics to make him proud.

"What are you going to do?"

"The million-dollar question, huh? Bennett wants me to give him physical therapy during the tour. But I have obligations, like working with contractors on our third location and scouting out a fourth. Despite what you told me before, I'm not really in a position to leave these important tasks behind, given the new media landscape. Plus, Ma's not getting any younger."

Court laughs. "Your mother's going to be around forever. She hasn't aged a bit since I met her!"

I grin at my friend. "You're right. Gives me hope for my own, long future." I can see it yawning before me. An image of Bennett with me appears, each one of us holding a child in our arms. I blink it away.

"Maybe filled with a certain tall, green-eyed singer with luscious caramel locks?" Her eyes sparkle.

"Court!" I smack her. "Stop it. I've had enough of band members to last me two lifetimes." My vision notwithstanding.

Her expression becomes serious. "I'm fully aware of what you went through with Darren. I was there, remember? He swept you off your axis, but you remained your level-headed self who I love. But, as I told you before, Felipe and I can take care of things here. You deserve a break from this reality for a while. Get pampered on tour."

"You don't know how tours go. I only joined Darren a few times with the band before, and here are my top ten annoying things about touring—smelly bus, long hours, fast food, laundromats, sound checks, groupies, bumpy roads, radio interviews, boy fights, and too much guitar hero." I rattle off this list in quick succession.

"Seriously?" She focuses in on my last criticism. "They really play that game? I would think they'd have enough of it in real life."

I raise my hand. "Word."

"Jenna." Her voice lowers. "How are you doing? For real?"

Her concern brings me to tears again. I grab another tissue while I try to get myself under control. After Darren's death, I haven't cried more than a few times. All within these past weeks. With Bennett.

"It's been awful. The reporters are ruthless." I wave the tissue toward the front door. "They're here again."

"I know. If you didn't notice, I hired security to protect our patients. We've got it under control here. It's you I'm worried about."

Her simple statement tugs at my heartstrings. "You're a great friend, Court. Honestly, I have no idea how I'm doing. I'm a mess."

"Anyone who knows you can't believe the lies online."

"Lissa seemed convincing." The woman Bennett was in love with all those years ago. Who broke him with his best friend. If I could redo that dinner, I'd yank out her damn hair extensions with my bare hands for the damage she's caused him.

"I have to admit," Court declares. "Even I was shocked about her accusations. But she's not a problem for you, right?"

If I weren't interested in the lead singer, my answer would be a resounding no. If I didn't know how he kissed, what his body felt like, or how he tasted, I could shake this off. But I can't. "There's something buried in Bennett that speaks to me," I confess. "Despite being at the pinnacle of his career, he's isolated. Alone. The worst part? He doesn't even recognize it."

Her tone doesn't betray the scary truth I just shared with her. Instead, she says, "I want you to live again, Jenna. If that means going back out on tour with the band who brought you to your knees, then I'm all for it. So long as your eyes are wide open."

Do I belong with UC? What damage would my presence bring to the band? The better question is what damage would Bennett suffer if I *don't* go? He confessed he loved me. Heaven help me, all the damaged parts of him—not the cocky frontman he portrays—draw me to him.

I toss the tissue, watching as it floats downward. "I believe they are."

"Do you want to start something with their lead singer? Bennett?"

That ship has sailed, but I don't share this with her. Even with Darren, I refused to get involved romantically until his therapy was over. With Bennett, I was powerless to stop myself. The pull between us is unlike anything I've ever felt before. *I tried to ignore it but couldn't resist the depths of his soul calling out to me.*

Because this is Court, I tell the truth. "I think so."

"This is so out of character for you, Jenna. I'm happy. Live out loud, screw the assholes."

I chuckle at her apt description.

"If this guy floats your boat, you need to see where it leads. Together. Screw all the ethics crap."

I try to let my head take the lead. "There are rules for a reason."

"Don't you know? Rules are meant to be broken." She stares at me. "I've never seen you act this way before about any guy."

Her words strike a chord. "Well, he is unlike any other man I've ever met." So warm. Caring. Putting up a front to hide deep wounds. "I like him a lot."

"Exactly what I've been waiting for you to admit!" Squealing, she pulls me in for a hug.

When we break apart, another worry pops into my mind. "What about my business, though?"

"Do *not* worry about At Your Service PT. Felipe and I will deal with the build out."

Back on firmer footing, I say, "I was thinking of tapping Sylvia to lead the third location."

"Sylvia?" Court adjusts her glasses. "I like her, but I'm not sure she's ready for that much responsibility. What about Greyson?"

"Let me think about him." I consider her suggestions. "I don't know what to do here." Should I leave these huge details in Court's hands? How will my other manager, Felipe, react? Then there's Austin, Sylvia, Greyson, and my other therapists. This is wrong. I sit up. I need to be here directing everything.

Court ignores my posture. "You're allowed to have a life of your own. Whether it means you travel with Bennett or settle down here with the head librarian, it'll be okay. You deserve love and happiness."

Her words sink into my overcluttered mind, and I bring her in for a hug. Court's always stuck by me—one of the many reasons I made her the manager of my first clinic. Not to mention she's amazing at what she does. "Thanks. But I don't know. All this has happened so fast. I probably should stay here."

She crosses her legs. "So I guess you'd be fine if this Lissa takes up where she left off with Bennett?"

"What? No way. She's terrible." I wiggle in disgust.

She laughs. "That's what I thought. You've got it bad for the lead singer."

"But it's not only him, Court. The press would lose their minds if I joined UC on tour. Especially since Bennett's kept his injury on the down low." I shudder. "They'll make up awful stories about how I'm going to kill each one of the band members."

"They wouldn't do that, would they?"

I nod. "Worse." I find it hard to imagine what they'll concoct, but it was terrible after Darren died. This would be degrees worse. "I can't see how this is a good idea."

"Except for the fact you're half in love with the guy."

Am I? He did say he loves me, but I'm so confused. Yes, his soul speaks to me. I want to help him conquer the world again, in his own style. I want to see him heal the wounds of his past. I want to revel in his happiness. Plus he's made me come like no one else, including Darren. But is this *love?* I swipe another tissue. "I'm such a mess."

Court lets me cry for a few more minutes, lightly tapping my back. "You'll figure it out, you always do. How much longer is Bennett in town?"

I pull back. "He's leaving at noon today." I glance at the clock. "In an hour." This realization sets me off again. My world could return to its controlled way, which should make me feel better than I have since Bennett burst into it. But it doesn't. The desire to spend more time with this challenging rock star tweaks my heart.

I want to insert order into his chaos. Introduce him to love and friendship, the latter of which I'm sure he already has in spades but doesn't know it. The way his mind works intrigues me.

The whole man intrigues me.

Can I do this again?

How can I not?

My shoulders slump. "Court, I want to go with him."

"Then let's see what I can do to make this your reality."

# Chapter Two

Buoyed by the plan Court and I put together, I return to my car with the intention of stopping by Ma's house. As soon as I turn the corner, paparazzi follow me.

Instead of giving up, I do the opposite. They are *not* going to get the better of me this time! As if Bennett were sitting next to me, I make quick turns into small streets. These reporters are, after all, in my playground.

One thing's for sure, I can't bring them to Ma's house. I press a button on the screen and we're connected. "Hey, Ma. I want to come see you but the media's being a pain and following me. Think you can pick me up in town at Russo Real Estate?"

"No problem. I'm in the middle of something, though. Is it all right if I meet you there in about an hour?"

"Sounds good."

Using some fancy evasive maneuvers, I dash to Angie and King's agency and park. Fisting the steering wheel, I exhale all the air in my lungs. What am I going to do for an hour? Property listings line the window in front of me. Might as well use this time to my business's advantage.

I scoot out of my car and zip into the nicely appointed real estate office, ignoring the tenacious reporters. A sweet lady greets me and I ask to see Angie, whom I felt a camaraderie with while touring the mansions. I'm led to a seat directly across from a messy desk, and Angie appears two minutes later. She takes one look at me and gives me a hug.

"I hate those horrible tabloids."

As I thought, a kindred spirit. "No argument here."

"Try to do what King and I do. Ignore them."

"I'm trying. It's difficult."

She nods. "So, what brings you over here? Don't tell me you're on the lam from the paparazzi."

"Sort of." I shrug. "But I do have a reason for bothering you. I need to find a new location."

"You're never a bother." She rearranges some papers on her desk. "Are you moving?"

"No. I want to open another clinic, but don't have a clue where to look."

She twirls a lock of her hair. "You've come to the right place, Jenna. We have some great listings. Tell me what you're looking for."

Without thinking, I rattle off the requirements for my next location. I give her my top ten list of hopes and dreams I've developed while searching for my other three locations. Angie takes copious notes, asks questions, and consults her computer. When I've finished my laundry list, she holds up a finger and leaves her desk. A moment later, she returns with printouts in her hand.

"Here you go. I think any one of these would make an excellent location for your next clinic." She passes me a stack of papers.

"Oh, wow. I didn't expect all this."

"Goes to show that you should've been working with me all along." She smiles, her brown eyes dancing.

I flip through the pages. "I have to agree."

She places her hand over mine. "I'm glad we met," she removes her hand and I feel a sudden emptiness. "You and Bennett make a great pair."

At her mention of the man who's taking up so much of my head—and heart—space, I wince. "He should be whisking away to the City in under fifteen minutes."

Angie's eyebrows pull together. "Why on earth are you here with me, then, and not with your man?"

"He's not my man. Not really. I don't know." I lean back into the chair. "The tabloids came out with some awful stories today."

"I saw."

"Lies."

She does a slow nod.

"I'm trying to figure out my next steps." I hold up the papers. "This is part of it." Ma's car pulls up to the sidewalk and I stand. "Thanks for listening to me, Angie, and for giving me these options. My ride's here, so I have to leave. I'll be in touch soon."

"I'm here for you, anytime. As a woman who has gone through this before, I can at least commiserate."

I hug her first this time. "I may take you up on your offer. You'll probably be sorry you made it."

"No way. I'll always be your wingman." She pauses. "Wingwoman."

With a jaunty wave, I exit her office and hop into Ma's car, kissing her cheek in greeting. We caught a break since the paparazzi tired of waiting. Or ran off to the helipad for Bennett. "Thank you for picking me up."

"No worries. I can guess what's got you rattled."

"The tabloids have a knack for doing that." I tuck the paperwork Angie gave me into my bag. "But I'm here now."

Her lips tick up. "Let's get you home."

We enter the small but orderly ranch house Ma moved into a few years ago. It doesn't hold the memories of the home I grew up in, but framed photos on every surface and on the walls go a long way toward recreating the old place. Ma said the four-bedroom was too much for her now that my sister Kara and I had left.

"Let me get you some tea. Ginger, peppermint, or hibiscus?"

I love that she rattles off a variety of herbal teas. "Peppermint, please."

Her eyes crinkle as she smiles. "You got it."

While she's preparing the tea, I wander around to the various photos. My sister and me playing in the sand on a beach when I was five and she was fifteen, two weeks before our parents announced their divorce. I move to the next one, of the three of us sitting in front of a tent in the backyard. In the stands when Kara graduated high school. Me waving to Ma from the stage holding up my physical therapy degree. Simpler times. Before the media twisted me into some sort of villain. And now, a killer arachnid.

I collapse into "my" chair. How did my life get this messed up? Ma comes into the room and passes me my tea. I blow on it while she drags her chair closer to me.

"Talk to me, Sweet Pea."

Her use of my childhood nickname calms me. "I really hate that my original diagnosis of Bennett was wrong."

"As I told you before, you didn't have any machines or anything to verify your instincts. Plus, it's a low-grade stage three, right? Almost a two."

Gotta love Ma. She always sees the best for me. "You're right. Still, it eats at me that I got it wrong."

She places her teacup into its saucer. "I wouldn't know you were my daughter if you weren't a perfectionist." She smiles to take away the sting of her truth.

I grab a throw pillow with a gerbera daisy embroidered on it and place it over my lap. "I've been Bennett's physical therapist for almost two weeks now."

She nods. "He seems nice enough."

I rush in. "He is. He works really hard at his therapy and has come so far in such a short time. Then something catches him off guard and he reinjures himself."

"Again. Not your fault."

"You're right, but I hate seeing his progress upended. It's like one step forward and three back sometimes."

"That's the nature of therapy, right? Healing the issues and offering coping mechanisms for the unexpected."

I take another sip of my tea. "I've taught you well." Staring into the hot liquid, I add, "I made a commitment to him when I took on his case. I promised he'd be stage ready."

"I'd say you've upheld your end of the bargain. Doesn't he have his opening concert tonight in the City?"

"He does." I toss the pillow onto the sofa. "However, he's not even seventy percent healed, no matter what the stubborn man would tell you."

"What are you saying, Sweet Pea?"

I glance at a framed photo of Ma and me smelling flowers in a local botanical garden. "Bennett's asked me to go on tour with him to continue his PT."

"Oh." She picks up her tea and puts it back down. "His idea?"

I rush in. "His doctor prescribed physical therapy for the next three months, and Bennett says he wants me to do it." In more ways than one, but I'm not going to share this with her.

"How do you feel about this? What about your clinics here?"

I switch the cross of my feet. "I'm the one who started his therapy, and I should continue it. Especially since I misdiagnosed him at the beginning."

Ma gives me a pointed look. "You know what I think of that crap."

"Fine." I recross my legs. "I still began his therapy."

"You did. Another therapist could read your notes and start up with him."

I flick my fingers but don't respond. After all, she's not wrong.

Since this truth remains unchallenged, she prods in a different direction. "Your clinics?"

"Are stable at the moment. Court has a handle on one and Felipe the other. I got the bank's go-ahead for the third, so it needs to be built out, which will take a minimum of four months. With my pay for working with Bennett, I can open a fourth clinic." I point to my purse. "While I was waiting for you to pick me up, I met with Angie Hunte of Russo Real Estate and she gave me a few different options to check out."

"You've been working really hard ever since . . . well, since Darren died. You haven't taken any time away, you just threw yourself into creating and expanding your PT empire."

My cheeks inflate at her descriptor.

"A vacation might not be the worst thing."

"It wouldn't be a vacation, not by a long shot. For one, I'd be working with a patient. Two, I'd be away from home and would miss you like crazy. Also, I'd be back on the UC bus, dealing with lack of sleep and laundry, fending off the paparazzi, and awful groupies, At Your Service PT would only be on autopilot, and not growing." I finish my almost top ten list—ignoring the big fact of facing the other members of the band.

"What does your gut tell you?"

I close my eyes. "To complete what I started." My eyelids rise.

She tips her teacup upward. "I loved Darren. I loved his jokes and his great sense of humor. Most of all, I loved how he loved you."

Memories of our time together wash over me. "He was amazing."

Darren was the definition of fun. Always with a ready prank. When I was around him, I was the center of all his attention, which was heady. Our happy memories are replaced with more recent ones of me with Bennett, who is less engaging with the world while being more real. Grounded and guarded. He's hiding more than he's shared with me, I'm sure of it. Instead of being repelled, though, I want to peel back his layers. Even in such a short time, our relationship is much deeper than what I had with Darren. I'm impelled to find out why.

"Darren was one of a kind." Her eyes turn soft for a brief moment. "However, it sounds to me like Bennett needs your physical therapy expertise and you need a break. Three months isn't all that long in the overall scheme of things."

A yearning to uncover more about Bennett compels me to reply, "That's true."

"If you go, I do have one word of caution for you. There's something off about this Bennett. He's concealing some truths. Plus, you said it yourself during dinner, he's reckless. I mean, he pulled his groin doing a crazy jump onstage. Darren never would've done anything bonkers like that."

No. He only overdosed.

Ma continues, "The things he said about not being close with his mother worry me. Every son needs his momma."

"I have no idea what went on between the two of them," I reply truthfully. "I've been working on him about her. I'm sure he blew a situation way out of proportion."

"How deep are you in with him?"

He told me he loves me. He stirs something up in me I've never felt before. He's played my body unlike anyone else, including Darren. I whisper, "I'm not sure."

"I was afraid you'd say that. Darren was an amazing man, and you both were so in love. Like Kara and her husband." She beams at how far her family has risen—from the ashes to a PT owner of soon-to-be four clinics and a husband-and-wife cosmetic surgeon and anesthesiologist power duo with two kids. "Be careful with Bennett. He looks as if he could rip your heart out and eat it as pâté."

"Ma!" Her analogy shocks me.

"What? I'm telling you how I see it. He has danger written all over him. He doesn't get along with his mother. Seems to be a loner in the band. My daughter doesn't need to be mixed up with someone like that. Not after what you had with Darren."

"But, but . . . you were so nice to Bennett at dinner."

"Because I'm a lady. I don't think he's right for you, so if you think by going off on tour you're going to coax him into marrying you, I don't want you going."

I rub my left arm while her words soak into my heart. Is he as bad for me as she's portraying? "I'm not looking to marry the guy. My goal is to help him heal properly."

"So long as that's all it is, fine."

"Fine." We stare at each other for a minute. "I have to admit the idea of taking a step away from all these responsibilities is alluring."

"A break you deserve," she concedes. "I don't want to see you end up the way you did before, though. The media's all over you already. Are you sure this is the best decision for you?"

"I hate the reporters for contacting Darren's family and stirring the whole mess up again. Seems like their job is only to create head-lines and get clicks. I'm trying to ignore them."

Ma stands and walks to me, placing her palm on my cheek. "I know you'll do the right thing, Sweet Pea." She gathers our empty cups and disappears into the kitchen.

*But what if the right thing means giving in to my feelings for Bennett?*

# Chapter Three

After kissing Ma on her cheek, I leave her car outside Angie's real estate office and walk to mine. At least those damn reporters haven't returned. I place my hand on the front door handle, but the ocean's roaring waves call to me.

Ma's car has long since turned the corner, confirming I'm alone. Fixing my scarf and wrapping my coat around me, I walk toward the boardwalk. I need to clear my head.

Court wants me to go on tour with UC. So does Ma. Both for different reasons. Court thinks Bennett is good for me while Ma does *not*. What do I want?

I check my cell. It's already six o'clock. UC must be gearing up to take the stage for their first major concert. How is Bennett feeling? How's his pulled muscle? Will he be able to perform and cover up his injury?

What do I want?

The top ten cons I described to Court about touring flip over in my mind. What are the pros? Spending more time with Bennett, reconnecting with the rest of UC, seeing the world, being free from Aroostook responsibilities. I come to a stop.

What do I want?

The ocean pulses against the sand, highlighting today's cold weather. I bet some of the tour stops are at warm places, so that'll be another pro.

Even though I can't get to ten, I know which one has more weight. The one with the gorgeous, injured man who's brought me more pleasure than anyone ever has. I want to help him heal—not only in the PT sense—and I think he might be able to help me, too.

Darren's face comes rushing to the fore.

Without a doubt, he loved me and I loved him. My time with him was idyllic, a fantasy. Even back then I suspected we had an expiration date. With Bennett, it feels like anything but.

The lead singer's tortured soul calls out to me. I have an unquenched need to peel away his protective gear and help him correct everything wrong in his life. For a man who appears to have it all—looks, money, fame—he's so broken. I get it.

How will the rest of UC take it if I join their tour? The newest member—Tristan—and I don't have a past, so he should be fine. Well, except for the whole he-took-Darren's-place-in-the-band thing. Correction. He's their new keyboardist. No one can replace Darren, and based on the movie, it doesn't look like that's his ambition.

In truth, it's Río, Coop, and Pierce—007—I worry about, with the last one raising the most red flags. He was Darren's best friend, the first one to discover he had died, and knows I had nothing to do with his overdose. From the message he left me a week prior to that fateful day, which I haven't been able to bring myself to delete, Pierce probably knew more than anyone about what was going on with Darren. He may be surprised, perhaps standoffish, but he'll come around since he knows the truth that Darren was the only one at fault for his death. *I hope.*

I continue down the boardwalk, past the summer concession stand, now empty. A blonde woman walking her dog passes, and she reminds me of Lissa. Gosh, Bennett's ex is a real winner! Claiming

UC's songs were about her and he's been pining for her is unbeliev-able. Does she not know he's been a manwhore for a decade now?

Still, the fact remains I'm going to have to deal with the likes of Lissa for a long time. He was the most promiscuous of the band, for sure. Groupies and fans alike won't sing my praises for joining the tour—if I do.

I kick a pebble across the wooden boards and turn toward my car. Can I go on another tour with UC, this time without Darren? My stomach churns harder than the ocean. The Bennett I've come to know, the man whom I have feelings for and who professes to love me, is so much more multi-faceted than my ex-boyfriend. Not to disparage Darren in any way, but Bennett's just . . . well, Bennett.

I'm so lost in my thoughts I don't hear someone approach until it's too late. "Fancy meeting the Black Widow herself on the boards of Aroostook."

Michelle.

Great. Today lacked only her.

I bundle my coat closer. My voice is dull when I ask, "What do you want, Michelle?"

She falls into step next to me. "How's my tall, dark, and sexy man doing?"

"Bennett's gone." I rub my left arm over my right.

"What?" She cackles. "You couldn't keep him for two full weeks? Must be a new record. You were with my high school boyfriend for a month before Thaine saw the light and came home to me."

*Three months.* But who's counting? "Your point?"

"Oh, I don't know," she says brightly. "Your first boyfriend in high school dumped you, another boyfriend died, and this one bolted. Seems you've definitely earned your nickname. Black Widow." She hisses.

As if spiders hiss.

I pick up my pace and don't bother engaging her. Maybe she'll take the hint.

Faster footfalls follow me. "I guess you don't have anything to say to me because you know I'm right."

"There she is!" A man wielding a massive camera yells at me. He's followed by five others, each with cameras and their own questions. I can't make out any of them, thankfully.

I calculate the distance between here and my car. Too far. A diner's across the street, so I pick up my pace to a jog and beeline for the "Open" sign, uncaring of Michelle's fate. Let her pose and spew her lies to anyone who'll listen. Don't count me as one of them.

Pushing against the door, I almost fall headfirst into the local eatery. The few heads inside turn toward me. A server, barely out of her teens, approaches me, waving her arm. "Sit anywhere you'd like."

"Thanks." I glance around and choose a table far away from the windows and sit in the corner. From my vantage point, I see Michelle talking with the reporters. Wonderful.

When the same server approaches, I order a Diet Coke and run through my options. I could walk back to my car, but reporters would be all over me. I could call a car service, but that seems extravagant. I could ask Ma to pick me up, but after our little tea, I don't think that's a good idea.

The server drops off my drink, for which I thank her.

There has to be a way out of here. Court's shining face bubbles in my mind, but she's busy with patients.

*Angie.* She'd be excited to help me evade the media, I know it in my bones. After a quick call, she pulls up outside the diner. Leaving some money on the table beside my half-empty glass, I prepare for the onslaught. With fluid motions, I dash out of the diner's protection and dive into Angie's car.

"Buckle up!" With this only warning, Angie steps on the gas and we fly away. "I'm not taking you directly back to my office, as I want to shake these vultures off your tail." Her evasive driving rivals Bennett's. Within ten minutes, she pulls into an apartment building's quiet parking lot off the main drag.

She puts her car into park. "What happened?"

I reach for my ponytail, only to remember I left my hair loose today, because Bennett prefers it this way. Was our bath and shower only this morning? Resting my head against the headrest, I say, "I was out for a walk checking out the ocean when the paparazzi appeared out of nowhere."

"They have a knack for doing that."

"I know. One minute I was enjoying the waves, the next Michelle came up and was harassing me, and then the media showed up."

"Wow. You've had quite the day."

I roll my head toward her. "You don't know the half of it."

"I know we've only just met, but I like you, Jenna. I feel what you're going through. Can I offer you some unsolicited advice?"

Why not? Everyone else has. "Sure."

She turns to face me, tucking her leg behind her. "Leave. Go out on tour with Untamed Coaster. Get out of this town until some new celebrity diverts the media's attention. You'll also get an added bonus."

I can't resist wading into the open-ended statement. "What's that?"

"You'll be able to control the media from the inside."

---

After a sleepless night, I finally come to a decision. I make an early morning stop at the office, confirming I can follow through with it. "Ensure you make an appointment to have the air conditioner checked by early spring."

"On my list," Court replies.

"Double-check to see if salt needs to be added to the water softener every month."

She salutes me. "Aye, aye."

"And—"

Court raises her hand. "I got this. Stop worrying."

"I know you do." I pace across the floor. "I've never left my baby for months."

"You were smart. You've structured At Your Service PT to run without you. I promise you, it will. If something unforeseen happens, I know how to reach you."

My legs keep moving. "You'll keep an eye on Felipe at the second location, right? Based on your astute observations regarding Sylvia, and the way Austin failed on Bennett's skater jumps, I've decided to tap Greyson for the third location like you suggested. Of course, that won't happen until I get back, so you don't have to worry about telling anyone."

Court laughs. "You need to get your head out of Aroostook and focus on your one patient about to tour the world. I can't even imagine touring with my man across the globe." She fans her face. "If only I had a man. I have to live vicariously through you."

"Bennett isn't my *man*," I correct her. "He's my patient." This reminder is more for me than for her.

"Whatever. If it were me, I'd be all over that fine man like moss on a tree." Using the bottom of her shirt, she cleans her glasses.

"Not. Going. To. Happen." I don't add in the last word, again. No matter how much he excited me or played my body to perfection, it can't happen again. "Two words—Professional. Ethics."

Court waves her hand. "I'd never tell."

"Ride or die," I repeat our catchphrase from school, causing us both to laugh.

"Knock, knock." Austin doesn't wait for our response and breezes into Court's office carrying a manilla folder. He stops short. "Oh, Jenna, I didn't expect to see you here."

His surprise seems a bit disingenuous. Bennett's less-than-positive appraisal of him may have colored my thoughts, though. "Hey. I just told Courtney that I'm going to be going away for a few months so she'll be in charge. Keep on doing what you're doing and you'll be great."

He looks as if he ate a sour pickle. "Where are you going?"

It's none of his business. However, the media won't keep my whereabouts secret for too long, so I decide to get ahead of them. "Bennett's doctor prescribed three more months of physical therapy while he's on tour. Since he's been my patient from the beginning, it makes sense for me to continue with him."

The folder slaps the top of Austin's thigh. "If you're going to be away, who's going to take the lead on your third clinic?"

I know he's angling to be the manager, but I'm not about to spill the beans. I play coy. "I don't think this is a decision that needs to be made right this second."

He juts his chin upward. "I'd like to throw my name into the ring. I'm a good manager, can meet deadlines, and my clients love me."

Except Bennett. "Those are excellent attributes," I tell him, needing to stroke his ego. "Remember I told you I think you may need some more practical experience before moving up into management, so keep working on your connections within the community."

"I will." He rubs his eyebrow. "Bennett, huh?"

"She's going to be working with her patient," Court jumps to defend me. I shoot a grateful glance at her.

"Yeah, right," Austin grumbles. My hands land on my hips. He turns to face Court, holding up the folder. "I actually came in here to ask you about this patient."

"I'll take this as my cue to leave, as I have several loose ends to tie up." I nod at Austin, then address Court. "I'll be in touch."

Ignoring our audience, she gives me a big bear hug. In my ear, she whispers, "You better check in. Only to let me know how things are going with your *patient*."

Because of Austin, I simply offer them a wave and leave the office. I hide my smirk until I'm well out of their line of sight.

My next stop is at home. A few intrepid reporters are camped out on the sidewalk, whom I ignore. Inside my house, I pull out a couple of suitcases and begin to fill them with my favorite pieces of clothing. Which need to last me three months. I stop. I'm going to be away for ninety days? How is this my life? Unfathomable before I met

Bennett Hardy. Even with Darren, I was away only a night or two at a time.

I need to get myself organized. Not only in the clothes department. I sit at my desk and write out lists of what I need to do before joining Bennett on tour. Stop my automatic food deliveries tops the list. Double-check that all my bills are on autopay. Cancel streaming services that I won't be here to watch. When I'm done, I stare at the final three—tell Angie, Ma, and Bennett. A big sigh overtakes my body. No time like the present.

The first item is easily accomplished. Angie's excitement for me buoys me to make the next call. Ma picks up on the second ring. Stomach churning, I tell her of my decision.

"I'm glad to hear this, Sweet Pea. Just promise me you'll be careful."

"I will. You know me."

"Better than you know yourself, I fear. Enjoy this hiatus and see the world. Just don't get caught up in Bennett's drama." She pauses. "For lack of a better word."

"Ma. Nothing can happen, because he's officially my patient. You know this is the best time for me to get away and regroup. I'll be ready to tackle offices three and four when I return."

"I know you will, Sweet Pea. I love you."

With those three words, I know she's given me her blessing. "Love you more."

A timer beeps in the background. "I have to run. I can't wait to hear how things are going!"

"I'll call you—" my words are cut off when she disconnects the line. I stare at my cell for a moment. *You're being weird, Ma.*

After a minute, I return to my bedroom and complete packing. Against my body, I hold up a new dress Court gave me, saying I'll need the sexy outfit to fit in with a bunch of rock stars. With a sigh, I add it to my suitcase filled with leggings and tunic tops. Can't hurt.

Shoes are easy, since I don't own anything remotely akin to what groupies wear. No six-inch heels, no booties. I toss a couple of different pairs of Sketchers into the bag. The pumps I wore to the movie premiere dare me to take them along and I toss them in as well. They do match Court's dress.

When my luggage is packed and everything's crossed off my list except for the last item, I take a seat in my family room. Remembering what Bennett and I did in here, warmth suffuses my cheeks. I shake my head. Circumstances are different now. "Never again."

Who am I trying to convince?

I pick up my phone. He hasn't sent me any texts since he jetted back to the City yesterday. *Does he still want me to be his therapist?* I shrug this thought off as nonsense. He couldn't kiss me and do the other stuff we did and not want me with him. Right? Oh God, what if he does that on the regular? He always was picking up women when I was with Darren.

Maybe this is for the best. I can do a job, get paid very well for it —enough for my fourth clinic—and return here without worry. Bennett could've already forgotten me. With this "delightful" thought, I dial his number.

"Jenna!" I can barely hear him above all the background noise.

"Hi. Are you still looking for a physical therapist?"

"I never started."

His simple statement sends me reeling. He hasn't discarded me. *Get it under control.* "That sure of me, were you?"

"I was hoping. Did you see the press from our gig last night?"

Might as well be honest. "I read a couple of headlines. Seems like it went well."

"It was amazing being back onstage. You'll be happy to know I took things very slowly. No running or even dancing." He chuckles. "I may have moved my hips a little bit."

I glance at the floor. "Can't take you completely out of your element."

"No way. But enough about me. When are you coming on tour?"

This is it. The moment of truth. Bees fly around my stomach. "Where are you now?" As if I didn't already know.

"We're still in New York City. We have two more gigs at Madison Square Garden, then we go to Philly."

I could stay away for a few more nights and meet him in Philadelphia. Grant myself a reprieve. Before I can chicken out, there's one last thing I need to know. "How's the pain level?"

"Right now, I'd give it about a six." *Which means at least a seven.* "I have the leg up with ice on it."

I sit up. "What were you doing a half hour ago?"

"Well, I might have tried out some lunges." My eyes slam shut. "To see how they'd feel, if I performed them onstage." He huffs. "Not my brightest idea."

I open my eyelids, giving a final glance around my house. "No, it wasn't. Bennett, if you keep doing things like this, you're only going to reinjure yourself and delay healing."

He protests, "I was feeling better."

*Because you didn't have PT for a day and a half.* I slump against the chair. "Can you please send a helicopter for me?"

"You're coming? Today?"

"Someone has to keep you safe from yourself."

"I know what else you could do to make me feel better."

I can practically see his eyebrows waggling. At least this is the opening I need. "I need to make this crystal clear. If I agree to join you, this will be our reset. There will be no more extracurricular activities between us. You can't kiss or hug me—or anything. Do you understand me?"

"Can I hug you hello?"

Because I want to savor one last time in his arms, I relent. "Once." In my mind's eye, he's wrapping me against his hard body, pulling me in so tight I can feel his heart beating against my cheek. My shoulders square. "Then never again."

"I'll take what I can get." He pulls away from the phone. At a distance, I hear him requesting my air transportation. Then curse. "Okay, the helicopter schedule doesn't work, so a car will be to your house in an hour instead. You'll be with me in around three hours.

All I'm going to say is 'strapped, locked, and loaded, are you ready to roll with Untamed Coaster?'" The phone disconnects to the sound of a whoop.

The exact words the band says before taking the stage tug at my heart. I can do this. I'll remain strong, abiding by the professional ethical requirements. Even if the simple sound of his voice makes me want to strip off my clothes. And let him deep into my soul.

Standing, I say, "Providing him the best physical therapy will give At Your Service PT unprecedented advertising. Four locations won't be able to handle all the patients." It doesn't matter our misguided history, I'm all about business from now on.

If only my heart would get the message.

# Chapter Four

The car stops in front of a swanky hotel, where the band's manager stands at the curb with a luggage trolley. "It was a pleasure driving you, Miss. I hope you enjoy your stay."

"Thank you so much. You made this ride a lot more pleasant than I anticipated." The driver's funny stories sure distracted me.

He tips the brim of his New York Yankees baseball cap. "I'll help unload your bags."

Luke opens my door as blood pumps through my body at an increasing tempo. I inhale the distinctive city smell of Manhattan. I can do this—practice physical therapy like I've been trained. Doesn't matter if my patient were a schoolteacher from Aroostook or one of the biggest rock stars on the planet. Heal him, collect my honest fee, and return to my life. Nothing. More.

I step out of the car, watching the two men load my few mismatched bags onto the trolley. My life contained in two large suit-cases and a carry-on. The driver wishes me well and drives away, leaving me with Luke. Well, I guess I am the hired help.

Plastering a smile on my face, I say, "Thanks for coming out to meet me, Luke, but I don't want to be a bother." I lift my hand, palm up. "If you could please give me my key, I'll push my luggage into the room and be out of your hair." Which is darker than Bennett's by a couple of shades, and much longer, touching his shoulders.

"Oh no, B would have my head if he thought I made you push your own luggage." He waves off the doorman and positions himself behind the trolley. "Besides, you have to check in. They wouldn't give me your room key."

His honesty causes me to giggle. My hand slaps across my mouth. "Sorry. Totally not funny."

Luke pushes the luggage cart in the front door. "I know you're not laughing at my being your bag boy." He makes a turn and grabs my carry-on before it hits the floor.

Something about this man dealing with my luggage is giggle worthy. "Absolutely not." I smother another giggle.

"Well, it is sort of funny. But don't get used to it. From now on, you're responsible for getting your luggage in and out of the bus."

The use of the word "bus" stops me in my tracks. "Will the bus be like last time?"

"Buses," he clarifies. "The band has two buses, but Bennett usually rides alone. The crew share a few buses among the roadies, sound techs, instrument techs. You'll be on one of those."

I relax. I'm not expected to be on Bennett's bus—I can't believe he *de facto* gets one all to himself. I stop myself from wondering why. "Sounds good. I'll only need one bag at a time, and depending on the schedule, I may be able to get by with only the carry-on."

We stop and Luke catches said carry-on from falling again. "Sounds like a plan."

He escorts me to the registration desk where I get my key, and we make our way to the elevators. While we wait, I ask, "Where is Bennett? I need to give him some PT before tonight's concert."

"We have a few hours before showtime." Luke checks his watch. "Impressive. You lasted ten whole minutes before asking about our lead singer."

My spine snaps straight. The elevator dings and we enter. "The only reason I'm here at all is to give him physical therapy."

I swear he mutters, "Have you run that by B?"

"Excuse me?"

"Nothing." The elevator stops at my floor and we approach my room. After pressing my card against the keypad, the door opens and I let Luke push the cart into the room.

"Thank you. I'll unpack from here—we're staying in this hotel two more nights?"

He pulls out his cell. "Yes. I'll let B know your room number."

"You don't have to do that. I noticed the hotel has a gym. Can you ask him to meet me there in thirty?"

"Of course, I live to be his personal secretary." He smiles to lessen the sting of his words, but message received that I'll be doing my own scheduling from now on. After sending a text, Luke leaves me alone.

My first order of business is to set my alarm for the gym. Next, I wander around the sterile hotel room. Nothing fancy, just a bed, television, closet, bathroom, and a longish counter hosting the television on top and some drawers plus a fridge beneath. I bet Bennett has the presidential suite, complete with a bedroom complete with an en suite bathroom, a living room, and kitchen. *Not that I'll ever find out.* With efficient movements, I unpack three days' worth of outfits and change into leggings for the gym.

Someone knocks on my door. Bennett couldn't wait another ten minutes? I open the door prepared to tell him to meet me in the gym.

Only it's not Bennett.

Pierce DeLuca stands in the doorway. Darren's best friend. Bennett nicknamed him 007 because Pierce Brosnan was playing James Bond when he was born, and they have the same coloring. For what it's worth, I think the nickname fits.

"Hi." I widen the door, allowing him to enter the room.

"Hello, Jenna." Controlled anger vibrates off his body, which does nothing to calm my nerves. Have I made a mistake touring with

UC again? In the middle of the room, which seems to be smaller all of a sudden, he turns and waits for me to close the door. His fingers rest on the studded belt he's wearing—my stomach flips when I recognize it as Darren's favorite. "I understand you're touring with us as Bennett's physical therapist."

I walk toward the counter with the television, covering my racing heart rate. "I am."

His jaw tics. Not a good sign. "I'm only going to say this once. I don't like it. There are plenty of other therapists that don't have your connection with the band. You should recommend someone—a school friend, close colleague, hell I don't care, *anyone*—and leave now. Before things get ugly."

*Get* ugly? My head ticks up. "I don't mean to make things difficult among you guys. I'm only here because I was tagged to check on Bennett's injury when it happened and have been his physical therapist for the past two weeks." I tighten my ponytail holder, keeping my hair bound. "It's my professional duty to see him through his rehab."

He turns his back to me and faces the window. "I want to believe you think you're doing something for his good. But you're not. We all —except Tris—were here when Darren died. You being on tour with us now reopens these wounds."

"I don't mean for that to happen. I only want what's best for Bennett."

He whirls to face me, his face a blotchy red. "What's best for Bennett is to seek treatment from some other physical therapist. I don't know why he can't see that. Or why you can't, for that matter."

I dissect the words he's flung at me. "I might agree," I begin cautiously. "If I wasn't the one to diagnose his injury when it happened. I didn't go with him to the doctor the first visit, but I was there for the last one. He needs more time to rehab than the measly two weeks—less than, actually—I've been working with him. I know his routine, his exercises. I can read his tells and know when he can be pushed harder."

"Someone else could do the same."

He's right. Didn't I make the same argument to Court? Am I allowing unprofessional feelings toward Bennett cloud my judgment? I stew a moment, but the certainty I'm the right therapist for the job is inescapable. More than that, I *need* the money to open another clinic. Bennett and I simply will not cross any more lines.

"You're right. Someone else could read my files and pick up his therapy. But they won't have the background I do with him, nor the time in on his rehab. While you may disagree—and I'm wary about being back with UC, believe me—I am the best therapist for him at this juncture."

"Darren would have something to say about this."

I take an involuntary step back, as if he'd slapped me across the face. "This has nothing to do with Darren." When we were together, I loved him, and he loved me. He made a series of bad decisions the night he overdosed. Pierce needs to mourn his passing and move on, as my therapist urged me to do. I am quite aware how big of an ask this is.

He crosses his arms. "Or have you already decided to hook up with Bennett as a way to stay connected with UC, Miss Black Widow?"

"What? No." I shake my head. Guilt prods that he's half-right because we already have hooked up. However, the reason definitely was *not* because of Darren. If anything, the fact Bennett's in the same band was a real turn off. I force myself to glare at the band's bassist. I hope it appears convincing. "I'm only his therapist."

"Keep telling yourself this, Jenna. Just know I have my eyes on you." His blazing blue gaze latches onto me. "If he so much as gets a hangnail, your ass will be out. Feel me?"

"I'm only here to help Bennett rehab. So he can perform as your frontman like he used to do."

His lips form a solid line. "See to it you get this job done. No other." He breezes by me, tagging my shoulder, as he exits the room. The door remains open.

I sag against the wall. If I had any doubts about where Pierce stands, they're all gone now. The need to convince him I'm here for Bennett's physical therapy, and nothing else, reinforces my resolve to keep things strictly professional with the rock star.

My alarm goes off, giving me a five-minute warning. Wonderful. With Pierce's venom swirling in my head, I close the door behind me and follow the signs to the gym. When I enter, the rest of the band—sans my recent visitor—is working on various machines. Bennett stands by a workout bench.

"Jenna!" the frontman exclaims, and limp-walks to my side. My body buzzes with excitement at seeing him again, which I tamp down when the other band members stop their exercises and encircle me.

Bennett reintroduces me to Tristan, whom he calls Tris. I extend my hand. "Nice to meet you under more normal circumstances," I say. "You seem to fit right in with the band."

"Thank you. I'm happy to be able to make your acquaintance formally. As you can imagine, I've heard quite a lot about you."

What can I say to this? "I hope we can forge our own friendship, free from any preconceived notions."

"It's a deal." He rubs his dark five o'clock shadow, a friendship bracelet around his wrist.

Coop and Río join us, cups of water in their hands. "I heard you're coming on tour with us again. Couldn't keep away, huh?" Coop grins to ease the sting of his joke, his hoop earrings even smiling.

"Call me crazy—"

A shirtless Río interjects, "Crazy." Everyone laughs, including me.

Shaking my head, I continue, "I was making a nice life for myself without you boys. Then Bennett here had to go hurt himself and *voilá*, here I am again."

"He's made a lot of progress," Río notes. "Nowhere near the showman he used to be, but at least he's been walking without too much of a limp."

I turn my head to acknowledge Bennett for the first time. "I saw you limping a second ago."

He shrugs. "Only sometimes. Not onstage."

"Yeah, only when you think you can get away with it," Río adds.

I stand straighter. "You shouldn't be limping. If you are, that means you've been pushing yourself too hard, which will only delay your recovery." The other band members snicker. I don't care. Bennett needs to hear this, loud and clear. "Which leads me to the inescapable fact that you were doing lunges. Of all things. Why do you insist on aggravating your injury?"

All eyes turn to Bennett. I refuse to allow my body to react to his nearness. How his hair falls at the precise right angle to highlight his amazing features. Straight nose. High cheekbones. Unusual and oh-so-sexy green eyes. This is all above his neck. The buzz centered in my chest that started when he entered this section of the gym intensifies. Maybe it's lower.

"Can't blame a guy for ushering his therapist here faster." He grins. "She was taking her sweet ass time."

No, no, no. I will not fall under his spell again. "Well, your wish seems to have been granted because here I am." I rub my hands together. "Are you ready to get started?"

"Born ready."

"You say that now." My thumb and pinky rub together at his suggestive phrase. "In that case, let's start off with the first round of exercises."

Bennett looks like he wants to argue with me, but his band members razz him, which I allow. I need to establish I'm in charge, so I simply cross my arms and wait for him to get to work. Which he does after all the guys give their parting shots and depart. Tristan remained rather quiet, but he was the most accepting of me. Although Darren's missing presence is felt, I do appreciate their new keyboardist.

Our first session goes pretty well, but I'm not about to tell

Bennett this if I expect him to continue working as hard. He still has a long way to go.

Bennett interrupts my thoughts. "Maybe having a full day off was what I needed?"

What is he getting at? Better put him in his place, and not as the frontman of the band. "Not if you truly want to heal faster. I can give you days off, though, if you'd prefer. Maybe fly in once a week for a quick session."

"No way," he growls. "I'll keep up the PT."

I bury my smile. "Thought you might see it my way." I do want to praise him for his focus during the session, though, so he keeps it up. "I'm aware of how hard it is for you to pay attention, Rock Star."

He eliminates the distance between us. In the middle of the gym, he looks as if he wants to either throttle me—or give me a hug. *Or rub his sweat-covered body against mine.* I'd prefer none of the above. *Yeah, right.*

Our standoff ends when he asks, "How did Austin take you coming on tour with me?"

"All right, not the question I was expecting." I consider the best way to respond. "He was surprised. He did take the opportunity to put his proverbial hat into the ring to be the manager of my third clinic."

"Did you tell him to fuck off?"

"No," I enunciate the word clearly. "He's good at what he does, he just needs a little more time to develop all his skills. Like teaching patients how to do skater jumps."

Bennett mulls over my response as he walks to the water fountain. "He sure does. I stand by my opinion of him, though. He wants in your panties."

My head shakes. "Seriously, he does not. You have an overactive imagination."

"Oh yeah?" He pours himself a cup of water, offering to prepare one for me as well. When I put up my hand, he downs his cup. "If I truly had an overactive imagination, Jenna, I'd position you so your back's against the corner, like so."

He walks forward, which causes me to retreat, my back in the corner of the gym, away from the machines.

"Then I'd hold up a cup of water between us, as if offering it to you to drink." His movements follow his description. "I'd do it to prevent anyone who's looking from figuring out my lips were covering yours in a devouring kiss I've been dying to have with you since you fled my bedroom in nothing but a towel. After, I might add, you had my cock down your throat and I made you come in the bathtub so hard I was drying the marble hours later."

As he talks, my breathing becomes more labored. His gaze eats me up like my body clamors for him to do. My core contracts, pleading for his fingers. Or more.

None of these things can happen.

"One hug," I choke out. As much to remind him as me. "Nothing more."

"If that's all I'm allowed." His palm skims near my overheated cheek, not quite touching. "Then I'll wait until we're alone." He steps away, and it takes all my concentration to remain upright.

I press into the corner, willing my boneless legs to support my body. When I've regained my equilibrium, I walk past Bennett as if I don't have a care in the world. "Make sure you ice it."

"What? Aren't you going to help me with it?"

"I have faith in you."

"Will you be at sound check? I don't practice my moves then, but I am onstage and you never know what could happen."

I stop. Is this a challenge? Should I be there, as his therapist? I *suppose* he could get himself into some sort of mischief, especially if he's looking for it. Twirling toward him, I ask, "What time?"

His gaze bounces between the clock and me. "Starts in an hour. I'd definitely like you to stay and meet everyone. Plus, Luke and I are interviewing guitar tech candidates and I seem to remember your wanting to see what our process is, to help yours."

Dammit. How can he be so sweet when my mind is still in the fog he created? "Thank you." In order to keep any semblance of an upper hand between us, I take even steps to leave the gym with my head held as high as possible.

Even if my entire body screams to rush back to him.

# Chapter Five

I stand off to the side of the stage, watching UC do their sound check in the famed Madison Square Garden. None of them are wearing their rock star gear. Not a ring or guyliner or whiff of hairspray. (Be that as it may, Río's still not sporting a shirt.) It's just five guys on a massive stage, ensuring their music will reach all the ears at tonight's concert.

Up there with their buds, rocking out.

Could be in a garage or on this stage—a group of talented men doing what they love. I can only imagine how their fans would react to such an intimate look at their heroes. My heart pings.

I push these sappy feelings to the side and examine Bennett's movements at the microphone. He's being careful not to exacerbate his injury, which is good. My vision slides over to the keyboard, where Tristan plays.

In my mind's eye, Darren's there. Laughing and hamming it up and hitting the keys. His beautiful smile gleams at his bandmates. His brothers.

Over the loudspeaker, a discombobulated voice says, "Think we almost got it, guys."

Onstage, they stop playing. My eyelids blink in double time and I'm returned to the present where Río stands from behind the drum kit and lumbers to Coop, who punches Pierce on his shoulder. Tristan joins the group, and someone laughs. Probably Río. Bennett stands among the guys. Not friends, my ass.

"So, Jenna, right?" A male voice asks from my right side.

I turn and am greeted by a mountain of a man. As tall as he is wide, with tattoos on both sleeves. Hoping he's on the side of good, I reply, "That's me." I extend my right hand and we shake.

"I'm part of the crew. Name's Jeb."

Good, then. "Nice to meet you, Jeb. What are you responsible for?"

He points to his chest. "I'm on staging. We do setup and break-down for all the guys' concerts."

I examine the stage, with catwalks that extend above the audience. "What you're saying is you really don't have too much to do?"

He chuckles. "Oh, a little bit of this and a little bit of that." He rubs his massive chest. "So, I heard you're Bennett's personal physical therapist."

Supposedly confidential news travels fast. "I've been hired to help him rehab an injury."

He places his palms on his back. Glancing around the venue, he lowers his voice, "Do you have any suggestions about how I could strengthen my back? I pulled it while we were setting up."

My therapist antennae spring up. As I can tell Jeb's embarrassed about his injury, I need to address his question with care. "Back injuries must happen often in your line of work." His nod encourages me to continue. "I can give you some exercises to do before you report for a shift, which should help strengthen your back. I also can provide you with some things to do at the gym on the regular to address your back muscles."

His eyes widen. "You could do that for me?"

"Of course." I pull out my phone. "What's your number? I'll send you a suggested gym workout." He gives me his digits and I text him mine. "Give me a couple of hours and I'll text you some exercises. Feel free to reach out with any questions."

"Appreciate it." The teddy bear of a man envelops me in a big hug.

A tenor voice booms, "What's going on here?"

Jeb releases me and we turn to face the inquisitor. Not wanting to get the roadie into any trouble, I say, "I'm meeting your crew, Bennett. Jeb here has a big job, making sure your staging is perfect." Not going to share Jeb's secret.

Bennett tilts his chin and he stares at the ceiling. A sure tell he's annoyed. "Hey, man. Everything going alright?"

The roadie, unknowing of Bennett's simmering ire, puffs his chest. "Sure is."

"That's great. Thanks for all you do." Green eyes skewer me. "Can I speak with you for a moment?" He doesn't wait for me to respond. Grabbing my arm, he tugs me toward an empty row of seats.

When we stop, I yank my arm free. "Jeb deserves more than a perfunctory thanks. He's part of your crew that makes sure your staging is perfect for your performance. He does important work."

"Don't you think I know this already?" He bends his knees to be level with my sight line. "I've hired every single person on this tour."

I'm not going to be pushed aside. I square my shoulders. "Then you should be more appreciative of the work they do."

"Who says I'm not grateful? Maybe I didn't like the big guy monopolizing your time."

Oh shit. Why did I think we could reset? When he goes all alpha male like this, I see desire simmering right up to the surface. Well, so what? We all have jobs to do. "How's the leg?"

He blinks. "It's a four. Not the issue at the moment."

"It's the only issue." My thumb and pinky rub together as I control my anger. "Aren't you needed for a sound check or something?"

He eliminates the space between us. "My part is over. We

already played here last night. Since I don't play an instrument, they only have to make sure my mic is working properly."

"That's what the control board meant before?"

"Yeah." His hands skim my body, from shoulders to my waist, without actually touching any part of me. "I'm sorry I went all caveman on Jeb over you. You do strange things to my head."

"Right back at 'ya."

Luke's voice comes over the speaker system. "B, ready?"

Next to me, his arms drop. He yells, "I'm just collecting Jenna and we'll be there in a minute." He licks his lips. "It's time to interview a new guitar tech to replace Chico. Are you ready to see how we do it?"

"Of course." I nod, trying to get my wayward breathing under control. "Lead the way."

We meander through a maze of seats until we meet up with Luke in a side corner. I check out the stage from here. "People sitting here will have a good vantage point if they bring binoculars."

Luke grins. "That's why we charge less for these seats. These guests will be able to enjoy the concert and see everything that's going on, plus be part of the balloon drop at the end. Unfortunately, they won't get as up close and personal with the band as people who pay more and are seated near the stage or catwalk."

The elaborate staging is impressive. It was created for maximum interaction with the fans. "Jeb and his crew do an amazing job."

"That they do," Luke answers. "We pride ourselves on hiring the best roadies and techs. We're a damn traveling family!" He chuckles, and I follow suit. Bennett does not. *I need to get to the bottom of his trust issues.*

That is, when the lead singer isn't trying to come on to me or prevent me from talking with the crew.

Bennett refocuses us on the work at hand. He flips through a stack of papers, then hands me an identical one. "These are the resumes of the guitar tech candidates we're going to interview. Our team has reviewed all applicants and shorted them down to the top five, who we're going to meet now."

They have five prospects? I usually start with ten, fearing I'll miss someone good. I make a mental note to review this policy as it would save me time with physical therapists in the future. My need for a top ten list is strong, however. Should it be broken?

Shaking my head, I peruse the resumes. "They all look impressive on paper."

"That's why we're meeting all of them." Luke glances at the resumes. "By the time we're done, we'll have picked the newest member of our crew."

I sputter. "You're interviewing all five *now*? What's that going to take? Like ten hours? Don't you have a concert to put on?"

Bennett chuckles. "Things go differently with us, I suppose. These interviews will be around thirty minutes each. We meet, talk with them to get a feel for how they operate, then make a quick gut decision."

"A what?" His words don't compute. "Don't you have to, I don't know, have them play or something?"

Bennett looks like he wants to talk, but Luke is quicker on the draw. "That's already been done in the previous rounds. We have a team who reviews all the resumes and invites interesting candidates to come in and do an initial meeting. The top of the crop is then invited to come back to show off their experience with guitars. In this case, B and I are the final round. Within thirty minutes of meeting someone, we know if they'll be a fit or not."

"Sometimes we pick different candidates, but more often than not, we agree," Bennett adds. "The entire process will be over, including an offer made, within three hours."

"Wow." I can't imagine being so streamlined. I'm the one who vets and interviews all job applicants. Maybe I could involve the managers on the front end rather than the back? Definitely something to consider. The two men stare at me. "So different from how I do things, but I like it. It takes me hours upon hours to hire someone."

"Glad to put your brain to work. Hope you can buy back some time using our method." Luke shuffles the resumes and holds up the first one. Kieron Malone. He whispers to a stagehand to bring him to us.

While we wait, I read his CV. He's toured with a couple of other bands, once as a backup guitarist and other times as a guitar tech. He also plays keyboards and can do backup vocals. Seems like a pretty talented guy.

A tall, lanky man wearing a pair of jeans is brought toward us. He has long blond hair, with the unfortunate distinction of being a similar shade to mine. He's also wearing it in a ponytail. He sports a goatee, wears a nose ring, and has one sleeve covered in tattoos. In short, he looks like a member of a band.

Luke takes the lead. "Hi, Kieron is it?"

He smiles, his light blue eyes scanning the Garden. Not surprising, it's an amazing venue. "That's me." He's introduced to all of us.

"It says here you've done some touring," Bennett begins. "How did you like your experience?"

"It was good. I mean," he brings his attention back to us. "It wasn't Madison Square Garden good, but we hit up some decent-sized venues."

"Tell us more about it," Luke requests. In response, Kieron details his experiences—from setting up the tour bus to meeting some groupies.

"I'd like to hear about your time onstage. And writing songs. How did that go?" Bennett asks.

"Of course, that was the best part. I mean, it was the reason we were doing it all, you know? Writing was more of a group effort, although I'll admit our lead singer did the heavy lifting. I added in some pretty good guitar licks, if I do say so myself. I could've created even better keyboard tracks, if we had keyboards." He chuckles.

Kieron seems affable and good-natured. Two things that will put him in good stead if he joins UC. Three pairs of eyes spear me, waiting for me to ask a question. I ask the first thing that comes to my mind. "Why UC?" My eyes slam shut. I hope I didn't sound too much like a physical therapist, asking a newly minted one why they want to work with me.

"Good question." This from Luke, which makes me feel as if my contribution to the interview wasn't dumb. Or at least he's being nice, for Bennett's sake.

"I've followed you guys for a few years now. Darren," he makes the sign of the cross, "Was a fantastic keyboardist. I modeled some of my licks with a nod toward his skills. I appreciate the way you five get along so well onstage and play off each other."

He continues with his answer, but his mentioning of Darren is like a gut punch. Darren was phenomenal. A truly great man. My gaze strays to Bennett, who's concentrating on the interview, as he should. How is it Darren never made me feel the way Bennett does? Am I betraying what we had?

No. I stop myself from going down this path again. But for his passing away, I wouldn't know anything about how Bennett kisses or feels or tastes. The two men are polar opposites of each other, even though they were founding members of the same band.

I tune back in to Kieron. "I think I'd add a new dimension to your crew, bringing my own experiences into the mix."

Luke and Bennett nod and shake his hand. I follow suit. Luke concludes the interview by letting him know he should hear back before the concert tonight. "If you're selected, will you be able to join us on tour immediately?"

Kieron smiles broadly. "Definitely."

After he leaves, we interview four other candidates with me repeating my new hallmark question. The process really does only take thirty minutes per candidate.

Luke claps. "Good job, team! We need to clear out of here so our fans can start finding their seats. Want to go to dinner and pick a new guitar tech?"

"I could eat a horse," Bennett replies. They both get to their feet.

I'm starving, but unsure whether the invitation includes me. I stare at my hands folded on my lap. "Jenna." Bennett extends his hand. "Coming?"

My palm meets his and the connection is so strong, I just might. That's not what he meant. *Head in the game!* "I'm definitely hungry."

"Great!" Unaware of the tension building between Bennett and me, Luke hops up. "I made reservations at a restaurant down the block. Feel up to a walk?" He places his hand on Bennett's shoulder. "Elias and his team will provide security."

"Let me get my hat and glasses. Meet you at the exit." Bennett takes off with a purposeful, yet steady, stride.

"Are you really ready to join UC?" Luke asks as we walk toward our rendezvous.

His question strikes a chord. "I hope so. Pierce truly isn't over-joyed to have me on the tour."

Luke gives me a solemn glance. "He, out of everyone, is going to be the hardest nut to crack. He was Darren's best friend, which I don't have to tell you. Took him a long time to warm up to Tris, but now they're all getting on well. Give him time."

What other option do I have? "Do you think the media knows I'm here?" Reporters are another reason I'm not jumping for joy to join the tour.

"Nah, they don't know for sure yet. Only *The Gossip* printed their version of the story, and that's certainly not a reliable publica-tion. If other reporters knew, they'd be descending like locusts."

I huff out a breath. "Great. Something else to look forward to."

"Hey," he wraps his arm around me. "You're with Bennett and we take care of our own. The UC PR team is on it."

I bristle. "I'm not 'with' Bennett." I make air quotes around the word, emphasizing how wrong his assumption is. "I'm his physical therapist. You, out of everyone, should know this. You were with us at the doctor."

"Honey, I know the truth. You know it. So does Bennett, the rest of the band and the crew. Beyond these people, reporters are going to do what they do best. Make up whatever they want. You know the game."

We stop by an exit. "Honestly, I don't know if I can handle all this attention again. It was one thing when I was dating Darren. Being here in a professional capacity is a whole other level."

"We'll protect you." He taps against the wall. "Might as well warn you, though. Our next stop is Philadelphia."

"I know."

"There's no easy way to say this. Darren's mother and sister live near the stadium. We've offered them VIP tickets. I wanted to let you know this so you can prepare yourself, after the article the other day."

Great. As if working with Bennett and dealing with Pierce weren't enough. Now I get to rub elbows with Mrs. Hilliard and Darren's sister, Marni, in the flesh? I haven't seen the two women since the funeral for a reason. My stomach lurches. "I'm not sure I can do this."

"Why? What did you say to her?" Bennett hits Luke in the back.

Without facing him, I reply, "The truth."

"C'mon, B, she had to know about Philly."

"Fuck. We'll keep you apart." Bennett walks toward the exit. "Let's go eat. Hire a guitar tech over nachos."

My feet follow the two men but my mind repeats Bennett's question: *What did you say to her?* I'm still close enough to home that I could call it quits and no one would be the wiser. Besides, Pierce probably would do a happy dance right onstage.

In the restaurant, I sit. Fidget. Stuff one chip into my mouth, repeat. I rub my palms against my thighs. Bennett and his manager review the five candidates we met this afternoon, discussing the pros and cons of each. I follow their conversation but don't contribute. My world is too full of recriminations and worry.

"What do you think, Jenna?"

I force my face to focus on Luke. "For the guitar tech?"

"No. For the exotic dancer—of course for the guitar tech." Luke shovels a couple of chips into his mouth, slathered with salsa.

I ignore the rumbling of my stomach. "I liked all of them. I think I would go for the last one."

"Really?" Bennett challenges. "I favored the second guy we met." He was good too. I shrug.

"You know who I liked?" When we don't take the bait, Luke answers, "Kieron. He seemed to have his head on his shoulders and gave off a down-home vibe to me. The second candidate seemed a bit too fussy. You know, with his list of dates he needed off."

"Only two of the tour dates," Bennett reminds Luke. "He was positive, something we're sorely lacking."

Crunching on more chips, Luke says, "Maybe a touch too much? Kieron seemed to have struck a good balance between being helpful and posting cat videos on your timeline."

"Fine," Bennett relents. "My pick probably needs to marinate another five years before he'd mesh with us anyway. How about Jenna's selection?"

"I didn't know I had a say." I pick a chip out of the basket and crunch, managing to swallow it over the tumult in my brain. "I liked how the last guy maintained his composure, even when Tristan walked over to talk about the music lineup for tonight. He didn't seem starstruck over Bennett, either. You need your employees to assimilate into your group and not fall over themselves to give you what you want."

"Good points," Luke says. "I only have one issue with him. The last band he worked with imploded. I'm not sure we need bad juju brought over to UC."

"Didn't know you were superstitious." Bennett shoves a fully loaded chip into his mouth.

"I'm not, but I also don't want to tempt fate when I have a choice. Which we definitely do—Kieron doesn't come with such baggage. Plus, he seemed like a cool dude."

Bennett weighs his manager's opinion. "I liked Kieron. He has a great resume. I could see him with the band, especially Coop. Let's introduce those two tonight, plus 007, and see how things go."

Makes sense, considering Coop plays lead guitar and Pierce is on bass. Luke voices my thought. "I like it. Assuming they hit it off, we've got our new guitar tech. Chico can work with him to transition throughout the week."

Chico was funny, always cracking Darren and me up with his off-color jokes. I bet he still makes the crew laugh. Personalities aside, the speed of this interview process astounds me. Perhaps I can pick up some tips for my own business model with UC? Wow.

Luke holds his hand in the middle of the table. "Are we in?"

Bennett looks at me, his eyebrows furrowed. *No way is he seeking my approval.* "Are we?"

Kieron seemed like a nice enough guy. He's been vetted in two other rounds. I'll give him my blessing, as if he really needs it. "Sure." I place my hand on top of Luke's and I feel . . . nothing.

When Bennett places his hand on top of mine, though, my nerves explode. "Count me in," his distinctive tenor announces.

Just like that, a new member of the crew is hired. Luke texts him to meet up with Coop and 007 tonight. Assuming all goes well, he'll let HR know of the decision as well as have the dubious honor of telling the finalists they didn't get the job. It impresses me that Luke extends this courtesy instead of letting someone else handle it. Or worse, ghosting them.

Our plates arrive. Luke digs into his steak burrito while Bennett dives into his hard-shell tacos. Me, I pick up my fork and play with my chicken quesadilla, my mind too busy with thoughts of Darren's family and reporters to relax and enjoy.

"Not liking it?" Luke wipes his hands on a napkin.

"It's good. I guess I'm not as hungry as I thought." Even if my stomach rumbles, thankfully not loud enough to alert my table companions.

"Well, I loved it." Bennett drops his fork onto his empty plate, and sips his hot tea. This time, he ordered peach.

I play with my own tea mug, filled with soothing chamomile. The need to escape raises its ugly head, and I don't second-guess myself.

Standing, I say, "I'm going back to my room to make sure I'm ready for tonight. I'll see you both in a couple of hours."

Without waiting for their replies, I take off at a fast clip to the hotel. A short time later, I'm sitting in a comfy chair in my room, figuring out how I can get a replacement therapist at this late date.

I grab my phone. "Hey, Court."

"Jenna! How's everything starting for you? Have you seen Bennett yet? What about the rest of UC?"

"Yeah. I've been thinking this might be a huge mistake. Want to switch places? I'll manage the first clinic in Aroostook as well as oversee the expansion, and you can tour with the band. I know you'd do a fabulous job with them."

"Jenna, can you hear yourself?" A pen clicks. "What's spooked you?"

"Things you don't give a damn about. Reporters. Darren. Darren's family. None of which would faze you. I don't know why I didn't think of this sooner. If you could pack your bags, I'll stay for tonight because there's no way you can get out here in time. Then, you can take my place tomorrow." Tidy. Orderly. Perfect.

"No."

I must not have heard her correctly. "What?" I stand and begin pacing around the small room. "I know for a fact you enjoy Untamed Coaster's music. You've commented about Coop and Río enough to let me know being around them won't be a hardship. You don't have anyone tying you down to Aroostook, and I can do your job with At Your Service PT until you return. What's your issue?"

"I don't have an issue. Your scheme would work fine but for one major flaw. Bennett is your patient. Need I remind you that you said you want him to have continuity of service—which he wouldn't have if I take over."

I stomp my foot. "We went to school together. We have the same philosophy and follow the same protocols. I don't think it would be an issue."

"The fact I'm Court and not Jenna is the only issue that matters."

I stop behind the upholstered chair and pick at its back. "I'm sure this could be overlooked," I mumble.

"I think my unflappable Jenna is scared. Scared about dealing with reporters. Scared of having to deal with the various personalities in UC, and the one who is no longer with it. Scared of how Bennett makes you feel."

I complete her list. "Scared of the loss of control, the travel, the tour bus, overwhelming logistics, the judgmental fans, crappy food, and Darren's family in two days." The list repeats in my head. "Well, maybe the food won't be so crappy, assuming I have the capacity to swallow it."

"Did you say you're seeing Darren's family?"

Leave it to Court to pick up on that gem. "Lucky me. They'll be at the tour stop in Philly in a couple of days."

"Shit."

"About sums it up." I delve into the recent article in *The Gossip*. "I can't face them. They hated me when I was with Darren. Now they think I'm some sort of groupie who only wants to spend time with the band."

"We both know that couldn't be further from the truth. I think you need to say it to their faces. Flat out."

"Oh, I forgot about Lissa and Michelle, too. No, Court, this was a bad idea. If you're not willing to take my place, I'll call Felipe. I bet he'd do it."

"His boyfriend might have something to say about it."

Rats. I forgot about his partner. "Then that leaves you. Start packing."

"I won't do it. You need this, Jenna. You need to explore whatever it is between you and Bennett."

"There's nothing—"

She continues as if I didn't object. "Plus, tell those reporters where they can shove it. This is your life, Jenna. Do you really want someone else telling you how to run it?"

"Well, no. But it's too much."

"It's a lot, I agree. How did the sound check go?"

I shrug. "Bennett didn't do anything stupid and the band sounded great." When don't they? "I met this roadie, Jeb. He's huge! Seriously, a giant built like a Mack Truck." I pause. "Anyway, he works setting up and breaking down the staging. He confided about back issues, and I promised him I'd send him some exercises to do." Which I have to do as soon as I get off the phone.

"That's pretty cool. Think you could give him PT while you're on the road?"

"I never considered that. Maybe?" Could others in the band and its entourage need therapy? I should explore this avenue.

"I think you need to stick it out, Jenna. Yes, meeting up with Darren's family could suck, but maybe you could clear the air? No matter what, you'll only have to deal with them for one concert, right?"

I sigh. "It's going to be bad."

She repeats. "For one day."

"I guess so. But the reporters are forever. They were relentless when I was with Darren, remember? He wasn't as in demand as Bennett is. Plus, I wasn't branded the Black Widow back then." Guilt summoned by the phrase still makes my stomach clench.

"I get it, Jenna. Try to turn things around on them. That'll make them back off."

I remember Angie's suggestion for me to fight the media from within. "You're not the first person to suggest this to me." I slump onto the bed. "Guess I'm stuck here. I'll try."

"That's all anyone can ask of you. Now go and send Jeb his exercises and get Bennett ready to hit the stage."

I stare at my phone. It's not Jeb I'm worried about.

# Chapter Six

Later, I join UC and what seems to be a million crew members in a conference room that's been labelled "The Closet" in Madison Square Garden. The sheer amount of people doing their jobs in this chaos is astounding.

Absorbing the controlled disorder, I approach Bennett, who sits with an ice pack on this thigh. "Are you looking forward to tonight's concert?"

I clear my jumble of thoughts about the hubbub going on around me. "It'll be nice to see you guys performing again. To see how things have changed with Tristan." Before a gig, Darren used to hold his own comedy session for the band and crew. Come to think of it, I remember Bennett standing apart yet laughing at his jokes.

"We're a different band now. Our vibe has shifted but we're still all about the music."

On what I consider to be safe territory, I sit across from him. "What's Tristan like?"

My question brings Bennett up short. He taps the ice pack. "He's pretty laid-back. He doesn't like to rock the boat, which I guess makes sense, considering why he joined UC. He's a good guy, though. Damn fine keyboardist, too."

I nod. "I've heard him play a little. He sounds like Darren did, only with a slightly unique twist." Goes to show everyone's replaceable. *Remember this.*

"He has his own take on our songs. He's been an integral part of writing our new stuff." He grins. "He's willing to try anything. For instance, he joined us at a rock climbing wall when we were filming the movie. He was scared shitless, and we all saw it. We tried to break down his walls and, surprisingly, 007 was the one to breach them first." He chuckles. "It was a good time. A turning point, for us as a band."

"I remember the scene in the movie." I scan the room and locate Tristan talking with Pierce. "He seems like a good fit." He's not trying to be Darren, which is a relief. While his job can be replaced, the man himself cannot. The new keyboardist needed to bring his own personality to the group, and it sounds like he did. "I look forward to getting to know him."

"I'm sure he'd like that." He waves at a woman sporting a pixie haircut and an eyebrow piercing. "Guess it's time for me to put on the leather pants."

"By all means. Turn into the rock star that you are." I take the ice pack and slink into the background, which is more difficult than I imagined given the number of people in the room. I'm standing by the snack table when my heart stalls. Bennett is now clad in black leather and fiddling with a leather cuff. Instead of four total like before, he's now wearing five rings on both hands.

"How's this? Do I look stageworthy now?"

"Yeah," I manage.

His lips tick upward.

I clear my throat. "You look presentable. I'm sure all your lady fans will scream." Or pass out. I tamp down the urge to impersonate a guppy. But damn.

"Glad you like what you see, Sweet Pea."

His use of Ma's nickname for me reminds me I forgot to let her know I got to the City safely. Which brings me to our last discussion about how she doesn't trust the rock god standing before me. "Don't let it go to your head, Rock Star," I grumble.

"What if it goes to my other head?"

Damn. Now I'm right back in the shower at Secluded Rest. With nothing between us but water. I step backward. "That would be a problem, especially since you're due onstage in twenty minutes."

"I know you could take care of it for me."

"Reset, remember?" Am I reminding him or me? Does it matter?

"Ah, yes." He skirts the table and takes two steps in my direction. I resist the urge to move, so there's barely six inches between us. "I suppose a reset prevents me from reaching out and running the pad of my thumb over your full bottom lip."

I bite said lip.

"A reset most certainly won't allow me to drop my fingers down the front of your shirt to squeeze your delicious boobs. Or nibble on your pebbled nipples."

I cross my arms across my chest.

"A reset—"

I hold up my hand. "Enough. Don't you have a job to get to or something?"

He smirks. "Only wanted to make sure we're on the same page." He steps away from me, and my body sags. Not two seconds later, his palm lands on my back. "Ready?"

How can he look so cool after the heated words that just came out of his mouth? My spine straightens. Two can play his game. "Lead the way." We move through the jumble of people all working to make tonight's concert a success.

Before we leave The Closet, he pulls me into a quiet corner. "If I didn't say so before, I want to thank you for coming on tour with me. I'm fully aware of the cost to you—leaving your family and friends and growing business behind, plus dealing with defamation in the media—and I truly appreciate it."

When he says stuff like this, how can I maintain any righteous anger toward him? I inhale. "You're welcome. For better or worse, you're my patient and I want to guide you through recovery. Are you sure you want me here with UC?"

"Without a doubt." He tips his head. "Are you ready?" He doesn't wait for me to respond, simply enters the relatively quieter backstage area. As I watch, Bennett straightens or expands or somehow grows bigger. His face alters. Before my eyes, he morphs into the lead singer of Untamed Coaster.

Things are much calmer in this room. I tilt my head. "Do you need me?"

"I always need you."

"Not what I meant."

"It's what *I* meant," Bennett says. "I'm going onstage and think it would be smart to have you watch from the wings. See what I do, how I interact with the crowd, so you can make suggestions about how I can do things better."

Damn. Can't argue with his logic. "You make a good case."

"You mean B made sense?" Luke approaches, slapping Bennett on the back.

He shrugs. "Happens sometimes. How's the audience tonight?"

"As good as last night. The opening acts did a great job, but they're clamoring for the real deal."

The other members of the band approach. Río asks, "Who's the real deal?"

"That'd be us," Bennett replies.

Tristan points to himself. "I'm a real deal now? Cool."

The five of them continue in the same vein as I back away. I *am* Bennett's physical therapist, not groupie, manager, or member of the crew. I'm not part of this repartee. My back hits a wall, which steadies me.

From this distance, I observe the band's interactions. Luke is part of the mix, laughing with them, exchanging fist bumps. To the outside world, they seem to be a close-knit group of friends about to embark on a shared experience, as Darren described.

Río pulls Bennett aside, and they have what appears to be an intense conversation—or at least an intimate one. A protracted discussion between friends. They end with bro hugs. If this isn't a sign of friendship, I don't know what is. Bennett needs to understand an ex-best friend from high school isn't the be all and end all.

Suddenly, the air shifts. Becomes charged. The five group members form a circle, raise their fists into the air. Bennett looks at each guy. In a booming voice, he yells, "Strapped, locked, and loaded, are you ready to roll with Untamed Coaster?" The band lets out a collective whoop and turns toward the stage door.

When he reaches it, Bennett's head goes in all directions before he zeroes in on me. His index finger extends toward me, and wiggles. Of their own volition, my feet take me to him. "Have a good time out there," I offer.

"I will, knowing you're here." He points to the black drapes. "See you on the flip side." With that, he disappears onto the darkened stage.

Anticipation among the crowd reaches fevered heights.

Clapping and stomping and whistling reverberates throughout the arena.

I relocate to the side of the stage, on the other side of the black curtain, next to Luke and some others I haven't yet met.

Río pounds his drums three times and the lights flick on, illuminating all five guys at their instruments. Well, four plus Bennett who stands at the mic stand. It's as if the crowd gets permission to lose their minds, because pandemonium ensues. They knew what to expect, yet they were joking and laughing backstage as if they were going to a ball game. My mind can't compute the juxtaposition.

For the first part of the concert, I enjoy the music and interactions with the audience. I also detail how Bennett moves with care, taking turns slowly. He's cautious out there, not that anyone cheering for their favorite musicians would notice the difference. But I do. And I appreciate it.

"They're on fire." Jeb walks up to my side. "I love watching them play. An energy lights up in each one and together they're magic."

"For such a big guy"—I physically turn toward him while keeping an eye on the stage—"you sure do have some amazing observations."

His stomach bounces while he laughs. "How does one preclude the other?"

"You've got me there."

"I wanted to thank you," he continues. "The exercises you sent me are tough, but I know they'll work. I promise to do them twice a day, like you recommended in your email."

"Happy to help. Please let me know if you have any questions or need clarification on any of the moves." I cringe as Bennett takes a turn too fast, winces, then sings while standing in place. After a full chorus, he covers the rest of the catwalk, without any disruption to his gait. If nothing else, his body will dictate how much he can handle.

"I definitely will. Is it all right if I share your exercises with some of my buddies? We all have back pain."

"Of course. Share away!" *I really should examine each one.*

His ask does make me feel all fuzzy inside. Something I haven't felt in a long time, since I was dealing with patients. Darren's death altered my trajectory. I no longer was able to be in the field—I was out of my mind with grief and guilt. The need to be an administrator, opening ten clinics, called out to me. A promise I made to Darren at his grave.

Another man says hi to Jeb, and I'm introduced to him as well as five more guys on the crew. While we're talking, I keep watching the stage to ensure Bennett doesn't do some other careless move. He doesn't. Another woman joins us, introducing herself as Nese Dalton, the band's stylist. She's the one to whom Bennett waved when he got the leather pants.

"I like what you've got them wearing," I note.

She beams. "Thanks. I don't veer too far from their natural styles. Give them a bit of polish, you know."

I nod, watching as Bennett strips off the jacket he was wearing to reveal a plain white tank top beneath. His buff arms make the ladies in the front row squeal. I tamp down the emotions rushing through my body begging to be wrapped in them again.

Never again.

*Reset.*

"So, what's your deal? Are you here to do their makeup?"

"What?" I shake my head.

"I was trying to figure out your role here. The only thing I could come up with is makeup. However, other than some guyliner and powder, which comes off within the first ten minutes of them performing, they don't wear much."

I remember something Darren said. "A makeup crew is brought in for television and photo shoots. Otherwise, they'd be washed out."

Nese's eyes round. "So you are their makeup artist. Sly."

"Actually, no, I'm not." I was never warned not to tell the truth, so I go for broke. "I'm Bennett's physical therapist."

"Huh." We watch him work the crowd, seemingly without a worry in the world. "He's looking strong, so whatever you're doing, I say keep it up."

"Thanks." Because I want to get to know this woman more, perhaps because she's one of the few women on tour, I ask, "How difficult is it overseeing their image? I would think with five strong-willed men, your job resembles herding cats."

"Nailed it!" She laughs. "To be honest, they're not bad. Sometimes I pick out something and a guy'll mutiny. I try not to take it too personally. I simply made a bad choice for him."

"Healthy attitude." I watch Bennett as he does a call and repeat with the audience, swaying in time with the notes. Every time he moves to the right, my breath hitches. I make a mental note to discuss alternative moves with him to better protect his muscle pull.

"Will you tour with us, or are you only here for this show?"

Satisfied Bennett's out of the danger zone, I focus on my new friend. "I'll actually be on tour for the first three months, until Bennett's fully healed." After which I can go back home and concentrate on building my next two clinics.

"Nice. I'm from Georgia, how about you?"

"New York. Long Island, to be precise."

"So this was a natural starting point for you."

"I guess you could say that. How long have you been with UC?"

"This is my first go-round with them." Her answer tells me why I didn't meet her before and why she doesn't know who I am. Or was. To Darren. "I assume you haven't been with the band before either?"

My stomach plummets. I hope she doesn't think badly of me, but I can't see a way out of telling her the truth. I screw up my courage. "Actually, I was with the band a couple of years ago."

"Oh. Who hurt themself back then?" She blinks several times. "Oh. Oh." She plays with her hoop earring. Dropping her voice, she asks, "Are you the Black Widow?"

I flinch, then switch the script on the assholes who gave me this name. "While that's what the media calls me, I prefer Jenna Westfield. I was the physical therapist who helped Darren rehab his wrist —and after he was deemed recovered, we started dating." I extend my hand.

We shake. "I'm sorry for your loss."

Tears prick my eyeballs. She's the first person in years to offer me sincere condolences over losing Darren. I swallow. "Thanks."

On the stage, Bennett roars a guttural note. With fear, I turn to watch what's going on and am rewarded by seeing him leaning backward with the mic held upright. At least this sound wasn't borne out of pain. I sag in relief.

"Oh, this is my cue. They're going to pop backstage for a quick change of clothes before going back out for their encore. I better get into place. It was nice meeting you, Jenna. I look forward to hanging with you."

"I'd like that."

She bolts to a table with the band's change of clothes. A minute later, they bound off the stage. Well, all of them minus Bennett, who takes his steps carefully while stripping off his tank top. His body glistens, begging for my fingers to explore every divot.

To staunch the drool, I focus on the audience before me. They hold up signs I can't read from here while continuing to celebrate UC. It warms my heart to see them welcomed back after their long break. Darren would be proud.

Bennett, now shirtless and dry, smiles at me. Guess he used his tank top as a towel. "Enjoying yourself?"

"I am. You guys are killing it." He's on a performance high, like all the band must be. Having thousands of people adoring you has to unleash rampant endorphins.

"High praise." A crew member hands him a bottle of water, which he opens. His Adam's apple bobs as he drinks the entire thing, some droplets landing on his chest. So much for the makeshift towel. I could offer my tongue as tribute.

"How long's the encore?"

"We do another three songs, ending with 'Crushing Blow.'"

Darren's song. Which, if *Untamed Coaster Unleashed* was accurate, includes some new runs by Tristan. "Oh. Great."

"It's our most difficult song to play, but still so popular. We like to put it at the end to honor Darren."

"I'm sure he's playing along with you all up in heaven."

"That's what we think too." Luke calls for him, and he gives a wave. "Gotta run."

"Walk," I chide.

His hand reaches toward me and I suck in my breath, awaiting our long-denied contact. I'm going to have to wait longer as he drops his arm to his side. "Not wasting my one and only hug when I don't have time to savor it." He stalks toward the band.

My heart hammers.

Working as a *professional* physical therapist to this man is going to be the biggest challenge of my life.

# Chapter Seven

U C's entrance backstage is announced by their fans' screams bouncing off the walls. The band high fives each other. Río exclaims, "That was better than last night!"

"Friday nights always rock," Bennett pronounces.

"They sure do," Luke agrees. "You guys were amazing tonight."

Coop says, "That's because we got our opening night jitters out of the way. I, for one, am ready to party it out. Who's with me?" All of them agree. "Alright, let's get changed and meet back here in thirty. New York City isn't going to know what hit it tonight!"

"Leave the leather pants in The Closet, Bennett," Río admonishes. "We don't want to cause another incident."

"Hey," Bennett fake scowls. "Not my fault." The five of them erupt in laughter, including Bennett, holding his sides.

I'm wondering what that scenario was about when Bennett snaps his fingers in front of my face. "You're joining us." It's a statement, not a question.

I don't want to be in his orbit when the pheromones are flying this high. "I'm kinda tired."

"Oh no, you don't. You can't make me do all those exercises at the ass crack of dawn and refuse to join us for some fun now." He crosses his arms, causing the muscles of his tattooed biceps to bulge over his still naked chest. Which leads downward to the aforementioned leather pants.

My tongue swishes in my mouth. "Noon is not the 'ass crack' of dawn."

"Whatever. Come out with us."

If he doesn't lower his flexing arms soon, I might be forced to climb him like a tree. *Professional.* However, the opportunity to be around a group of people so high on life is appealing. Especially considering the most exciting thing to happen in Aroostook over the past years has been the opening of a new Sephora.

"I suppose one night won't kill me."

He raises his arms in the air, causing his lean torso to dance. "Now it's a party. Stay here, I'm going to change."

Too curious for my own good, I blurt, "What happened with your leather pants and an 'incident' before?"

His hands settle on his waistband. "You need to earn the rights to the story." With a laugh, he disappears toward The Closet.

Nese appears at my side. "Some patient you have there."

"Yeah." As soon as I realize my tone is wistful, I correct myself. "He's a handful."

"My guess is more like two." She pauses a beat, then lets out a huge guffaw, drawing the attention of some of the band members still at the threshold.

"Nese," I chide. "I'm his physical therapist."

After the rest of the guys leave, she says, "Fine. Then you won't mind if I'm his bed warmer for the night." My brows pull together, earning another loud laugh from her. "Just kidding you, Jenna. I wouldn't touch any of the band members with a ten-foot pole."

"Why?" My thought leaps from my mind into the air. "I mean, they're all talented and good-looking."

"*Too* handsome, if you get my meaning. Men like that are too high maintenance for me."

"Says their stylist."

"Which gives me all the insight needed."

"Well, these high maintenance guys are hitting a club in thirty minutes." Nese could provide the buffer I need. I crook my elbow at her. "Want to join us?"

"Us?" Her pierced eyebrow lifts.

"Bennett invited me. Since we haven't had time to discuss the show and how it affected his injury, I agreed. I don't plan on staying longer than an hour."

Her short brown hair bobs. "If I agree, will you let me style you?"

I glance down at my leggings. "Guess I'm not dressed for a club, huh?"

For the third time, she laughs. "C'mon. I'll make us both so hot the band will be panting. Then we can turn them away in favor of some normal guys. These boys need to be brought down to earth."

I giggle. "I like how you think." We walk toward The Closet, her domain. In here, there's a surprising amount of women's clothing, considering the band's all men.

At my question, Nese replies, "Back-up singers."

"All three of them?"

She shrugs. "They have to look good too, you know." After flipping through some hangars, she plucks a little black dress off the rack and holds it up to my body. "This should be good for you. I've got killer boots to match."

I take the garment from her. It's like an oversized scarf, much flashier than the one Court gave me. "I don't know about this. It's so . . . skimpy."

"All the better to taunt Bennett with." She holds up a deep purple fringe dress to her own body. "What do you think?"

"Looks like a cross between Donna Summer and a flapper."

"Then my work here is done." Another one of her hearty laughs ensues.

Now wearing her selected dress, I zip up the boots and stand. She exclaims, "Girl, you look fine."

Self-consciously, I skim my hands over my body. "This is," I search for the right description. "A lot."

Nese smirks. "Or not enough."

My hands race to the zipper on my back. "I don't think I can wear this."

Her hands cover mine. "Of course you can. You have a beautiful body, so show it off. Make the band pant with want. Then dance with someone in the crowd."

She makes it all sound so simple. I suppose it would be, but for Bennett. At the thought of him in those black leather pants, my mind seizes. "I guess I can wear this. I'm only going to be out for an hour anyway."

"That's the spirit." She fluffs her pixie cut and passes me red lipstick. "Here. I think this shade will look perfect on you."

Might as well go all out. In front of a mirror, I put it on, then blot. "How's this?"

"Fantastic. Keep the lipstick. I've been looking for the right person for it. Looks like you're the lucky winner." With a final scan in front of the mirror, she says, "Let's go turn some heads."

Together, we return to the main room, which is about half-filled. Crew members, techies, and roadies mill around Río and Pierce. "Holy shit." This exclamation comes from Río's mouth. Of course.

We pretend not to have heard him and approach the crew, where I'm introduced but know I won't remember a single name. "Don't worry," Nese says. "It took me a while too, but you'll remember their names. Wearing that scarf, they'll certainly remember you."

"Hey. You said it was a trendy dress."

Her palm cuts in front of her face. "My bad."

I don't have time to dissect her comment when the air in the room changes. My head flips from side to side until I land on the culprit. Bennett, now in a pair of ripped jeans, graphic T-shirt, and wet hair. My heart rate picks up.

Nese nudges me. "Yeah. Professional relationship."

"It is," I correct her, all the while my insides rejoice because he's walking directly to me.

*Get it together, Jenna. Professional. Nothing more.*

"Nese. Jenna. Nice to see that you ladies will be joining us."

I can't process much, as the bees inside my body have returned with a vengeance. Nese comes to my rescue. "Did our dresses tell on us?"

Without moving his eyes from mine, he answers, "Kinda the dead giveaway."

From inside the room, Luke's voice booms. "If you're ready to take this party on the road, follow me. Three SUVs out front have our names on them."

Bennett takes my arm and directs me out the door. In my ear, he whispers, "Not a hug. I just don't want you to get lost in the shuffle."

This is how I end up seated between Bennett and Río in the back of a black SUV, with Nese in the row behind us beside Coop and Pierce. Tristan and Luke round out our car, with a woman I haven't met yet seated between them.

I can't concentrate on the rest of the vehicle's occupants, as my mind is entirely focused on the fact Bennett's thigh is plastered against mine. Not like there's much room in here anyway—Río's is against my other one. He's still not wearing a shirt, despite the cold.

To take my mind off the seating arrangement, I say, "So. The call and repeat that you did with the audience tonight."

Bennett nods. "Was off the chain, right? They were screaming so loud back to me."

From behind, Coop whacks Bennett's shoulder. "I don't think I've ever heard them so riled. Am I right, 007?"

"Yup."

No one comments on Pierce's lack of enthusiasm, as Río interjects. "It was fucking awesome!"

From the back row, Tristan adds, "I don't know what it was like for you before, but I've never heard anything like it."

With all five band members talking about the concert, I decide now is not the right time to discuss physical therapy alternatives. I fold my hands in my lap, allowing the conversation to swirl around me. Jibes, laughter, and accolades are bandied around. Even Luke offers his own assessment—they're only going to improve with each gig.

Río gets on his knees and faces the back of the SUV, leaving Bennett and me in sort of a bubble. The lead singer takes another swig from his water bottle. "Were you going to make a comment about the call and repeat, or were you opening up a topic for conversation?"

Damn perceptive man. "I was going to offer you a suggestion."

He cups the ear closest to me. "I'm all ears."

Glancing around, I confirm no one is paying any attention to us. Río and Coop are engaged in a deep discussion about what seems to be a drumbeat, punctuated by laughs from Nese, with the two in the backseat offering their two cents. I can't see or hear Pierce. Maybe if he overhears us discussing Bennett's physical therapy progress, he might believe I'm here for work. Nothing more.

I pluck at the bottom of my dress. Here goes nothing. "I was thinking that instead of taxing your right thigh with the movement you were doing to encourage audience participation, you might do cross-body points with your hands. You'd get the same look, without the possible downside of reinjuring your thigh."

Bennett performs a modified version of my idea from the confines of his seat. "I think I can do that. The old way did hurt," he admits.

I nod. "I saw your cheek twitch, which is one of your tells that you're hiding pain. I know this isn't the best solution, but it should get your point across without involving any twisting motions below the waist."

From his perch above us, Río addresses us. "What's going on below the waist?"

"Nothing, asshole," Bennett shakes his head, although his smile betrays him. For my ears only, he adds, "The night's still young."

Once Río resumes his conversation with the rest of the band, after dropping a "that's what she said" on us, I mutter, "It was an idea I had. We can put more meat on the bones during your PT session tomorrow, if you'd like."

"I appreciate the fact you were thinking about me while I was performing."

"Correction. I was thinking about your rehab and ways not to set it back." Not telling him I was enjoying his show. *Professional.*

"You say tomato, I say tomaaato. Yeah, let's go over this in therapy tomorrow. Which won't happen before noon." He stares at me, his green eyes daring me to object.

I don't. "Sounds good."

Following honking, random switching of lanes, and innumerable stops and starts, we pull up in front of a club with a line around the block. "We're here," Río announces. "Let's go par-tay!"

I don't think I ever had his energy.

The vehicle's doors open and we pour out. Bennett offers me his hand to exit, which I gladly take due to the spikey-heeled boots Nese gave me. As soon as I'm on the sidewalk, though, I pull my hand free. Gentleman that he is, Bennett helps the stylist out as well. I will my heart to stop thundering.

Luke leads us, plus the people from the other SUVs, toward the front doors of the club, much to the shouted delight of the people in line. After all, it's not every day they get to see their favorite band up close and personal. Río and Coop assess the crowd with more than a little interest.

"Guys, c'mon," Luke waves us on. "Let's get you inside."

Elias, head of security, ushers us past bouncers, who appear unfazed by UC coming into their space, despite the raucous cheers from those in line. We're escorted up the stairs into what I believe to be the VIP area, given my past experiences with Darren. Sofas and club chairs are set up around the periphery, allowing for a dance floor in the middle. The room is already three-quarters full, which should give me the ability to slip out in short order.

"Drink?" Bennett mimes holding a glass.

Not one for drinking, I shake my head. At his insistence, I relent, "Pinot."

He nods and disappears behind me, to the bar we passed near the front. Nese wraps her arm around my middle and pulls me over to the group I was introduced to earlier today. It's so loud in here, we can't hear ourselves talk, which suits me fine. I don't have the energy to people right now.

An alcove area, filled with comfy chairs, beckons. "I'm going to grab a seat," I tell Nese, motioning with my chin.

"I'll join you once I get my drink."

With strides as long as the boots will allow, I make my way over to a chair and sink into it. Now comes the fun part—observing people. Those on the VIP dance floor capture my attention first, grooving to the music played by the DJ. As usual, I don't know the artist, but they have a good rhythm and the crowd here seems to like it.

My gaze scans the rest of the room, where some people are hooking up either right out in the open—like Río—while others are in more discreet corners. From my experience, UC has always enjoyed this type of scene. Get drunk, dance, hook up. Rinse and repeat.

Not me. Give me a nice, quiet club where you can carry on a conversation despite the music any day. The rare times Darren took me to a jazz or blues club were my favorites. I sigh. Better prepare myself for these types of places for the next three months. The idea of any of these people going to a blues club is farcical. *Or I could choose to stay on the bus.* Wiser option.

"There you are." Bennett cuts a path toward me, a glass of pinot noir in one hand and a tumbler with something amber in the other. He passes me the wine.

"Thank you. I just needed to get out of the melee for a bit." I get to my booted feet. "Ready to mix and mingle?" Tonight's for him, and I know this is what he wants to do. Besides, I'm outta here in forty-five.

"No. Let's sit."

To my surprise, Bennett sinks into the chair I was occupying.

To my utter distaste, at least three women plop down on the sofa next to him.

Not wanting to fight off the women vying to warm his bed tonight, while he knows it's against his doctor's orders, I move to the side. Women fawn all over him.

Needing a break, I tell him, "I need to use the restroom."

"Hurry back."

As if. I skirt a couple of high-top tables as I zigzag toward the back of the club.

"Hey there, baby. Are you here alone? I could fix that for you." A nice-looking guy stands in my path. He has visible tats on his neck and fingers and a killer smile. Too bad he doesn't have tattooed sleeves like Bennett, or his cheekbones or his wicked green eyes.

*What am I doing?* No comparing my patient to club patrons!

"I'm actually with the band." I wave my hand toward where they are. "Gotta use the restroom."

"Oh." His eyes widen. "Lucky girl." He backs away to let me pass. I guess chivalry isn't totally dead.

My pleasant thought is interrupted when I hear Bennett's voice boom over the music, "Smart move."

I do a quick turn and see Bennett standing next to the nice guy. Who does he think he is? Staking a claim where none is needed because I'm not hooking up with *anyone* until my physical therapy gig is over and I'm away from UC! I give Bennett my evil eye to confirm the guys won't come to fisticuffs, spin on the too-high heel of my boot, and clomp into the bathroom.

When I'm washing my hands, Nese enters. "There you are. Are you having a good time? I saw you speaking with a hottie a minute ago."

This is how rumors begin. "We were like two ships. He let me pass to go to the restroom. Nothing more."

"Then why was big, bad Bennett going all Thor on him?"

I lean against the sink. "Please tell me you're exaggerating."

"Maybe a little." She lets out one of her laughs. "He did go up to the guy, though."

My eyelids close for a second. "You're crazy, you know that Nese?"

"So I've been told." She pulls out her lipstick and grabs a paper towel to blot. "Want to join me in a game of air hockey?"

"I didn't notice a table."

"It's in the back, around the right corner." At my frown, she adds, "Across from here."

"Ah." My feet scream to be relieved of the boots. "Nah, I think I'm going to head back. It's been a long day."

She tosses the paper with a perfect lipstick kiss into the garbage. "We just got here."

"Maybe another time. When I didn't start working for UC that same afternoon."

Her face falls. "Fine. I'll hold you to it."

"Don't worry, our agreement to leaving the club after making a one-hour appearance is void." We bump fists. Guess UC is rubbing off.

At the bathroom door, we separate. Phone in hand, I pull up a rideshare app, but Bennett steals it from my hand. "Hey! Give that back. I was ordering a car."

"Which is why I'm not giving it back to you until I've had my dance."

I squeak. "Dance? What about the ladies on the sofa?"

Without an ounce of recognition, he shrugs. "I only want one dance with my physical therapist. I promise no touching."

"Excuse me?"

"Not wasting my one and only hug in a cramped room filled with too many people. When I call my card, it's going to be you and me. Alone."

My knees almost buckle. What have I started? "I'm not a challenge."

"Never said you were, Sweet Pea. I'm simply telling you the truth."

Damn. "I guess my feet can stand one dance. But no more."

"Understood."

The classic "Love Rules" by Hunte starts to play. The sultry beat, combined with lyrics about how the band's lead singer got together with his wife, plays over the dance floor. In front of me, Bennett sings the words directly in my ear.

It's as if we're the only two people out here. Bennett's gaze caresses me with a hunger I've only experienced in his arms. He doesn't make any quick movements or do anything to hurt his muscle pull. No. He's taking it slow and steady.

Not touching my face, his palms skim the air in front of my cheek. Breaking the barrier, he pushes some of my hair behind my ear, then lets his hand fall down my back. The only way I know this is because I can feel his body heat. He's back to avoiding actually touching me.

Deciding to test his willpower—more out of curiosity than anything else—I raise my hands above my head and move my hips in time with the sexy beat. In front of me, Bennett growls and takes a step back. I twirl around, giving him a good view of my backside, unleashing my inner bad girl. The one who let this man play me with his fingers not once, but twice. The woman who sucked him off in the shower. For one more moment, I want to be her.

Only with this man.

I twist my head around, taking in the gorgeous rocker behind me. Long and lithe with muscles begging to be licked. I turn to the other side, still keeping my back to him.

"No, no, no," he admonishes. "You're not going to trick me into wasting my one and done."

Standing in front of him now, I chide, "You know how good it could be."

"Which is why I'm not wasting it in a room filled with strangers."

"You know Luke. And Río. And Coop, Tristan, even Pierce."

"Not gonna happen." He closes all but one inch of the gap between us. In my ear, he whispers, "I will, however, take this opportunity to kiss and bite and nip down your body with these." He wiggles his fingers. "Only they won't touch you."

He demonstrates what he means, running his hands up and down my body—half a finger distance away. In response, my breathing picks up. I jut my chest toward his hands, in a blind offering. One he traces from a millimeter away.

My core clenches. It doesn't care we're in the middle of a dance floor in New York City. If it could, my core would tackle Bennett to the floor right here and now. I bite my lip to keep from inviting him.

The song comes to a climax as Bennett's hands drift lower, almost giving my weeping core what she wants. But not quite. My entire body pulses with need at the spell he's created around me.

Hunte belts out the final note as Bennett's face approaches mine. My mouth drops open, waiting for his kiss to destroy me. It never comes.

"Next time," he husks. "When we're alone, I'll give you a proper embrace." He waits a beat. "Maybe."

I can't compute his words, too caught up in the air he blew into my ear. How his teeth clamp down on my lobe.

Oh wait. That's not him—it's my own fingers tugging on my borrowed earring. My face radiates heat. Little pants beg for more.

"Crap, guys. I need a shower after that display."

Luke's taunting words refocus me. I take one look at the man in front of me and bolt out of the club.

# Chapter Eight

I remain as long as I can in my hotel room, embarrassed over what happened last night. Who was that woman dancing with UC's lead singer? Perhaps she should've worn a sign proclaiming she works for the band around her neck. Or on her forehead.

With all the determination in the world. I pack up my tools of the trade and leave to meet Bennett in the gym. Physical therapy. Something I went to school for and know enough about to mentor up to forty therapists once my third and fourth clinics open. This, I can do.

In the gym, men and women are on the various machines. No one pays me any attention as I commandeer an empty side room. Perfect for therapy.

Quiet. Peaceful. Out of the way.

We need to talk about what happened on the dance floor. Or maybe not? Why do we? *Because you're running scared and giving him mixed signals.* I sigh, setting up the various stations around the room.

Bennett enters the quiet room in a pair of shorts and a tank top.

Of course he's wearing another tank top. All the better to taunt me with. "Hi, Jenna." He walks over to the third exercise station.

"Hey." I point toward the first station. "Why don't you start here?"

"I'm feeling this exercise. I'd prefer to do this one first."

Is he challenging me in order to be obstinate? "There's a reason for my procedure," I explain. "We need to warm up the muscles in a certain order."

"All of these exercises work the same muscle group."

My hands fly to my hips. "It'll work better if you start with this one."

He raises his hands. "Not trying to pick a fight here. We'll do it your way." He adjusts his trajectory and begins his therapy. Why can't the man simply listen to me the first time?

I offer him slight corrections, but for the most part, he's got a great handle on things. When I pick up the bands, he eyes them skeptically. After I go over the positives of using them and demonstrate how to use them in a couple of exercises, he relents.

"Damn." He wipes sweat off his brow with the back of his hand. "These are tougher than I anticipated."

"They're good for you." I bring him over to do skater leaps, encouraging him to add a small jump to the steps he's been doing. Hesitation is written all over his face. "Let me show you again," I offer.

With measured steps, I do the exercise. My leap, if you could call it that, is akin to a glorified hop. If he can start adding these to his rotation, it'll build up more muscle around the pull. Not going to force him, however.

He leans over into the proper position and does them with a step.

"Good job. Now try to add in a slight little baby jump."

His mouth pulls in concentration. He adds a step-hop to the next one and I clap. "You did it! Good job!"

Bennett grins. "I did it? I really did it?"

"You did! Next time, feel free to add an even bigger jump. Not too much. I don't want you overtaxing that muscle."

He nods and repeats the exercise with little jumps. After ten times, I call it. "Great! You don't want to overdo it. What's your pain meter?"

He rises to his full height, his six-foot-two body towering over my five-foot-six-inch frame. "I'd give it about a five."

"Six," I correct. "Not too bad."

He glances around for a table to end his session. "Should I lie down on the floor?"

"If you don't mind. You could go into the main gym area, but I think that would cause more of a stir."

"True." He swipes his bottle of water and glugs down about half. "Good session today. Surprisingly, I liked the bands."

"Which you balked at," I remind him, starting to massage his thigh. His muscular thigh. Attached to his extremely fit body. While his external appearance is off the charts, it's what's inside that's truly sexy. All he's overcome.

Dare I get lost in another rock star's life? What will happen to everything I've built over these past years? No. I simply can't allow myself to get lost in him and the messy world of UC again.

Finishing his massage—during which he's been blessedly quiet—I busy myself with the next order of business, ice. When the ice pack is in place, I walk through the room, collecting the therapy items. All the weights and bands and towels soon are piled near the door.

He pats the floor next to him. "Sit."

Because I don't have anything left to do, I fold my legs and sit next to him. By next, I mean about three feet.

"You really like being in control, don't you?"

His question catches me off guard. "Nothing wrong with control."

"I agree. I mean, if I didn't take the reins, who would for the band? Guess it takes one to recognize it in another."

Silence extends.

When I can't take it any longer, I say, "There's a reason why I like things in a certain order. For your exercises, we were taught to take them one by one because each builds upon the prior one."

"Makes sense." His fingers play with the ice pack before dropping them to the floor. "Like last night?"

Oh God, don't make me go back there. When I lost my inhibitions on the dance floor with him, and I can't even blame alcohol. "What about it?"

"You were letting loose. Enjoying yourself." I shake my head, but he interjects. "Don't bother lying to me. I was there, remember?"

"Hard to forget," I mutter.

He chuckles. "Damn straight. I saw it the moment it happened. When you realized you were having fun and getting lost in the music. A second before you bolted."

No escaping this conversation. My shoulders lower. "You have to understand something about me, Bennett." I glance away from his too-handsome face. "I'm responsible not only for Darren's death, but my grandmother's too. When I don't keep a tight lid on everything, it all spins out of control. You know what happened with Darren."

"He overdosed. You weren't responsible."

"I knew he was taking Oxy."

"Did you pour the alcohol down his throat?" I shake my head. "Make him take several pills throughout the day and night?"

A tear falls. "*No*. But I was on the phone with him the night he" —My lips purse.

"He was a grown man. He made his own choices." Bennett throws the ice pack to the side. "Listen, he was a ticking time bomb. It was bound to happen. None of us were aware, or even able, to stop it." He tilts my chin. "Not even you."

"That's not what happened with my grandmother."

His arms go next to his hips, and he leans his weight onto them. "Tell me about her."

I close my eyes and begin sharing all the happy times we enjoyed together. All the baking we did when I was little. How she was diagnosed with breast cancer when I was seven. I gaze into his understanding green eyes. "When that happened, I took it upon myself to ensure she went to every appointment, including chemo and radiation, and made sure she took all her medicine."

"Cancer is a bitch."

"Yeah. But that's not what happened. Well, it did, but not then." My lips close.

Bennett chuckles. "You can't leave me hanging like this. What happened to your Grandma?"

I look to the side, my fingers playing with the scrunchie at the back of my head. "She got a clean bill of health. I'm positive my daily visits helped her." I drop my arms into my lap. "Once she was healthy, my visits became more sporadic. First I skipped a day, then a few days. Eventually I went to her house only once a week."

"I'm sure you had lots of things going on at school. You were exploring the big world. I'm sure your Grandma understood. She probably even wanted that for you as you grew up." He reaches out as if to run his palm down my arm, but his hand drops to the floor before making contact.

I stare at his large hand. Without raising my gaze, I say, "Three years later her cancer came back with a fury. She died the next year. All because I didn't keep visiting her daily to make sure she was taking her meds." My fingers cover my tear-stained face.

I can't stop from flinging myself into Bennett's arms, where he pulls me against his chest. He rubs my back in a soothing manner and I unravel against his hard torso. "Her death wasn't your fault either. I'm sure you were her bright light." He continues with circular motions. "I can picture you—all of ten years old, in pigtails—fussing over her. Baking cookies. Bringing light into her life."

"I still failed."

"Hate to break it to you." He kisses the top of my head. "No one gets out of this life alive."

Which brings us right back to Darren. I cry for Grandma. When those tears slow, new ones fall for my ex-boyfriend. "It wasn't his fault."

"He had a disease."

I nod against his chest. "One he caught because of me." There. I said it out loud for the very first time. My absolute guilt.

Bennett's hands close around my shoulders and he pulls me up to face him. "You're wrong. You didn't cause Darren to become an addict."

I swallow. "I encouraged him to take the pills to help his recovery. He didn't want to."

"Why did you do that?"

"Because the doctor prescribed them, and I knew he wanted to get back on tour as fast as possible. He needed his wrist to play the keyboards. Oxy made rehab more tolerable. Wrist injuries are extremely painful, you know."

"A groin pull is no walk in the park either."

My head shakes. "No, it isn't." Heat flames on my cheeks. "Yet here you are working your way through therapy without the help of any drugs."

"Because of Darren." He scoots away, leaving me unanchored. "I saw what happened to him and don't want that fate for myself, although—unlike him—if I took his route out, no one would be left to mourn me."

"You're wrong." I get to my knees. "Your mother, the band, your manager, your fans. They all would be bereft." I scoot over to be in front of him.

Bennett shrugs. "He also had his mother and sister. And you." His index finger traces my tear-stained cheek. "All people who loved and grieved over him. I wouldn't have any of you. I guess this makes me more selfish than he was." He clasps his hands in his lap. "I did suspect, you know."

I can't even begin to parse his confession, so I latch onto his final statement. "You suspected what?"

"That he was getting addicted. I didn't insert myself into his private life to question him, though. It wasn't my place. I figured he'd kick the habit when he was ready. I didn't imagine it would kick him instead." His body tenses.

"You're not a doctor. You couldn't have known."

"And you are?"

"I was his physical therapist. I should've seen the warning signs." My gaze darts to the man before me. "Medicine can help a patient heal and bring pain level down to manageable levels. That's all I wanted for him." I yank my ponytail holder out of my hair.

"I was with him twenty-four seven. You weren't. I could see his behavior changes—not to mention how his pupils constricted when he was high." At my gasp, he adds, "He was good. He hid it really well. But I could tell, and I did nothing."

I whisper, "How?"

"My mother has been on various prescription medications throughout my life. Taught me some signs. I wondered." He shakes his head. "Again. Not my place."

"He was your friend." The words are out of my mouth before I realize my mistake. Bennett doesn't do "friends." I rush ahead. "If you had confronted him, what do you think would've been the outcome?"

"I don't know. Hopefully he would've gotten treatment."

"If I had known, I would've insisted he go to rehab. Maybe he'd still be here."

This answer is unknowable. If he were still here, would I be with him now? Life with Darren was exciting because he was larger than life, yet we were very different people. He told me he was drawn to my down-to-earth practicality—but when he died, I was already starting to understand how incompatible our lives were. I mean, a therapist and a rock star, really?

I glance at the man in front of me—another rock star. But with Bennett, things are different. He's a different man who speaks to me on a deeper level. Not merely on the physical, which has been beyond any of my experience. He's hiding some painful scars.

"Why was your mother on medications?"

Bennett's long eyelashes blink several times. "It's a long story."

I glance at the clock on my phone. "We have time."

"I don't talk about her."

"I know." My phone rings, and I quickly send Ma to voicemail. I'll call her back. What Bennett's opening up to me about is important.

He watches my movements but doesn't comment. "My mother's always been delicate, as Dad used to say."

"Delicate? How?"

His shoulders raise then fall. "Mentally. I understand she became increasingly unstable when they had trouble conceiving."

I reach out and grab his hand. "But you're here now."

"Yes." He squeezes my fingers. "That's the problem." He stares at our entwined hands. "They went to extreme measures to conceive and finally succeeded with IVF." He takes a deep breath. "Mom became pregnant with me. And my twin."

My mind puzzles at his response. I don't remember hearing Bennett having a sibling. I keep my lips shut.

He continues, "As happens often with IVF, she lost my sister early. I survived."

"I don't know too much about pregnancy, but how far along was she to know she miscarried a girl?"

"She was only a few weeks in. There's no way to know the gender. The only reason I call it a girl is because that's how Mom refers to my twin."

My palm covers my gasp. "That's terrible."

"Whenever we speak, there is the invariable sentence that begins, 'If you'd let your sister live' or, if she's being more charitable, 'If your sister were here.'"

How could any mother say such a thing to her only surviving child? Obviously, Bennett's said she isn't in her right mind. I can't process the pain he must carry with him because of her. Without thinking, I crawl the remaining distance and wrap my arms around his broad chest. "I can't imagine. It wasn't your fault."

His arms rise and clamp down over mine. "Like the deaths of your grandmother and Darren weren't yours."

Heat seeps into my body, from the front and the back. Both my cheek, pressed against his hard pec, and his arms wound tightly around my back, welcome his comfort. I hope my body comforts him in the same way.

I remember his comment about Darren's drug use. "Is your mother getting help?"

His chest expands against me. But for being pressed against him, I might not have noticed. "She is."

"Your father's gone, right?"

"He died when I was seventeen. A few weeks before I joined UC."

No wonder I feel a kinship with the lead singer. We've both known death. I handle mine by controlling my environment. He chooses to remain an outsider looking in on his life. I squeeze him tighter.

"I'm so sorry you've had to go through all this," I tell him. Still on my knees, I adjust my weight.

He brushes hair away from my cheek. "You've had it rougher than anyone else I know."

I gaze into his green eyes, the color of leaves after a rainstorm. "Except for you."

"This doesn't count, you know. You started it."

My head tilts, my chin brushing against his shoulder. Confusion runs through my veins until it hits me. I pull away, all the while craving his warmth. "I'll let you off the hook. This time. You still have one hug left."

His smile carries with it a hint of sadness. "I plan on collecting, but not now."

*Not when we're so raw* I supply. "Do you want to talk any more about all of this?"

He shakes his head. "I've had more than enough for now. You?"

"Same." I rock to my feet and stand. "See you at sound check?"

"Don't you know it."

I return to my room, all the while wondering which one of us is looking forward to the evening's gig more—him for the screaming fans, or me, to watch over my patient.

Or is there a third option I never considered—where we both help the other heal?

# Chapter Nine

From the backstage wings, my gaze follows Bennett as he makes his way across the stage. Not with his prior running from side to side, but still covering ground at a faster clip than I'd prefer. My lips purse.

"What's he doing wrong out there?" Luke nudges my side. "He's looking pretty good from where I stand."

"He's pushing it," I reply without taking my gaze off the lead singer.

"I'm sure he knows his limitations."

"Bennett's amped on adrenaline. When he clears the stage, I predict he's not going to be feeling quite so euphoric."

Silent, we watch the band perform for another half song. "B's cut it back quite a bit. My guess is the fans close to the stage think he's spending more time with them." Bennett's arms flap like wings, riling up the crowds. "They're loving it."

"I'm probably being too cautious. I don't want to see him reinjure himself and have to use a cane." Although I can picture him using a cool one ending with a handle in the shape of Untamed Coaster's logo. "He'd probably make that look sexy too."

Luke chuckles. "Figure that out already?"

As if. The man is sexy personified. "Still, I'd be happy for his rehab not to go backwards."

"I'm sure B would agree with you on that score. How *is* our patient coming along?"

"He's doing most of the exercises without too much problem. Can't quite do the jumps, but that's to be expected so soon after the injury."

"How much longer will he be doing therapy, do you think?"

"The doctor prescribed three months. This time period includes weaning him off from twice a day to once daily, then dropping down to every other day. I'm thinking he'll be ready to step down to once a day in a week or two."

"Great. I'm going to need him for interviews and radio shows starting after Philly. When we're in the City of Brotherly Love, though, I've arranged for the whole band to visit Darren's mother and sister since they declined tickets to the show. Understandable."

My stomach twists. How bad would it look if I don't visit the Hilliards? We always put a shiny face on things when Darren was alive, despite the tension between us, but now—especially after the article—I refuse to go near them.

*Proceed with caution.* I dip my big toe. "I think I'll leave the visit to the band." At this moment, my phone vibrates. Using the universal symbol for wait a moment, I check the screen to see Ma's face. Even though I want to talk with her, since we haven't had a chance to connect yet, given the overwhelming sound being produced by Untamed Coaster from the stage, I decline the call. I send her a quick text, saying it's too loud at the concert and I'll call her in the morning. I return my attention to Luke. "Where were we?"

"You were about to tell me the true deal between you and Darren's family."

I tip my chin toward the band. *Doubt it.* "Not much to tell. Darren's not here any longer and I was his last girlfriend. I'm an easy mark for their ire."

"That's fucked up. You had nothing to do with his death."

Luke's the second person to tell me this today. Not to mention the discussions with my own therapist. Guess if I hear it another hundred times, I may consider the possibility. But I'm not there yet. I seek comfort in my usual response. "I was his physical therapist. I should've recognized the signs."

"Well, I was their manager when it happened. Think I should be on the hook as well?"

I face away from the stage. "What? No. Don't be silly."

"By your logic, the entire band should be indicted and put into prison for aiding and abetting."

I move my body toward the stage again. "That's dumb."

"So is blaming yourself. Or letting his family do that to you. Maybe if you get together with them, you can settle the air? Prevent terrible stories like the recent one from coming out?"

I sigh. "His family never liked me, Luke. After all, I was a mere add-on to his glamorous lifestyle. Darren always overlooked it, but I could tell they wanted me gone from his life. When they got their wish, but not in the manner they'd hoped for, let's just say it was a less-than-amicable break."

"I didn't realize things between you were so strained."

Returning to face the stage, where Bennett's leaning toward the fans in the front rows, "It's best if you go without me."

He rubs his chin. "Perhaps." Off to the side, Kieron chats with a man who has his back to me. "Chico and Kieron," the manager notes. "Our longtime guitar tech seems to be working well with the new hire."

"I remember Chico working with the band." Taking my time, I observe the pair. "Must be difficult for Kieron to come into an already established unit."

Luke's shoulder rises. "It can be. UC tends to form a bond among the band, techs, roadies, and crew. We understand why Chico had to leave now—after all, he's going to be a father soon—and we're hoping this transition is smooth."

My chin bobs. "Understandable." My focus switches from Kieron to Bennett, whose stride appears steady. "I know Darren used to think of you all as a huge family."

"Huge and dysfunctional," he corrects, with a grin. "I'm not sure I would still be here but for how fantastic it is to hang with these guys. The band is tight, and I feel honored to be their brother. Which was cemented when Darren died." He eyes me with caution.

"The band definitely closed ranks when it happened."

"Yeah. I can't imagine going through such, uh, sadness, with any other group of guys. From that moment onward, we became even tighter. Some managers would've let the band members sort out their feelings alone, but UC invited me into their inner circle. It was rough going from then to where we are today." His chin juts toward the stage. "We pulled through. Even brought Tris into the fold."

My gaze switches from Bennett at the mic to the band's new keyboardist. My heart bleeds at watching a new man play keys, but Tristan adds his own flair to their songs in a much more demure way than Darren did. Still effective. "They're more subdued since Darren—"

"Yeah." Luke shifts his weight between his feet. "There's less laughter now, more true support and love for each other. We've been through hell, as have you, and we've come out of it closer."

I absorb what he's telling me. "So you're all closer than friends?"

"With the exception of Tris, who's melding in great, we're closer than most brothers."

Not for my sake, I push, "You and Bennett?"

His grin stretches. "The band's manager and lead singer make quite the pair, don't you think? He's my closest friend."

My heart grows for them. I just need Bennett to understand it. "You're both lucky."

We watch UC perform for half a song. "Can you believe it? They're already gearing up for their encore. Better make sure every-thing's ready for them. Catch you later."

I wave and Luke disappears into the blackness. How can I help

Bennett accept the love from his bandmates and manager? Get over his feelings of failure toward Darren? Deal with the awful things his own mother spewed at him? All the while allowing him to heal all my wounds? I choke out a laugh. We make quite the pair—ahem, non-couple.

Before the last song's over, Nese appears with arms overloaded. I spring forward. "Here. Let me help." I grab the towels from beneath her arm.

"You dry. I'll dress."

We're giggling when the band rushes off the stage, already stripping out of their wet shirts. I pass a towel to Coop, "Here you go." The guitarist smiles as he opens the towel.

Next up is Tristan. I hand the terrycloth to him. He takes it with an "Appreciate it."

An already shirtless Río snaps it out of my hand, saying, "Don't mind if I do."

The bassist approaches me, eyeing the towel as if I put itching powder on it. I extend my arm toward him. "Here you go."

Pierce's gaze bounces between me and the towel, sweat overcoming his dislike of me. "Thanks," he mumbles. He can't get out of my space fast enough.

Bennett's the final member of the band to approach me. Damn man is shirtless and dripping from either the water bottle I caught him dumping over his head or performing under the lights. Or both. I offer him the last towel. "Here you go."

He licks his lips. It's all I can do to keep my traitorous body from rubbing all over his wet one, savoring all the ridges of his hard muscles. Opening his arms wide, he says, "Care to help me out?"

"What? No." I scrunch it up and shove the towel at his ripped midsection. "Dry your own damn self."

He chuckles and does as instructed, ending by rubbing it over his head so his hair spikes in all directions. Nese walks over and hands him a new shirt, for which he thanks her. The asshat has manners when he wants to use them.

"Enjoying the show?" Bennet slides his clean shirt over his torso, eliminating my view of his muscle-laden chest.

"It's been amazing," I admit. "How's your leg feeling?"

"Pretty good." He punches his thigh. "Barely any discomfort at all."

Luke yells, "All right, guys. One minute before you close down fucking Madison Square Garden!"

The other members of UC, except for Pierce, whoop it up. Bennett turns his head and adds, "Hell yes!" In the corner, Darren's best friend fiddles with his belt.

Seems like my presence isn't welcomed by the whole band, although I'm not about to intrude on Bennett's high. I will, however, remind him to watch his injury. "Try not to do too many side-to-side motions."

The lead singer salutes me. "Yes, boss."

"B, get your ass over here!"

"Coming!" Full lips blow a kiss in my direction before he takes off to Luke.

"That seemed cozy." Nese sidles up to my side, still holding the band members' wet clothing.

I play it off. "It's only Bennett. You know how he can be."

Her pixie cut bounces around her head. "I've only seen him in action for like a week. Do tell, how *can* he be?"

I wave my hand. "He's a cocky flirt. Thinks he's God's gift."

Her pierced eyebrow lifts. "Do you agree?"

"What? No! I'm his physical therapist, remember?"

The band runs onstage, with Bennett bringing up the rear. Which works, considering he's the lead singer and naturally would receive final billing. He greets the crowd again, "Hey there, New York City! You're still here?"

The audience laughs and cheers.

"Since that's the case, think we should play another song or two? What do you say Río?"

From behind the drums, Río's response is a drum roll punctuated by three cymbal crashes.

Bennett throws his head back and laughs. "What Río wants, he gets, right ladies and gentlemen?"

In the middle of the stage, Bennett points to the guitarist. "Do you agree, Coop?" The guitar riff is prompt, echoed by Pierce's bass.

"Nice way to answer my unasked question, 007!"

Bennett strides over to the keys. "My new man here, Tris, are you up for playing a little bit more?"

The new keyboardist, who sports more than a five o'clock shadow, smiles. "Sure am!"

Bennett executes a three-sixty, causing me to inhale. When he takes a steady step, I exhale. "Then I guess we have no option but for you all to *Take a Ride with Us!*" UC launches into their recent number one, a hard ballad about love and longing and wishes for the future.

"I like how he did that," Nese remarks.

My brain short-circuited when Bennett executed his controlled spin. "Did what?"

"Introduce the entire band without making it so obvious. It seemed rather natural." Her loud laugh would be heard across the room but for the fact the music drowns it out. "As intimate as a conversation among twenty thousand people can be."

The number boggles the mind. "You definitely have a point. There's no way on earth I could get in front of that many people."

"You and me both, sister. It takes a special person."

Bennett makes it all seem so easy. He crisscrosses the stage, trying to reach every single concertgoer. Even with his groin pull, he puts on a physical show. Unlike Tristan and Río, who are stuck behind their instruments, Bennett's out front. Coop and Pierce move more freely —and they do, sometimes back-to-back with each other. Other times, like now, Bennett strolls over to Coop as he wails on the guitar.

I note, "They make it look so easy."

Nese stays by me until the end of the song. "Well, I better go take care of these wet clothes. Are you coming out with us tonight?"

It's been a long day, filled with too many confessions. I need to regroup, rejigger my anti-Bennett armor, and prepare for tomorrow's trip down to Philadelphia. "Not tonight. I'm beat."

"You know where to find me if you change your mind." Nese disappears behind the black curtains.

Within minutes, the concert draws to a close. From the ceiling, balloons fall. Bennett's silky voice attacks the last notes. His fist raises into the air while the rest of the band hits their final notes.

Bennett's wild out there. Uncontrollable. His entire frame lowers as if he's about to jump high in the air. "Don't do it."

Time stands still.

So does my breath.

I will him to keep both feet on the stage.

At the last moment, he punches the air and the song ends.

My entire body sags in relief. His muscle isn't ready for such a leap, even if he's feeling no pain at the moment. Adrenaline and all.

I watch as the guys come together in the middle of the stage and bow. The audience is wild, screaming and clapping for their idols. I don't blame them. The band was next level tonight.

Following more waves, they exit and return backstage. Once again, a wall of amped-up testosterone precedes their actual bodies. They're laughing and fist-bumping. Río and Bennett seem to be in deep conversation, which I observe from afar. The way Río leans in toward Bennett, punches his shoulder, and throws his head back speaks louder than words. Without a doubt, Río believes they're friends. If not good friends.

This interaction, plus my conversation with Luke earlier, leads me to believe Bennett's absolutely wrong. The band is a tight-knit group of friends.

I'm drawn to watch Coop, Tristan, and Pierce. As with Río and Bennett, they also high-five. Tristan even puts Pierce in a headlock, which surprises me. If they can accept the quote-unquote new guy—

especially Darren's best friend—my belief in their friendship with Bennett is cemented.

I trail UC into The Closet, where Nese stands at the ready to hand out after-party attire. Eyes shining, Bennett approaches me. "Come out with us."

"Not tonight. We have a big day tomorrow, between therapy and traveling to Philly. I need to get some rest."

"Sleep is overrated."

He strips off his second wet T-shirt. Trying to maintain some degree of propriety, I turn my head. Only to see Río across the room in only his underwear. Next to him, Coop's stripping off his shirt while Tristan's pulling a clean one over his head. Are all these men exhibitionists? I spin in Bennett's direction. His hand is at the fly of his leather pants.

My eyes climb to the ceiling. "Geez. Are all of you not shy?"

Bennett laughs. "It's usually only us guys getting changed, and we've seen it all." His hands drop to his thighs. "With you and Nese around, though, perhaps we should be more careful." He walks away from me. From the center of the room, he announces, "Guys. There are ladies in here. Maybe we shouldn't strip?"

Río's "Yeah, right!" comes hard on the heels of Luke's, "Good luck with that."

Bennett raises his hands. "Only a suggestion."

Damn if the man doesn't lower his zipper. My cheeks become hot, and I spin to offer him my back.

In my ear, a tenor whispers, "Nothing you haven't seen before."

"Mistake," I strangle out. "Never again." I manage to say this over my body's begging to turn around and wrestle him to the floor. His deep chuckle flies through every bone in my body.

After a minute, Bennett announces, "You can turn around. I'm decent again."

I suck in air and turn toward him. His long legs are now covered in a pair of dark jeans with holes strategically placed. This man could make a garbage bag look good.

"Do I meet with your approval?"

My eyelids close.

"You sure do meet mine. Did anyone tell you how sexy you look in that outfit?"

Hardly. I'm in a pair of black jeans and simple top. My hand skims my hips. With my gaze locked on the floor, I reply, "Ma gave me these for my birthday."

Because I'm staring at the floor, I can see his boots take a step closer. "I like them. But I like you more."

My chest rises and falls. "You can't keep saying this stuff to me." I count the scuffs on the tile floor.

"I'm only saying the truth." When I don't move, he shuffles closer. "Another truth is I'd prefer to see those jeans on my bedroom floor. And then I'd like to take off your panties with my teeth. Caress your—"

I raise my hand. "Stop." My head pops up, only to realize he's less than a foot away. "You can't do this. We can't do this."

"Maybe it's exactly what we should do. No one has ever made me feel like you do, Jenna. You hear me, and not only the notes I sing in front of thousands. No one knows about my mother. How she treats me. No. One. Else. And you don't judge me on it."

This poor, beautiful man who's only known hardness and abandonment is being vulnerable to me in a sea of humanity. He's so loved, if only he could accept it. From Luke. Río. The other guys as well.

"I'm impressed by what you've overcome."

Big green eyes blink, masking his embarrassment and pain.

No matter how many times I tell him—and myself—we're in a strictly professional relationship, this moment feels different.

My entire being calls out for him. It's a physical yearning.

It doesn't matter that all of UC is right around us. I can't stop myself.

I launch my body at him, wrapping him in a big embrace and kissing his hurts away.

With no hesitation, his arms close around my waist.

I'm lost in the battles he's fought and lost and won and is still fighting. Our mouths meld. Our tongues duel. He's offering me the same sort of comfort that I'm giving him. It's intoxicating.

A flash goes off behind my eyelids.

Noise intrudes from outside my bubble where only Bennett and I exist.

Luke's angry voice yells.

Bennett breaks our kiss. Forehead to mine, he murmurs, "I *still* didn't hug you first."

# Chapter Ten

My alarm goes off, waking me out of a deep sleep I only fell into perhaps three hours ago. I need more sleep. And tea. Lots of tea.

After Bennett kissed me last night—whoa, if I'm being honest, *I* started it—all hell broke loose. Luke kicked the paparazzi out of The Closet. A new member of the Garden's security team confessed to letting them enter, thinking it was routine protocol. The whole incident has been labeled a misunderstanding between the Garden and UC.

In the melee, I slipped out and hopped into a cab to the hotel, where I've hidden out ever since. Ignored knocks on my door. I'm aware of Bennett's upcoming physical therapy session, but it's not in the hotel. This morning, we'll be doing it on his tour bus as we travel down to Philadelphia. Thankfully it's only a short ride—can't deal with the possibility of riding on his bus overnight right now.

I've beaten myself up a million times over initiating the kiss last night. Bennett's story simply speaks to me on such a deep level. He's been through hell. Is still going through it. I jolt upright realizing he may consider me to be the closest person to him.

All this is compounded by the fact that he sees my warts and doesn't judge me for them. The way he held me when I confessed my deepest truths over my guilt about my grandmother's death. And Darren's. He understands me. This realization makes me fall even harder for this amazing man.

The need to help him overcome more than his groin pull almost drags me down. To make him understand he is loved by the band. Show him through my own parental relationship that other mothers don't treat their children the way his has.

As if I conjured her, my phone rings. "Hi, Ma."

"Jenna, so good to actually hear your voice. I know you only are starting with Untamed Coaster, but how are things going?"

I can only hope this means the reporters haven't published anything about our kiss last night. Our *very* inappropriate kiss. Bennett could charm underwear off a nun, I swear.

Grinning, I reply, "It's good. I've been working with Bennett and he's doing well, although I'm worried he's going to mess up his progress with how he moves around onstage. Other than that, I'm enjoying meeting the crew and the massive amount of people working behind the scenes to put on an Untamed Coaster concert. I'd forgotten how many are involved."

"I can only imagine. Have you made any new friends?" I tell her about Nese, and the process of replacing Chico with Kieron as the guitar tech. When she asks, "How's the press treating you?" I know she's buried the lede.

"How bad is it?" I Google Bennett's name and am rewarded with a full page of different views of our kiss last night. The headline "Black Widow Strikes Again!" says it all. I bang my head against the padded headboard as I create a protective bubble around the beauty of that moment.

Ma doesn't say anything, merely lets me process. A minute later, I say, "I hate the media."

"Can't imagine why."

Her sarcasm isn't lost on me. "I know you don't approve of

Bennett, but it's not what it seems. Yes, I gave him a kiss last night after his show, but it was more of a 'you can do it' encouragement." Actually, more like we were swept up in the concert high.

"From the *other* photos, it looks to me he's perfectly capable of bringing all of Madison Square Garden to their feet."

"Well, true." I play with my hair, which is messy around my head. "It's more personal stuff. Things he shared with me that I can't repeat, not even to you. It's his story to tell. Just know he's not led a perfect life like you might expect. And he has valid reasons for distancing himself from his mother."

"I'll take your word for it, Jenna. However, the media's turning this into a circus. I'm not sure how the banks will appreciate their investment being portrayed as a rock star groupie."

My shoulders slump. "I'm most certainly not a groupie. I'm a licensed physical therapist on tour for a reason, which is to get the lead singer healthy again."

"Maybe you need to tell the reporters this. And stop kissing your patient."

Her words hit their mark. "I wasn't kissing-kissing him, Ma." My lips were only covering his and my body stuck to his like glue. I pull up one of the photos. Hell, we shouldn't have done this in public.

Or in private.

"I'll speak with Luke, UC's manager. He'll get the PR team on it, to make this disappear." He better be able to. Of course, if I were able to keep my hands off Bennett, none of this would've happened. "Other than having your younger daughter's face plastered over the internet, how are you doing?"

"I'm fine." I can almost see her cheeks puff. She's always so positive, which makes this criticism all the more difficult to swallow. "Not much to complain about. Your sister won another award for anesthesiology, which is also being covered in today's newspapers."

"That's great. Pass along my congratulations to Kara."

"Will do. Oh, and Michelle is telling everyone in town that Bennett came on to her, saying you're getting her sloppy seconds.

Again." Over the phone, I hear something rip. She probably opened sweetener for her morning tea.

I roll my eyes. "Joy." I shove the blankets down my thighs. "Untrue on every level." Placing my feet on the floor, I stand. "Well, I should get ready to start the day. We're driving down to Philly and UC's going to visit with Darren's family."

"Oh," she rasps. "Are you joining them?"

I need to shut down the hopeful tone in her voice. Given how much she loved Darren, she's always wanted us to be something we'll never be—friends. "Bennett and Luke both invited me, but no. You know how things were between us—I think it's for the best that I stay behind. I'll give therapy to Bennett on the drive down and he can go with the band. I'll either explore Philadelphia or figure out strategies for his therapy while they're away. I'm planning for him to drop down to one daily therapy session soon."

She sighs. I wait for her to push me to visit Darren's family, but she finally says, "Sounds good. Have a safe trip and don't forget to text me."

After we sign off, I stand in front of the bathroom mirror. I'm paler than normal. Great. I take a lengthy bath to relax—newsflash: it doesn't work—and tie a towel around my body. When I glance at my phone, a new text has arrived.

COURT

You didn't even leave NYC before making headlines!

None of which are true

Didn't think they were but, OMG, that kiss! 😶

Not what it seemed.

My gut prompts me to admit my last response to her is a lie. I know it. Bennett knows it. Court probably knows it. How to convince the public it was only a friendly kiss? I shrug into my comfy work attire and head downstairs to the bustling restaurant, where I'm directed to UC's table in its own private room.

*Oh, great.* Pierce is the only other person in here. He glances up when I enter. "Hi," I say. "Do you prefer I eat breakfast in a different area of the restaurant?" *Or in a different state.*

He glances into the main restaurant. "You can stay."

From the tone of his voice, it feels as if he's making a huge concession. While I want to sit as far away from him as possible, I go up to the buffet and fill my plate about half full, then select an empty chair next to him. Smoothing the napkin across my lap, I say, "Thanks. I was dreading going out into the general population."

His cheeks inflate at my oblique reference to prison. "Perhaps staying with me might change your mind."

My trembling fingers pause in picking up my knife. With determination, I cut some butter and put it on my mini croissant. "I think I'll chance it," I reply with a bravado I don't feel.

Pierce's talented finger skims the rim of his coffee mug. "I see you've moved on to Bennett."

Of course he waited until *after* I'd taken a bite of my croissant to dump this on me. My gaze goes to his face. Instead of skewering me with vitriol, he's looking into his murky brew. I swallow while composing my response.

"Pierce, we both know I'm on tour with UC to give Bennett the physical therapy he needs to heal his injury."

"He seemed pretty damn good out on stage the past couple of nights." His fingers leave the coffee mug and he picks up a pastry.

"That's because he's using some coping skills I've taught him as well as avoiding making certain movements. You haven't seen him run across the stage, have you?"

His brows furrow. "No."

"Spin around?"

"No." They draw together deeper.

"When he's not performing, do you see him limp?"

He drops the half-eaten pastry onto the plate. "Sometimes."

I nod. "That's why I'm here." I still should address what the media captured last night. "He's shared some personal things with me, and last night's"—how should I put this?—"brief kiss was a way for me to encourage his growth. The photographers blew it out of proportion. Like they do."

He repeats, "Like they do."

We sit in silence, neither one of us daring to move.

Pierce is the first to break. "Good. Because I wouldn't think you could move on from Darren so fast. And with his bandmate, no less."

The bandmate comment I get, but fast? It's been two years. Pursing my lips to refrain from poking the bear any further, I take another bite of my croissant. Which tastes like sandpaper. Seeing as he needs some sort of validation, I nod in his direction.

Our awkward encounter is broken when Nese and some of the other crew bound into the room. Noise levels rise, silverware clanks against plates, liquids are poured. Nese sits next to me and I exhale. Forcing a smile, I ask, "How was last night?"

"Oh, it was amazing." She digs into scrambled eggs. "You should've been there. We were out dancing until three."

When I was tossing and turning in my bed. Maybe she's right. If I had gone, at least I wouldn't have wallowed all night. I finish my croissant. "Who was out that late?"

She giggles. "All of us. We're night owls—we'll make you one too. Touring does that to your circadian rhythm. Give us a few more days and you won't be seeing single digits on your clock ever again."

Even when I was with Darren, I always kept my work schedule. To be fair, I was usually only out with him one or two nights in a row. After a show, we were horizontal more than vertical. Although he never made me feel the way Bennett has. Once again, heat rises up my neck.

Nese nudges my torso. "I can see you're on board with this idea."

Not about to share my thoughts about Bennett, especially with Pierce at my side, I dig into my fruit salad. Conversation swirls around me, but I don't partake. When Tristan, Coop, and Río enter, some of the crew members give them their seats so they're now surrounding Pierce. Grabbing my quiet cell, I point as if someone's calling and flee the room.

Into the restaurant proper.

Too many eyes track my movements as I force myself to walk at a normal pace toward the exit. I take a deep breath when I leave, only to have my pulse ramp right back up as Bennett and Luke turn the corner.

"Jenna," Luke greets me. "Just the woman I wanted to see." The two men approach. Bennett remains unusually quiet. "B and I were talking, and we'd like for you to join us on our field trip to visit Darren's family."

"No."

The manager's hand lifts. "Now hear me out. It would be good publicity for you. And B. And UC, to be honest. Show some solidarity in light of the, let's say, challenging headlines from this morning."

"About them," I lick my lips. "Can you make them go away?"

"We've tried, but there are too many of them. The best way to combat their effectiveness is with a counter punch. Right, B?"

"Seems like it."

Why is Bennett being so quiet? He's never quiet. Maybe he hates this idea as much as I do? Holding onto this thought, I reply, "No. I'm not going. Believe me, it would make for a bad scene."

Bennett adjusts his stance. "I'll stay behind too."

Luke looks between us as if we were playing tennis. "No. B, you *must* be there. Jenna, while I can't control what you do, please reconsider."

I shake my head. "I won't. I would only make it uncomfortable for all of you and ruin the visit. Bennett, though, you should go."

The lead singer crosses his arms across his large chest.

Luke sighs. "Fine. But you will be coming, B. Like we discussed, Tris won't be going, but the original members of the band need to be there." The manager glances between us. "I'm going in for breakfast." Then he disappears.

"I hate leaving you behind."

Cognizant of possible eyes and ears lapping up our conversation, I place my index finger over my lips. "Not here."

Bennett's face swivels around. Grabbing my hand, he drags me through a door marked "Employees Only." We walk down a hallway and enter what I presume to be an empty break room since it has a coffee machine, a microwave, vending machines, plus some tables.

He begins, "I don't want to see the Hilliards. What do I have to say to them? Darren's no longer with us and I've moved on to mackin' out with his girlfriend?"

"Don't say it like that." I realize what he said and stomp my foot. "We're not 'mackin' out' You were friends"—I stop and correct my descriptor—"bandmates until the day Darren died. You wrote songs together, rode fame all the way to the top, won Grammys for UC. You shared a lot of happy memories. I'm sure they want to reminisce about the good times."

"I don't have to be there for that. 007 does."

"It seems to me it would be cathartic for all of you. Tristan too. He's never met them before, right?"

"No."

"How about this? You go eat breakfast, we do PT as the bus takes us down to Philadelphia, and UC can decide as a whole who should go visit the Hilliards." I run my fingers over a small cocktail paper napkin. "Band members only. I just can't."

"This right here is the reason I want you to come. Or we both should stay back."

"Bennett." I gaze into his green eyes, willing myself not to get lost. "This visit may help you all heal. The movie took you a long way, I saw it even from the audience. Being back on top also gave you a boost. It's okay for you to miss a, uh, colleague. I had a very different relationship with him and his family. I don't want to be the reason your good visit goes sour."

"I could talk you up."

A small laugh escapes. "I think the less you say about me, the better. My only worry is how you—as a band and singularly—are going to deal with the 'Black Widow' headlines." This right here is the only reason I should accompany him. So we can get to the bottom of it. *No.*

"If you come with us, you can sort it all out." He runs a finger down my cheek, causing me to suppress a shudder. "I hear you about the rocky relationship you had with his family. This might be a chance to correct it."

"To say what? I had a great time with your son, but now that he's gone, I need to stay close with UC, so I picked the lead singer. But don't worry, the replacement keyboardist is totally off limits."

"Wow." His finger tucks some of my hair behind my ear. I need to put it in a ponytail before our physical therapy session. "Guilt recognizes itself."

His thoughts about not picking up on Darren's drug use resurface. I offer a half-smile. "Yeah. Guess it does."

His eyes close and our foreheads touch. "I understand why you want to stay away. I'll keep you company."

His woodsy scent assails my nose. I shake my head, rocking my forehead against his. "No. You have a different relationship with them. Besides," I pull back, "one of us needs to defend our honor. Defuse the situation the media's portraying."

His eyelids raise with a slow pulse. "That we're together?" He glances downward. "I'm not touching you."

My eyes widen as I realize only our foreheads are in contact. "And you won't again." It takes all my concentration to take a step away from his intoxicating scent. "You straighten them out. I'll stay behind and work on your next round of therapy."

"Remember, Jenna, this wasn't my choice. But I'll do it for you."

He steps toward me, a wicked glint in his eye. "I think I should get two hugs out of this deal, though."

I bring my two index fingers together, making the sign of the cross. "Oh no, no, no. One hug. That was our agreement."

"Your demand," Bennett corrects. "I can wait to collect." He disappears down the hallway while I gather my scattered thoughts. How can this man make me forget everything, including my name, without even touching me?

*I'm in so much trouble.*

# Chapter Eleven

Turns out, all of the guys except Tristan left to visit Darren's mother and sister about thirty minutes ago. I'm in no mood to socialize with Nese or the other crew members or roadies. Nor do I want to talk with Ma or even Court. Better I keep my own bad company.

Inside Bennett's bus where we did our morning therapy session, I sit then stand. He's doing so much better than I expected. He'll probably be able to drop down to one session a day sooner than I had predicted. At least there's that.

I pace the bus, which isn't small by any means. It's not big enough, either. Maybe it's the fact the guys are visiting Darren's family, or the reality of touring with UC again, I have a sudden need to talk with my former boyfriend. I slip out of the bus, which is parked in the back of the stadium that will host the concert tonight. Using my all-access pass, I enter backstage and find myself standing on the stage, behind his keyboard.

I stare at the instrument Darren used to adore. In my mind's eye, I picture him playing in front of a massive crowd. My feet move forward until I'm so close I can touch the keys. I reach out but my hand falls to my side.

"Darren," I begin. "I loved you. You drew me into your life and opened my eyes to crazy experiences. I will always remember our time together with wonder." I lift my arm again, but it lowers. "I'm not sure, though, what I brought into your life except maybe a remembered sense of normalcy. With Bennett, it's different. He's been hurt deeply, which I understand more than you know. Because we never talked about my grandmother. You never shared about your addiction either."

I take a step backward. Now's not the time for recriminations. I've made peace with nearly all this with the help of my therapist. It was his life's path, not my responsibility. I advance to the keyboard again and my fingers lay atop the keys. "I owe you for introducing me to the vibrant colors of your world. I loved you, but I know it's time for me to let someone else into my heart. You'll be a part of me forever."

I gently press down and a light sound is produced. Tears flowing, Darren surrounds me in the place he adored. His fingers envelop mine, skimming over the ivory and black keys. I whisper, "I want to let Bennett into my life. Give me a sign. Please."

My heart jolts as if it were squeezed from within.

As if Darren kissed it.

He gave me his blessing.

"Thank you." My eyes continue to leak.

Behind me, someone says, "Jenna."

Half expecting Darren to have materialized behind me, I turn and am greeted by another tall guy, this time with the beginnings of a five o'clock shadow even though it's not even two. I swipe my cheeks. "Hi, Tristan."

He joins me at the keyboard. "The guys all went to visit Darren's family. I thought you went with them."

"Nah." I can't let my answer hang out to dry, so I add, "It would be way too weird." At his nod, I say, "Didn't you want to meet them?"

He mimics my response. "Nah. It would be way too weird." He shoves his hands into his back pockets, friendship bracelet pushing up his arm. "Do you play?"

"Huh?" I press one final key and shake my head. "No. It was Darren's thing. And now, the keyboard is yours." I allow Darren's approval to permeate my being and change places with the new keyboardist, who plays a melody I've never heard.

"Something I'm messing around with," he says, his neck tinged a light red.

"I like it." The band did well with their choice. Tristan's very talented.

After listening to him practice a couple of UC songs, ones I can hear Darren play with him, we leave the stage. As we enter the parking lot, I ask, "How do you like playing with Untamed Coaster?"

"They're great. I love performing on such a big stage with fans screaming our lyrics back to us. That's amazing. And UC's letting me test out my chops with writing. I appreciate everything they've done for me."

Seems to me there's a lot more behind his answer. "Is this your first stadium tour?"

"Hell, yes." He turns his head toward me. "Sorry. Didn't mean to curse."

"I appreciate it, but it's not like I've never heard the word 'hell' before." I elbow his stomach. Which is quite hard. Must be a requirement that all the members of the band be shredded. "Kidding. Feel free to speak as you normally would around me."

"Thanks. Momma would have my scalp if she heard me curse around a lady."

I stop walking and do a full turn around the parking lot. "I don't see any ladies here, so your secret's safe with me." It's hard to believe such a polite, well-bred guy has joined up with the rowdier men I know in UC.

"'Preciate it. So, you and Bennett, huh?"

"Go right to the heart of it, why don't you, Mr. Polite?"

Tristan's hands return to his back pockets. "Sorry. Last night's story's been plastered all over the internet, adding to the others from a week or so ago." He stares at the pavement. "It's none of my business."

He's right. It isn't. But talking it out with someone who never knew me with Darren is inviting. "It's fine. Hard to avoid." We walk in an oversized figure eight among four empty parking spots. "I met, rather examined, Bennett when he hurt himself at the end of the movie premiere. His doctor prescribed physical therapy and since I was a known quantity to the band, he came to my clinic. We're not together." Did I add this last part for him or me?

"How's our lead singer healing?"

"Good. He should basically be good to go in another week. The doctor wants him to continue therapy for three months, until he's fully healed." I lean closer to his frame. "Probably for liability reasons more than medical."

"Your secret's safe with me."

We both grin at the fact he's reusing my phrase. Tristan bends down and picks up a rock, tossing it across the lot. "So you two aren't dating? Or is it a fake relationship for the media's benefit?"

My protest rises without thought. "We're not dating. I'm his physical therapist." I continue walking and realize he stopped. When he catches up with me, I add, "It's unethical for a therapist to date her patient."

Tristan nods. "So if some other guy wanted to sweep you off your feet, you'd be open?"

Is he hitting on me? "Well, it wouldn't be against any ethical rules."

"I know. I wasn't asking for myself," he hurries to clarify. "I've heard things around the crew and wanted to see if I could help you out before things got out of hand."

My feet stop. This man, whom I've only barely met, is incredible. "You're looking out for me?"

He shrugs. "You're practically family. Wanted to make sure nothing bad happens to you."

The fact he's taking a big brother protector role over me makes tears tickle the back of my eyes. Again. Only a couple of days into the tour and I'm turning into a watering pot. I blink several times. "You have to be the sweetest man I've ever met."

His hands return to his back pockets. "Momma raised me right."

"She sure did." After a few steps, I add, "If you could dissuade anyone from pursuing me, that would be most appreciated. I'm not here to find a man." *Bennett checks all my boxes.* "It was a hard decision for me to come tour with UC again, but the fact the doctor prescribed Bennett's therapy tipped the balance. I've been working with him since his injury and want to see him back to one hundred percent."

"I applaud you, Jenna. Stepping back into this world after everything that happened with Darren."

"Yeah, well. The same could be said about you. Here you are, actually replacing him on the keys. I admire you, Tristan."

"It's been a long road, but I do finally feel as if we're jelling together as a band."

"I know." I grin. "I saw the movie."

"It's all out there, thanks to Quinn Walker. You remind me of her. Smart, talented, and you don't take any shit." He pauses. "Stuff."

"I try not to." Don't know how successful I am, however, given the way the media's calling me Black Widow. "Are things really as relaxed among you and the band as you make it seem?"

"Mostly," he replies. "Our struggles nowadays are about business and music things. I feel as if I've been accepted into UC by the original members. I make sure not to rock the boat."

"I get it. Please do me a favor, though. Be yourself in all your Mr. Polite glory. Don't let the rest of them take that away from you."

His white teeth glint in the sunlight. I follow their rays to his ears, where holes for earrings rest. I've never seen earrings in them. "You have pierced ears?"

Fingers cover both ears. "Yeah. I like how they look, but they're Coop's thing."

"So? Nese's eyebrow is pierced."

"Well, true."

"All the guys have tattoos, some more than others. I bet there are piercings you don't know about." Nor do I want to find out.

"I don't want to encroach on Coop."

He doesn't elaborate and I don't push. He'll come clean with the guys when he's ready. Why he's hiding this piece of himself baffles me, but it's his secret to share. Guess he takes polite to a whole new level.

A black limo pulls into the parking lot. "Looks like they're back."

I straighten my shoulders. I hope Darren's mother didn't badmouth me from here to kingdom come, but Darren's support from the stage buoys me. Walking and chatting with Tristan was a wonderful diversion, but now that they're back, my stomach churns with the unknown.

When the doors open, Luke leads the group out of the vehicle. Pierce is the first to say anything, and it's directed at Tristan. "Hey there. Want to play some hoops?" He points to the back, toward the roadies' buses.

"Sure thing." Under his breath, he asks, "Will you be all right?"

Tristan's concern for me overshadows the ruckus in my stomach. "I will, Mr. Polite. Go, have a great time." He takes a step away. "Wait!" He looks at me and I kiss his cheek. "Thanks for a great afternoon."

His hand covers where I bussed him. "Any time." He jogs to meet up with Pierce, Coop, and Rio.

Luke and Bennett are in deep conversation by the entrance to the lead singer's bus. Instead of intruding, I aim my feet toward my own bus. I could use some alone time to process before our late afternoon therapy session.

Unfortunately, Bennett has other ideas. I'm not ten feet away before he yells, "Jenna. Hold up."

Am I ready to face him and hear what Darren's mother said? Fight off my attraction to the too-sexy man whose kisses—and more —bounce in my mind? With Darren's consent, can I do this? My feet stall and I spin to see Bennett walking toward me at an even gait.

"Hey there. Have a nice afternoon with Tris?"

Not the opening line I expected, but I go with it. "I did, actually. He's a really nice guy. I'm happy you all chose him to replace Darren. He has mad skills, true, but he also brings an even pace to the band. I like him."

"He's good people. I feel like what you see is what you get with him. I appreciate his honesty."

When he doesn't say anything more, I decide to jump right into the deep end. "How was your visit?"

"It was good. Sad. She's still mourning her son's loss, as I expect she'll do for the rest of her life. His sister was there too and they're picking up the pieces and moving on. His mother wants to start a music scholarship in Darren's name."

My eyebrows go up. "This is a great idea. I'm sure Darren would've loved it."

"Yeah. Me too. Luke's going to take care of it from our end. We hope to have it ready to go by the end of the tour."

In about a year. "Sounds good."

Under his breath, he mumbles, "Still not hugging you," right before he grabs my hand. "Momma Hilliard also gave me stern advice to stay away from you. Said you'll only bring discord to the band."

Because my breath is shallow, I whisper, "What did you say?"

Bennett takes my other hand. "I told her that you're my physical therapist. Reminded her of the fantastic job you did with Darren, rehabbing his wrist, and that you're helping me heal." He squeezes and a shock only he can give me races through my arms. "I also told her to ignore the magazines. You're no more of a black widow than any of us for not noticing Darren's addiction."

My breathing accelerates with his every confession. Not to

mention his acceptance of his non-role in Darren's overdose. "How did she take it?"

"Marni, his sister," at my nod he continues, "Scolded their mother, saying she was being unfair."

The fact his sister defended me fills me with warmth. I nod, my gaze glued to our joined hands. "Still. His mother wants me gone."

"No."

My head bounces upward.

"Luke explained your role, while Coop said you're a steadying influence on me." He smirks. "Río added that you elevate the whole crew, and he's happy you're back with the band."

"I can't believe it." I take his words in. "What did Pierce say?"

He squeezes my hands again. "Even 007 refused to badmouth you the way Darren's mother wanted. Not going to lie, our bassist isn't your biggest fan, but he did say you know physical therapy."

Much more than I could have hoped for, especially after our interaction at breakfast. "Wow."

"So you see, we're all happy you're here. With us. On tour. No matter what our former bandmate's mother says. I also think her days of talking with the press are over."

"I can't thank you enough for everything you said to her. I've never been her favorite person."

"She had some choice words for me about you." Still holding both my hands, his knees bend so we're eye-to-eye. "I'm not letting her get between us, Jenna. What we have needs to be explored."

His declaration worms into my heart. The way he defended me to Darren's mother proves he has so much love to give. After everything that happened onstage with Darren, I realize I need to be the one to unleash it.

He waits for me to process everything. I offer his hands a tentative squeeze. "I agree."

Green eyes become wider. "Let's go inside my bus. What I want to do to you isn't fit for public consumption."

I trail him up the stairs. I'm tired of fighting him.

Others.

Myself.

He's awakened something within me I didn't even know was there. The fact he's my patient doesn't mean a thing anymore. With Darren's blessing, I'm finally ready to let loose.

He uses his body to push me against the refrigerator. With only a few inches between us, he asks, "Can I hug you now?"

I close my eyes. "Yes."

A growl emanates from him, more compelling than anything he rumbles on stage. "This is it, Jenna. You and me. I'm not going to be able to hold back."

I gaze into his green eyes, which have taken on a deeper hue. "You're not healed."

"Fuck that. I'm healed enough for this."

His lips crash down on mine, stealing my breath and all of my thoughts. He wraps his arms around my body, pressing his entire body into mine so his growing hardness juts into my stomach. His tongue traces my lips, seeking entrance into my mouth. Which I give him.

Because he's the man who defends and supports and heals me. As I hope I do him. In this moment, I'm all his.

My hands snake around his neck as I melt into his long, lithe body. We kiss like this for seconds, minutes, hours. Days. Time becomes meaningless.

Bennett breaks away from me, both of us gasping for air. He doesn't wait more than a couple of beats before kissing down my throat, lingering on the spot where my neck meets my shoulder.

"You smell of bourbon and vanilla."

I drop my head onto the wall. "It's my perfume."

He sniffs. "Plus something uniquely Jenna you can't get from a bottle. A hint of perfection."

His description makes my knees weak. But for the fact I'm holding onto him, I'd be a puddle on the floor. I interlace my fingers around his neck and absorb his own unique woodsy scent. "I'm hardly perfect."

"Maybe you are to me."

He recaptures my lips, his tongue immediately dancing with mine. More. I want more of this man. My hands slide down his torso to the bottom of his shirt, which I pull up. Our kiss breaks only to rid him of the offending material, then his naked torso presses into mine again.

My fingers skim his muscled arms, reveling in his defined shoulders. Needing air, I break us apart and stare at the way his chest rises and falls rapidly. How his tattoos dance on his muscular arms. I'm doing this to Bennett. Me. A mere physical therapist from Long Island. Which brings me to the reason I'm here. "How's the thigh?"

"Given all the blood flow to it, the muscle pull is at a zero. My groin, however, is hurting."

Mentally, I give his pain level a two. As for his perceived injury, I'm sure he's not feeling any pain there. I cup his junk. "This hurts?"

I'm rewarded by another growl. "You could use your magic on it." He does a slow blink. "To make it feel all better."

My fingers tighten around his expanding appendage, causing him to suck in his breath. "Sounds painful," I murmur. I tighten around him again.

In a whirl of motion, he steps away from me, yanks my shirt over my head and discards my bra. Then, he grabs my hand and directs me toward the back bedroom. Over his shoulder, he says, ' But for my stupid injury, I'd have you in my arms right now as I carried you to the bed. Better yet, I'd have picked you up and wrapped your legs around my waist as I navigated to any flat surface so I could get inside of you sooner. So, you see, I am making concessions."

A giggle bubbles up. "Your physical therapist appreciates it." A second later I step into the bedroom, both of us half naked and breathing hard.

Bennett pushes hair away from my face. "Damn. The things I want to do to you, Jenna. I want to make you scream *my* name so loud the people all the way in New Jersey will hear you. I want to make you forget *your own* name. I want to make you unable to remember anyone else who's ever been inside you."

My head spins at his words. When he closes the gap between us, I whimper. He doesn't waste a second, rather devours my mouth while his fingers knead both breasts. With one, he circles my nipple while the other squeezes my entire B-cup. With the right bra, though, I can almost be a C-cup. The way he focuses on them makes me feel like I have double-Ds.

"Bennett," I breathe. My next words are lost as he drops his lips to replace his fingers playing with my pebbled nipple. He takes it between his teeth and nips, shooting streaks of desire directly to my core.

It's harder and harder for me to stand on my own two feet. "Ah!"

I'm rewarded by a growly chuckle. In the time it takes for him to move from one breast to the other, he murmurs, "You're getting there. But you still know your name." He latches onto the twin and repeats his same moves. Sparks of desire intensify.

Not one to be outdone, my fingers undo the button at his fly. With as much care as I can muster given my raging passion, I pull the zipper downward with an electrifying zip.

"Two can play this game, Sweetheart." He tugs my leggings down my legs, leaving me in only my panties. "Open your legs for me."

I'm unable to do anything more than follow his directions. His left knee insinuates itself between my open thighs and pulls me upward, leaving me under his control. While he nibbles on my right breast, his jean-covered thigh pumps forward and backward.

My heartbeat increases. I want him naked. Hell, I want to shred my own panties. At this moment, though, I can't articulate any of it. I'm completely at his mercy. I glance at his face on my breast. I need to see his eyes. "Bennett."

Blown-out pupils rise to meet my gaze. "Damn. You can still talk."

He pulls his left knee up higher so only my toes are on the floor, then he rubs against me at the perfect spot. Can I come from this stimulation alone? I emit a low moan.

"Better."

I give myself over to Bennett, trusting him to give me what I need. His mouth covers my ear, into which he exhales. I tip my head to allow him better access while my lower half has no purchase to support my weight. No—it's all on him.

I glance down at his thigh, which now sports a rather large wet spot. From me. While I know I should be embarrassed, I'm not. He's turned me on more than ever.

He bites my nipple again. "Come for me."

I buck on his thigh, my core clenching around nothing. My head shakes. With a breathy whimper, I tell him, "I can't."

"From the stain on my jeans, I think you can." His thigh pushes against me, rougher than before. One hand returns to my breast while his lips cover mine again. Tongue deep in my mouth, he continues to play my body as if it were made for him.

Out of nowhere, an orgasm crashes over me. I cry out something unintelligible, not caring where I am or who could possibly hear me. Bennett continues his movements as I come down off the lust-induced high.

He doesn't allow me to recover for more than a minute. My feet are under me briefly before he ushers me to the side of bed, where my legs make contact. "Give me your panties."

I can't process, simply react to his command. One leg lifts, then the other, and I pass him the soaked bit of lace. He lifts it to his nose and inhales, then stuffs them into his back pocket. His hands come to my shoulders and push me downward, directing my butt to contact the soft mattress.

"Up you go."

He joins me on the bed as I urge my body up toward the head-board. A pillow is shoved beneath my butt and his fingers part my wet core. "You're driving me insane."

"Good," he replies. "I'm going to do that again right now."

He leans down. His tongue plays with my clit the way he was French kissing me not long ago. Up one side and down the other, causing my hips to buck.

"Yes!" At my exclamation, he continues but I want more. "I need you," I wail.

Bennett pulls back. "Do you need this?" One long finger enters me, around which I clench.

"More." Since when have I ever been this demanding? Only with Bennett. No one else.

"Will this do?" A second finger joins the first.

I undulate in time with his movements, begging for more. "I need—"

Whatever I was going to say is cut off when his thumb encircles my clit. He's sitting up, watching my every reaction.

Learning.

Gauging.

Adjusting.

It's as if he was created to bring me pleasure.

My hips circle, greedy for everything this man offers. When his free hand lands on my nipple and he pinches, I skyrocket out of the bedroom.

Bennett wears a smug smile. Meeting his gaze, he says, "Two."

I let all my weight rest on my elbows. "What are you doing to me?"

"Fulfilling my promise." His palm lands between my breasts. "Lie down. I'm going to make things even better."

Better? Any better and I'll be dead. My protest dies on my lips when his mouth covers my core, his tongue repeating what it was doing earlier. Only now, my clit is overstimulated. My head thrashes against the pillows. "No, Bennett."

He chuckles. "Before, you were begging me for more. Now's not the time to change your mind, Sweetheart."

He laps my sex again and something shifts deep within me. I jump from overstimulated to needy. "Yes!"

"That's more like it." His tongue dances around my clit while his fingers slip inside.

For want of something to hold onto, my own fingers grasp my nipples, twisting. My actions heighten those Bennett's creating within me. His gaze drifts up to lock on my own.

I've never felt anything remotely like this. Green eyes staring at me while his mouth and fingers own my entire lower half. His tongue presses against my clit and—as if I were on a roller coaster—I crest the peak and barrel down the long slope into blinding ecstasy, screaming all the way. When his fingers pull out of my body and he sits straight, I melt, boneless, into the bed. Watch as he licks himself clean.

Then, Bennett shifts to one side and reaches into his back pocket, presumably for a condom. Wrong. He pulls out my panties, which he brings to his nose, rubbing his finger over the material. "They're still wet." He licks the piece of lace. "I love how wet you get for me."

Mind. Blown. I try to rearrange my disjoined thoughts to form a coherent sentence. Or even a phrase. I come out with, "Taste you."

Using my panties, he outlines his dick. "All yours, Sweetheart."

Still unable to command my limbs, I direct him to remove his jeans. Standing at the foot of the bed, he takes his time to shuck his open jeans, pausing to remove his wallet. With his hands on the waistband of his black boxer briefs, he asks, "These too?"

"Yes. Now." Why is it taking him forever to get naked?

His sexy grin tells me he's doing this on purpose. Drawing it out to prolong the encounter. "Because you asked so nicely," he slides his underwear down his long legs.

Standing at the foot of the bed, his erection juts outward, highlighting both its size and need for me. I scramble to my knees and move to meet him. Licking my finger, I trace the protruding vein from root to leaking tip. He adjusts his stance.

My mouth waters. I want to give him at least as much pleasure as he gave me—three times. Slurping his essence, my lips encircle him.

His hips pump as his palm lands on the back of my head.

Following his direction, I suck him as far into my mouth as possible, rotating my hand at the base.

"Damn," he pants. "Don't stop."

I continue giving him head and soon he's no longer thrusting, rather rocking into my mouth. Owning Bennett Hardy the way he owned me turns me into a previously unknown wild woman.

"I'm close."

His warning spurs me to draw him harder, deeper, tighter. With an anguished yell, he pumps several times and spills into my mouth. I swallow every drop, then sit back onto my heels, a wide grin overtaking my face.

Something's off.

He's projecting both pleasure and pain.

I understand the pleasure. The pain dawns on me after a few heart-pounding moments. "Shit!" I'm off the bed and running to the kitchenette in an instant.

By the time I return to the bedroom, Bennett's sitting on the rumpled bed, his right leg outstretched. I place the ice pack on his thigh. "How bad?"

"Like a seven," he responds through clenched teeth. His hand clasps mine. "Worth every fucking ounce of pain."

Leaving our hands entwined, I crawl into the bed and snuggle against his left side. His arm covers me. "I'm so sorry. We shouldn't have done this."

"Jenna, yes we should have. The things you make me feel are amazing. I want to share the slightest hint of my pleasure." He traces my fingers.

All the reasons this is wrong—we're wrong—override my previous positivity. His groin pull. The doctor's order not to have sex for another week. My ethical prohibition. Ma's animosity.

A strangled sound twists from my soul.

# Chapter Twelve

"Shh," Bennett croons. "Talk to me." His arm secures me at his side, not allowing me to move an inch.

Keeping my eyes closed, I ask, "Is the ice helping?"

His chin bumps my head as he nods. "Do you want to hear what's helping me more?" I remain silent, so he plows forward. "You. How you see me as a person, not just the lead singer of UC. You want me as a woman wants a man."

This man, naked, holding me in place, is getting under my skin so deeply I toss all caution to the wind, no longer caring about ethical rules. "I've never done this before."

"What? Get so caught up in passion you don't care about anything or anyone other than sharing our bodies like an unending encore?"

I half-smile. Into his ripped chest, I admit, "Sort of." Sucking in air, I disengage from the cocoon he's wrapped me in. "You make me lose control."

"Who needs that anyway?" My face remains neutral, so he continues, "We're different, you and me. You crave order and rules while I do my best to avoid them."

"It's more than that. You thrive in chaos, while I wilt."

"Hey." He tilts my chin. "I've heard we can do all things in moderation. Some rules are good. Some disarray can lead to an exciting adventure. You don't have to be as buttoned up as you have been. I also don't have to flout authority at every turn."

"That's simply how we're wired, Bennett."

"My point exactly." His lips cover mine in a soft kiss. "Guess what? It's okay for us to be a little different than we have been." His shoulder rises. "Well, I kinda like making my own rules, but I know I should stick to at least some of the ones the powers above me hand down."

"I can't imagine anyone being the boss of you."

"Well, the label likes to think they can plot out my life. The PR team prefers I color within their lines as well." Two fingers rub over his nose. "The meeting today gave me pause."

I don't want to rehash what Darren's mother spewed. "Because of the warning she issued?"

He doesn't have to ask to which "she" I'm referring. "No." He brings me against his chest again. "Because of the scholarship we're going to set up. I want to make this succeed. In order for that to happen, I'll need to follow the rules."

"That you will. It's for a good cause."

"Wanna know what else is for a good cause? You letting go sometimes. I promise to be the one to catch you if your safety net disappears, but I doubt it'll come to that."

I shake my head. "I don't know—I thrive in structure."

"Because of all the bad things that have happened in your life. Your grandmother and Darren both dying before they should have. You crave control over the uncontrollable, I get it. I just don't want rules to suffocate you and keep you from having fun and letting your hair down a little bit."

I force my lips to tip upward. "Like with you?"

His eyebrows bounce. "I wouldn't say no."

My hand finds the ice pack. "See. This is why there are rules,

Bennett. The doctor told you not to have sex for another week and look what happened when you broke his rule. You got up to a level nine."

"Seven," he corrects. *Riiight*. His palm lands over mine. "Worth it. Besides, we didn't violate his rule. We didn't have sex."

I roll my eyes. "I had three orgasms. You had one. I'd say we had sex."

The gleam in his green eyes is unmistakable. "Were they good orgasms?"

I punch his shoulder. "You know they were."

"Good isn't great."

"Fine. They were great orgasms. Better?"

"But—mind-blowing, earth-shattering, body-melting orgasms?"

My phone rings.

I hold up my finger. "Don't get too carried away there, Rock Star. Not all parts were involved."

As I send Ma's call to voicemail, he gives a single word reply. "Yet." He pauses. "Telemarketer?"

"Nope. Ma. I couldn't answer her while we're both naked and talking about orgasms."

"And she's smart, too!" He kisses me again, as if I earned a reward. "Call her back later. When you're dressed in a parka."

I shake my head. This man is incorrigible. From out of nowhere, a yawn overtakes my entire being.

"Nap time," Bennett declares. "I don't care if it's midday, there's a rule that you have to sleep when your body requires it. We both know how much you adore rules."

"Oh there is such a rule, is there? I've never heard this one before."

He nods his head. "Definitely. I heard it from a grey-haired sleep doctor on late night television. Haven't you ever watched him?"

I giggle. "No, can't say I've ever heard of him. What station?"

"All of them. He's a frequent guest on the late-night shows, don't you know. The crew loves him because he encourages them to get more sleep." He opens his mouth and yawns. I'm sure it's a fake. "Now it's our turn to listen to the old doctor."

I can't resist this playful side of Bennett, so I force myself into work mode. Standing, I put the ice pack back into the freezer. When I return to the bedroom, the next thing I know, I'm horizontal. Muscular arms anchor me against an amazing man. My head tips back. "Thank you, Bennett. You knew I was ready to bolt, but you didn't let me."

"From now on, I'm not going to let you escape due to some crazy thoughts in your head. You've got me for the long haul, Jenna Westfield."

I kiss his chest. God help me, but I like the sound of this.

---

"Good job with these exercises, Bennett." I adjust my ponytail and ease him up to a sitting position. "Let me take this." For the second time today, I remove the ice pack from his thigh and return it to the freezer.

"Thanks."

After our nap, he went to sound check and then returned to his bus for another PT session. "Are you ready to heat up the stage tonight in Philadelphia?"

"You tell me, Miss Physical Therapist. I promise not to pull an Elvis, but I should be able to rile up the crowd."

"I have no doubt." I toss the towel into a hamper I secured for our sessions. "There. Back to normal in here. I'll bring this hamper back to my bus and you won't even know I've been here."

He holds up a finger. "One. I never want to forget you've been here. Two. I have more room in here than you do, so leave the hamper where it is. Three. I don't want you to go to another tour bus."

"You're very sweet, but I think it's for the best. Especially with all the media prowling around."

He waves his hand. "Fuck 'em."

"Such a Darren thing to say. Except he had the ability to fly under the radar, for the most part. You, not so much."

He plops onto the couch and pats the cushion next to him. I should go back to my bus and change. "I need to get dressed for the concert. Can't exactly show up like this, after all." I motion to my leggings and tunic top.

"You have time." He swallows. "I think we have one more thing to talk about." He examines my reaction. "Darren."

After what happened earlier on the stage, and on his bus, I'm ready. "Guess we need to exorcise his ghost, huh?"

"In a way. I wish you didn't blame yourself for his overdose."

"I wish the same for you," I protest.

His finger covers my lips. "I want to thank you. I was worried, at first, about how you'd be able to see me as Bennett and not as Darren's bandmate."

"I'd never—"

"I know. You never have. I want to tell you I appreciate your seeing me for me. You know about my mother. Hell, you've even met Lissa, who refused to give it up in high school because she was saving it for marriage, yet was crawling all over me the other day like a long-lost lover." He shudders. "You're aware of my unwitting role in Darren's death. And you still let me touch you. It means more than I can express."

His honesty washes over me. It's time for me to share some of my own truths. "Being with Darren was exhilarating and intoxicating. Flying to meet you guys, getting backstage passes. Being treated like his VIP. I was high on the life." I flick a piece of lint off my leggings. "I did love him. I wouldn't have had sex with him if I didn't."

"I understand."

I doubt he does. "I also remember watching the band back then. All the groupies. The innumerable number of women you each took into whatever rooms or alcoves were available. I'm not wired that way."

He kisses the top of my head. "I believe you. You did change

Darren in that respect, you know. Once you two were dating, that was it. When women approached him, he'd show them your picture."

My palm flies in front of my face. "Oh. I didn't know that. Well, he told me he'd show my photo, but not about the other." Back then I didn't want to know if he was faithful, so I pretended to be an ostrich and never asked.

Bennett nods, dropping his chin to his chest. "I think what we have is special. I want to explore where this relationship could go. But I don't know how to compete with a ghost."

Mindful of his injury, I restrain myself from straddling his lap. Instead, I rub my palm over his tatted arm. "You're not in competition. I did love Darren." I catch his gaze. "But—"

My heart races.

"But it never was the way it is between us. With you, I can give you physical therapy the same way I helped him heal. Only, you throw your all into the exercises and challenge yourself to improve, following my suggestions. Darren also was successful at therapy, but I never got the feeling he exerted more effort than was minimally required." I turn my head. "He had the help of pain meds, on which he relied too much. Obviously."

Bennett shifts in his seat.

I don't let him say anything. "It's more than that, though. I was younger and your rocker lifestyle is way too easy to get caught up in. Once Darren rejoined the tour, we only spent snippets of time together. I wanted more from him than he was able to give emotionally, which I overlooked."

"We were living the high life," he starts to explain.

"I know. Jetting from place to place, staying in fancy hotels, being catered to by everyone was new at the time. I understood it, even enjoyed your lives vicariously."

*Dare I share this next part with Bennett?* If we're going to have a shot, he needs to know. "Truth is, I was beginning to want to go to a deeper level with Darren. Dig deeper. Whenever I tried to bring up a topic—whether it be about his absentee father or my grandmother or future goals, whatever—he'd change the subject to something lighter. We were total opposites. It was starting to wear on me."

"Oh, Jenna." He opens his arms and I lean against him.

"I loved him, Bennett, I did. But I felt it was more superficial than I needed, and he didn't—or couldn't—dive deeper. He was very happy to hide behind his jokes. He excelled at living large." I take a deep breath. "Guess that's really what killed him in the end."

Bennett kisses my forehead. "Darren was full of life, always looking for whatever was next. Next song or next experience or next city. I never knew him to be too introspective."

"Agreed."

"I know he was smitten with you. Like I am." Bennett's lips meet mine for a brief second. "I need you to tell me I'm not competing against his long shadow."

"You're not. I don't care what the media or even Darren's mother say, you're a very different man than he was. I loved his attitude"—as soon as I say "love," Bennett's body tenses. I gaze into his eyes. "You have to admit he had a *joie de vivre* unlike most other people."

"Yeah."

Time to woman-up. I refuse to let this man slip from my fingers. I move so our thighs are touching. "As I said, he was my opposite in most respects. You. You're a different man. More introspective. I think you're harboring deeper pains than you've shared."

Bennett's head bounces backward, but his mouth remains closed.

"Tell me, if I asked you where your mother lives, would you answer me?"

I hear him audibly draw air into his body. "Yes." He pauses. "She's—"

My fingers cover his lips. In a low tone, I say, "I didn't ask where, only *if* you'd tell me. Reveal this horrible pain you've been carrying around with you, all by yourself. When you're ready, please share. Until then, all that matters is you'd answer the question." I wait for what I've told him to sink in. "Darren wouldn't even acknowledge a problem. I asked him, several times, to tell me about his father and he switched topics. Or cracked a joke. See the difference?"

He turns and brings his arms around my body, squeezing so hard my eyes water. I don't free myself, because I need his strength as much as he needs mine.

"I would tell you anything, Jenna. All you need to do is ask."

"I'd prefer you bring me inside on your own terms."

We remain locked together. Darren kissed my heart on the stage this afternoon, and now I take this time to truly allow him to rest in peace. He'll always be part of me, urging me to grow professionally or help with another injury. I've finally admitted out loud something I'd long buried—the fact we probably wouldn't have made it as a couple. Our personalities were too diametrically opposed. He'd never share with me his deep truths, beyond the curated ones he disclosed to the whole world. Nor did he show an interest in learning about mine.

Bennett, however, is the polar opposite. No matter what, he'll answer all my questions, which makes me not want to ask. Rather, let him reveal them to me on his own time.

My eyes close. In the silence, I allow Darren to fly free.

# Chapter Thirteen

S everal days pass. The guys do their pre-show ritual and then they run onstage, with Bennett taking his time, due to his injury. He's doing well with his therapy—I can't believe he pushed to keep his afternoon sessions this week. Tomorrow, though, I'm insisting he drops down to one. It'll fit better with his schedule anyway, since doing skater leaps on a moving bus is no joke.

Once they're performing, I return to the green room and call Ma. We keep missing each other, so I'm hopeful tonight will be a different story. I'm happy when she picks up. "You're a hard one to reach."

Her laughter floats through the receiver. "Takes one to know one. How's life on the road?"

"Good. It's challenging being with everyone again, but there are new faces. The band's doing well. In fact, they're giving a concert as we speak." I hold my cell out toward the stage.

"They sound good. How's Darren's replacement doing?"

"Tristan Lambert is his name. He's a really nice guy. Super talented. I like him a lot, and it seems the band does too."

"Good to hear. So, how does being on tour with this version of UC differ from before?"

"It is different, Ma, to be sure. You know how Darren was always cracking jokes and ready to try something new at the drop of the hat?"

She laughs. "Hard to forget."

"Well, that vibe's no longer here. The guys are less, I don't know, rowdy. But they're still very much into their music, which is all that matters."

"Sounds like they grew up."

I let Ma's observation sink in. "You may be right. Although Río is still loud with an oversized personality." They all follow Bennett's quieter lead, even if he doesn't believe me.

"How are *you* doing, Sweet Pea? Keeping your head amongst all the rock stars?"

More like losing it to the lead singer. Though I'm not going to share this with Ma—I need to ease her into our growing relationship. "I'm doing my best. Bennett's PT is going well and we're dropping down to once a day." To deter her inevitable questions, I focus on the new additions. "The tour has different crew members than I remember. I've made a good friend, who's their stylist, Nese."

"That's nice. Does she know your track record with the band?"

"With all the press, it would be impossible for her not to know. She's cool about it. I'm hoping to spend more time with her to see how she picks out different outfits for the guys that all work together."

"Sounds like a big job."

"It is." I move the discussion to the various crew members and roadies and their jobs, hoping to avoid anything about Bennett. Or Darren. Or my recent revelations about him. They're too raw for me to share, even with my mother.

"Well, it's getting late, so I should go. It was wonderful to hear your voice and not only in voicemail."

After we click off, I return backstage and watch the crew bringing UC to life. Sound, lighting, staging, Kieron doing his guitar tech work on his own now that Chico's gone. All of the members working in concert with the five men performing. It takes a village. I wonder how many in the audience realize . . . or care?

Bennett sings the final note to "Make Me Feel It" and the audience screams their appreciation. He drops the mic to his side, then stretches his arms wide as if asking each person in the crowd to give him a hug. Soaking up their adoration.

Am I ready to be with this man? While Darren was many things, he never was the face of the band. One that women from four to eighty-four want. Am I cut out for this type of lifestyle?

"Damn. Every time they perform, they sound better."

I glance to my left, where Nese now stands. "They sure do. Their clothes don't hurt, either."

She blows on her knuckles. "Glad to have a hand in their continued rise."

We both laugh. "So tell me, Oh Guru," I tease, "how do you dress each guy to their own style, yet make the whole look that good?"

She points at the stage. "What do you see out there?"

My gaze snags on the lead singer, standing with his back to Coop, who's making love to his guitar. "Well, Bennett's wearing his signature black leather pants, with a T-shirt over top that has some sort of geometric print on it, with his bracelets, rings, and his ever-present UC pendant on a necklace. Coop has on a pair of ripped jeans and white T-shirt under an open button-down, boots, sunglasses, and his hoop earrings. I can see a flash of his UC necklace at the top of his chest."

"Nice description of their outfits." Nese leans closer to me. "Let me tell you what I see. I see the leader of the band, UC's singer, capturing everyone's attention because of the sexy leather cuddling his muscular legs. He's highlighting the guitarist, whose ripped jeans catch the light 'just so' to expose his thigh to the audience, teasing them with the possibility of what could be."

"Oh wow. You dress them to seduce the audience."

"Damn straight. Haven't you heard that sex sells?" Her big laugh punctuates her description.

I take in the rest of the band's attire. Río plays drums *sans* shirt as usual—from this vantage point he could be naked, although I do remember gym shorts underneath. Pierce's muscular arms bulge out of the tight shirt tucked into his jeans held up with Darren's studded belt. Even Tristan's boy-next-door vibe is amped up by the multiple necklaces around his neck.

"You're a genius."

Her white teeth beam at me. "Not a genius. Only accentuating what I have to work with and subliminally projecting it forward."

We watch the show for a while. Nese tags my shoulder with hers. "So, anything more to share with your UC bestie about you and the sexy green-eyed beast onstage?"

My gaze travels to Bennett. The leather pants mold against his body, outlining every part of his musculature. Perhaps they're not the best choice after all? Shaking my head, I notice he's highlighting Pierce on bass. While I know he doesn't like the spotlight, Bennett's forcing him to interact, and I have to admit he's doing a great job.

Nese nudges me again.

"Huh?" I turn my head. "Do you think the pants are too tight on him?"

She bursts out laughing. "I ask you how things are developing between you two and your response is to ask about his *pants*?"

Heat rises up my neck. My palm covers my wayward mouth. "I'm sorry. You were fishing for information about me and Bennett?"

"Not anymore, girlie. Your response said it all."

Crap. "Please keep it between us."

"Don't worry. And, no. The leather encases his body to perfection but not in a lewd way. Your man is hot. With a capital H-O-T."

Is he my man? "I'm not sure he's mine though, Nese. Look at him out there. That's a different man from the one I know doing physical therapy. He's enticing everyone in the crowd to either be him or jump him." My finger taps my lips. "I don't know this man."

Her pixie cut flows around her head. "He's donned his public mask. The one he wears whenever he's onstage. I'm betting around you he drops it altogether. Then he's only Bennett."

I let her description sink in. Part of me is thrilled that she thinks he's himself around me. Another part feels sad that he has to hide behind a mask at all. Although, I do remember watching him put his mask on before a gig. "Do you wear a mask in public?"

"No. Then again, I'm not hounded by the paparazzi and don't have my every move scrutinized." Her whole body turns to mine. "Tell me, are you the same woman in front of reporters as you are right now?"

I remember the hordes of photographers hounding me at my clinic or my house. "Well, no. Because they don't deserve to know what's going on in my life. You do." I consider what I've said. "So, you're basically saying Bennett's had to learn how to protect himself and the way he does it is with this mask."

"Precisely."

If he weren't performing in front of thousands at this very moment, I would give him the biggest hug. "That sounds terrible."

"But necessary. He has to protect himself. They all do."

"Makes me glad to be a physical therapist."

"I hear you. I'll style them all day long, but don't put me out in front of the cameras. No thank you." The music takes us away. When the song ends, she asks, "Are you going to come out with us tonight?"

"I'm not sure. It's been a long day." She's given me so much to consider. "I'd like to get some quality sleep tonight." So long as I stay on my bus and away from the man hamming it up in front of thousands of people.

"Well, think about it. I, for one, would love to party with you. You haven't joined us in a while. Besides, I'm sure he would too." Her chin juts toward Bennett. "Well, I'd better get their encore clothes ready for their change. See you in a bit." She disappears behind black curtains that always are backstage.

My mind runs over what I've learned tonight. Bennett's mask.

Nese's costumes. I'm finally freed from any bonds to Darren—am I ready to dive back into an even deeper pool?

The band finishes their set and rushes backstage, stripping off their clothes. Bennett searches for me, his face beaming when he finds me in the corner. Naked from the waist up, he stalks toward me.

Preventing a disgusting, wet hug, I hold up a towel between us that Nese gave to me and shove it against his glistening chest. For good measure, I rub my palms over his pecs. Can't deny the excitement that pulses from his body, deep into mine.

"A guy could get used to this treatment." He steps back and rubs the towel over his back, all the while grinning at me.

I notice his smile reaches his eyes, which appear softer. This is the true Bennett—he's dropped the mask. I reach over and trace my fingers over his necklace, stopping at the UC pendant. "Your good omen."

"You're my lucky charm."

His words embrace me.

"Guys, guys," Luke calls for the band's attention. "Once you finish up the encore, you have your meet and greet, and then the afterparty at a local club. Be on notice that the radio station that's hosting the party invited twenty of your fans to be in the VIP area, so I need you to be on your best behavior." Luke's gaze spears Río.

The drummer holds up his drumsticks in the sign of the cross. "What? I'm always good. You must be talking about Tris."

We all crack up. Mr. Polite is the furthest thing from the trouble-maker of the band.

Nese passes Bennett a new shirt and whispers something in his ear. He takes the shirt and offers her a blinding smile. Then he comes over to me and grabs a lock of my hair. "See you at the meet and greet?"

"I'll be there," I confirm. "Then I'm going to bed. Have fun at the after party."

He yanks on the end of my hair. "I'll see what I can do to change your mind." He steals a quick kiss, slips his new shirt over his torso, and follows the rest of the band onto the stage, much to the delight of the audience.

After dealing with their dirty clothes, Nese joins me backstage, smiling like the Cheshire cat. After a minute, I can't control my nosiness. "What did you say to Bennett back there?"

"Wondered how long it would take you to ask." She focuses on UC's encore. "I dared him to get you to come out with us tonight."

"You didn't!" I think about our kiss, my fingers flying in front of my lips. "No wonder he didn't seem surprised when I told him I was going to bail."

"That man has it bad for you. Almost as much as you have fallen for him. I, for one, am looking forward to the fireworks."

Facing the stage, I square my shoulders. "No fireworks." When I turn my head, Nese waves at me as she walks away.

Alone watching the end of the encore, I think about everything Nese told me. Bennett's easy to fall for, but am I ready for this lifestyle? Onstage, he strips off his shirt and tosses it in my direction. I watch it land ten feet in front of me and, of their own accord, my feet take me toward it. Picking up the wet material from the floor, I scrunch it into a ball. He gives me a naughty grin, causing hearts to flick at him from my eyes. Yes, too easy.

Following the meet and greet consisting of about one hundred women with a sprinkling of men, the band congregates in The Closet to prepare for the next outing. Within seconds, Cooper and Río stand in their skivvies. Spinning on my heel, my overheated face points toward the door. Time for me to leave.

I take one step when a large hand lands on my shoulder. "What can I do to change your mind?"

Without turning, I reply, "Bennett, I can't go out tonight. Enjoy yourself." I slip through the door, half-expecting him to follow me. When he doesn't, I tamp down flutters of disappointment and use my all-access pass to gain entrance into the back parking lot and enter my bus.

The one I'm sharing with other crew members. Where I belong.

I make my way to my bunk. Leaving my shoes in the narrow hall-way, I climb into my bed and curl into the fetal position. The truth is I like Bennett way too much for my own good. He represents every-thing I'm not—undisciplined, chaotic, and free. *No he's not.* He may be the first two, but free? No way. He's bound by his own demons.

I guess we all are.

Not wanting to be stuck in my own head, I text Court. After a quick catch-up, I dive in:

> Bennett's amazing onstage, but he's a different man from the one I'm getting to know with PT.

How so?

> He wears a mask . . . whenever he's performing, in meet and greets, at afterparties, in interviews, photo shoots, or music videos. Not the same person at all. There, he's more flirty and arrogant. Not with me.

Well, are you the same amazing and warm woman you are with me when dealing with your other managers? Or construction teams? Bank officers?

> No, of course not.

Why are you demanding more of him than you require of yourself?

I flip over and stare into the underside of the bed above me.

I don't know.

Let me tell you what I think. I think you're falling for him, big time, and you're scared. He's not someone you can control. Sure he has responsibilities, like you do, but have you ever considered the pressure he's under? Maybe he sees you as the one person on earth that can help him cope.

Well, he does have pressure. Bennett's not only accountable for his own actions, but the band pays the salaries of all the crew and roadies. That's a lot. Like me magnified by a million.

Maybe not a million! Your shoulders carry a lot of weight too. All I'm suggesting is this isn't the reason you're not giving him a fair shake.

How do you know me so well?

You can thank me when I'm standing up for you at your wedding.

I cough.

Now who's getting ahead of herself?!

All I'm saying is don't run away from something good. Where is he now?

At a VIP thing.

And why are you texting me?

*All he did was ask me to go out with the band tonight.* Like the past few nights, which I've always declined.

Even though he doesn't need me to survive tonight's VIP event, he asked me to join him. Court's right—the least I could do is give him the little bit of help he requested.

Tossing my conscience aside, I slink out of my bed and change into the dress she gave me before the tour—seems appropriate. When I return to the green room, only the venue's cleaning crew remain. I enter the area designated for the band's exit, where a group of people are standing. I spot Kieron first.

"Hey," I say to the tall and lanky guitar tech. "Are you all waiting to go to the VIP event?"

"Sure are. The bus should be here any moment. I thought you rode over with the band?"

I shake my head. "Nah, had to change." I point at my less-than comfortable shoes. "Figured they'd look better at a club."

He nods. "Gotcha." A bus enters the parking lot. "Good timing. I'm ready to relax after the show. Not saying it's hard work, but it's frickin' good to be able to not be on." He winks as he gets in line behind me to enter the bus.

It must be good to be able to kick back without worry. Bennett and the rest of the band members don't have this luxury. The very reason I decided to attend tonight. I climb the stairs.

We arrive at the club soon and I follow Kieron to the VIP area. Given his height and long blond hair, he's an easy mark to guide me. After showing my all-access pass to the bouncer, I enter the VIP area and hug the wall.

Fans surround the band members. A camera crew wearing radio station garb circles the crowd. I identify a few guys, plus one woman, who look like they could be DJs for the station. Everyone has drinks and seems to be having a great time.

Especially the fans. They're hanging on everything coming out of Bennett's mouth. To be fair, they're that way with the rest of UC too, but the largest contingent surrounds the lead singer.

My gaze travels to him. His smile is painted on, not allowing for even a small glimpse into his real self. One woman in a tight black dress runs her hands over his arms, and I want to scratch her eyes out. Bennett, however, does no such thing. Rather, he removes her hand from his forearm, pats it, and drops it by her side.

Another woman with long, jet black hair, sidles in front of him. If he glanced downward, I'm sure he'd get an unfettered view of her cleavage. To my amazement, his eyes don't budge from her face. He does, however, step to the side and grab a passed hors d'oeuvre from the server. When he returns to the group, he chooses a different entry point.

He's learned how to deal with these types of gatherings like the professional he is. My heart wants to reach out to his, but I don't want to interrupt the fans as they get their UC fix. The DJs rearrange the groupings, so Bennett's now with the group that was surrounding Tristan. They seem much more mellow.

"You came?"

Nese holds up her drink to me, only I'm still empty. Shrugging, I raise an imaginary glass to her, causing her to giggle. "Changed my mind. Couldn't let you have all the fun."

"Let's get you a drink so we can do a proper toast." We weave through the throngs of people, finally ending at the bar. Ten minutes later, I hold up my glass of pinot noir and we toast to another great concert.

"The radio station did this up right," she notes. "The club is jumping, the fans seem nice, and the drinks are off the hook."

Her gaze drifts toward UC, mine follows suit. Bennett's now talking with the sole female radio DJ. Figures. "I remember back in the day. Darren used to drive their partying. Luke tried to get them to ease up but lost nine times out of ten."

"I can't imagine. This time around, things seem a bit more buttoned up. Take Tristan, for example. He's chatting with the group over there," using her drink Nese points to the cluster of fans who were all over Bennett a few minutes ago. "Seems like a civilized conversation. Río, on the other hand." She drink-points to him. "He looks about ready to do body shots at any second."

I laugh at her description. "You're pretty spot on."

As if on cue, the bunch with Río call for the server, who reappears a few minutes later with a tray of shots. Instead of sucking the liquid off various body parts, however, they all do them the normal way, much to my relief. Not sure Río would agree.

One of the male DJs claps his hands and announces the event is over. Fans hug band members good night, and then most of them leave. It takes the DJs a few tries, but they manage to wrangle all of their guests out of the VIP area, leaving the band and crew.

"What happens next?"

Nese downs the rest of her drink. "The band goes into the main club to choose their evening's entertainment. If they haven't selected a fan or two already."

"But they all left?"

"Oh, you have so much to learn. They may have exited because the DJs ordered them out, but if a guy, say Río, told them to wait by the doors, you can bet your sexy butt they're waiting."

"That's so . . ." I search for the proper word. "Skeevy."

"You were with the band a couple of years ago. I can't imagine they've changed too much."

My time with Darren was limited, and we never stayed at these types of things a minute longer than need be. Were they like this before? I remember enjoying a couple of drinks with a crowd but then Darren would spirit me away to his hotel room or the bus and we'd have our own private party.

A memory niggles at the back of my mind—the night I first met Bennett was at a bar. We talked about *The Godfather* movies. Plenty of fans milled around, but not this sort of organized meat market. Still, I do remember Darren talking about all the women the band took to their bunks. He told me he was happy not to be part of that scene any longer.

How does Bennett feel about all this?

I crane my neck, looking for him. Nese leans over, "He's talking with the bouncer."

My gaze jumps to the bouncer where Bennett stands. They seem to be in a deep conversation. "I wonder what they're talking about?"

Nese grabs me by the shoulders. "Listen. I know you've denied you two are together, but I'm not buying it. The Bennett I've heard of would be talking with the bouncer to select his evening's entertainment, if you get my drift. If, as I suspect, you've changed him, he's asking the bouncer for the fastest exit route."

I watch as the bouncer pulls something out of his back pocket. "I'm going to tell Bennett I'm here. Have a good night."

"I knew it!" Nese's smile conveys pure happiness. "Enjoy!"

As I approach, Bennett signs a paper and hands it back to the bouncer. "Tell your daughter she has a great father."

An autograph. He was signing an autograph. I tap Bennett's shoulder, causing him to jump. "Hi."

He swings around to face me, his professional mask firmly in place. The second he recognizes me, it hits the floor. "You came!"

He owes Court one. "I did."

With an "excuse me," to the bouncer, he takes my arm. "Did you enjoy tonight's concert?"

"What's not to like? You guys are great, and you didn't do anything to endanger your recovery."

One eyebrow raises. "That's all you saw?"

"No," I admit. "I also saw a hardworking man drawing thousands into his world, where nothing matters except the next note. You were the master out there."

"Wow. I was hoping you'd say you liked how I sang. But I'll take your review over those by Jeremy Davis any day." He kisses my hand. "I need a drink."

We're on our way to the bar when a server approaches with a martini glass on her tray. Her eyes eat him up. "Thought you might like this."

"Appreciate it," he takes the drink then turns to me. "Do you need one?"

I shake my head, holding up my wine. "I'm good."

The server loiters but when Bennett's attention remains focused on me, she finally departs. "You have people throwing themselves at you all the time."

"Yeah, but none as intriguing as my physical therapist." He sips his drink. "Wearing a sexy-ass dress."

I swallow, and not my wine. "Bennett, why?"

Instead of responding, he asks, "Would you give me your shirt so I could sign your tits?"

Ewww. "What? No."

"How about letting me take you from behind in the corner of this club?"

"Are you crazy?"

"If I asked you to pick two women and take me to your room, would you let me?"

"No way."

He sips his drink. "I rest my case. You wouldn't approve of such crazy behavior. You keep me on my toes." He shifts his weight between his now jean-covered legs. "You give me PT and don't let me get away with anything. You intrigue me more than anyone I've ever met. Have since the first time we met."

"And talked about *The Godfather*." I place my empty glass on top of a high table. "Still wrong, though."

"The original rocks."

I counter, "Second one is better."

He grins at me, and I grin back. He places his hand on the middle of my back, pushing me toward the exit. "Let's go back to my bus where we can watch both and make an informed decision."

"I already know the answer."

Luke stands near the exit. "Leaving?"

"You said we're driving through the night. Just abiding by your wishes."

The manager bursts into laughter. "Since when did you ever follow my instructions, B? Jenna, you're a very good influence on our lead singer here."

Not waiting for any further comments, Bennett steers me out the door and into a waiting SUV. "I'm ready to be proven right."

Once we're both in the vehicle, I say, "What do I get when I'm proven the winner?"

He kisses my cheek. "More orgasms than you can count."

# Chapter Fourteen

My alarm wakes me at nine o'clock. One eye pops open to confirm we're still in our clothes we wore to the club last night, *sans* shoes. The television is on, but we both crashed while the first movie was playing. Now it's the streaming service's homepage. Guess Bennett's challenge will have to continue another day.

I glance over at the man sleeping next to me, his usually styled caramel-colored hair falling over his forehead, scruff filling in more than usual. The perfect Roman nose. The only thing that could possibly make this man more attractive would be a dimple, but his face is clean of them. His butt, though . . .

"Morning, sleepyhead," his gruff voice rumbles, causing my core to clench.

Court's observation rings throughout my body. I *do* fear I can't control him. Manage, maybe?

He leans over and plants little kisses from my jawline to my cheek, ending with my willing mouth. Can I manage him? Do I want to?

On a moan, I fling my arm around his shoulder and settle onto his lap. His hiss reminds me why I'm here.

I leap off his thighs. "Oh shit. I'm so sorry!"

"Sweetheart, not a worry. I'll gladly take all the pain in the world if it means you'll straddle me." He reaches for my waist to haul me over to him again, but I scoot away.

"No way. You're down to having therapy once a day. I'm not going to be the reason it gets extended."

He strokes himself through his jeans. "I can show you something else that would like to be extended."

Ignoring the saliva pooling in my mouth, I give him a stern look. "Bennett. Behave."

"Said no woman ever." He pauses. "Well, except for Mom."

His mention of the woman who's treated him as less than because he was born hurts a dark spot deep inside. "Hey," I move so we're touching thigh to thigh. "Unlike what I know about your mother, I, for one, am thrilled you're here in this world. I can guess all the females at UC's concerts would agree. Not to mention the women in the meet and greets and last night's club. Although," My lips purse. "Some were a bit too familiar for my taste."

"I'm used to women being handsy with me, Jenna." He grabs my own hand and traces my fingers. "However, you're the only person I want to touch me." He places my palm over his hard hammering heart.

The bus rumbles down the highway, going to whatever city's next. At the moment, I don't care. Tossing my fears off the speeding bus, I want to be wrapped in Bennett's bubble. I lay my head on his pec. "Where are we off to?"

"Not sure," he replies. "Some place in the south? Georgia? Tennessee? I don't know."

"Is this how you live your life? Perform, drink, travel, rise and repeat?"

"Pretty much. It's better when we get a couple of days off. Luke sets up a nice dinner for us or sightseeing of some sort."

I rear back. "Really? Like what?"

"We've done museums, music studio tours, adventure things like rock climbing."

"Sounds cool. What about a culinary tour? You guys seem to have an expansive palate."

He chuckles. "Can't say that we have done one of those."

I file this option away for my next conversation with Luke. "So what do you think's on tap for today?"

His stomach growls. "Well, I'm hoping food is our number one priority."

I kiss his willing lips. "Stay here." I walk down the main aisle to the driver's seat, tugging Court's dress into place. "Hey, Danny."

"Miss," he replies without moving his eyes off the road. "What can I do for you? Everything all right with the big guy?"

I appreciate how he looks out for Bennett. Danny's as much a part of UC as Bennett or Nese or Luke or any crewmember. "Bennett's fine, but he's hungry. Any idea when we'll be stopping for food?"

Before I'm finished talking, he's on the walkie talkie. "There's a rest stop in two miles. I told the other drivers we'll be stopping, and they'll meet us there."

"Thank you so much." I return to Bennett, picking up a shirt along the way. "Here you go. We're stopping for some grub soon."

His head pops through the material. "You asked for me?"

"Can't have the lead singer of Untamed Coaster passed out due to hunger now, can we?" I giggle. Giggle? What is this man doing to me?

---

"Pass me the syrup."

Coop passes Pierce a glass dispenser. "Here you go, asswipe."

For his part, Pierce shoots the guitarist a dirty look, then pours a healthy amount of maple syrup over his Belgian waffles.

Tristan, sitting next to me, says, "Did you all check the internet this morning? When will the press let go of this stupid Black Widow thing?"

My blueberry pancake halts on its way into my mouth. Bennett clamps his hand around my thigh. "Total bullshit." He kisses my cheek.

I can only imagine the comments. How people have jumped on the growing bandwagon of bashing me. I drop my fork onto my plate.

"We all know the truth," Río says. "Don't let them impact your life, Jenna. They'll move on soon enough."

Yeah. I've heard that before. Like weeks ago when we first went out to dinner. Or while checking out property in Aroostook. Since I've joined the tour, things keep escalating rather than quieting. I catch Luke's gaze. "What can I do?"

He checks out the table. "I've talked with our PR team about this, guys. The media is like a dog with a bone with this story. It's too juicy for them to be put off, no matter how hard we try. The best thing we can do is ignore them."

Easier said than done. Especially for me, considering my previous exposure to reporters was when I was Darren's girlfriend. Back then, the media seemed to slant in my favor. When he died, the stories focused on his drug use and out-of-control private life—which I didn't challenge since I was dealing with his death. Now, however, their barbs prickle the guilt I feel over his death. Plus, I have a business to consider.

My fingers twist in my lap. Bennett says he wants me here with him, but all this negative press can't be good for the band either. I whisper, "Do you want me to go?"

"No." Bennett rushes to answer. "You're helping me get over an injury the media know nothing about. You even told me I'm doing better and dropped my therapy to once a day. Fuck 'em."

I glance up, and the rest of the band's glasses are lifted—coffee, OJ, water, or a Mimosa in Río's case—and they clink. "Fuck the liars!"

Seems like I'm staying. If only I could figure out how to tune out the media.

"Besides," Coop adds. "I bet the reporters are simply jealous. I mean, Jenna looks better than all of them put together."

I'm about more than my appearance, but I do appreciate his sentiment.

"Yeah," Río says. "Makes me want to hurt something so she can be my personal physical therapist too."

Everyone, except Pierce, laughs. I try to join in, actually managing a light chuckle.

Not to be outdone, their manager teases. "She has a hurt wrist and pulled groin muscle covered. What are you thinking of pulling out of joint, Río?" He glances at the floor. "Your . . . big toe?"

The rest of the table erupts in laughter. For his part, Río takes off his shoe and sock and places his foot on top of the table, ignoring how disgusting a foot amidst our breakfast is. He wiggles his toe in my direction.

"What do you think, Miss Physical Therapist? Can you fix me?"

The absurdity of it all is impossible to ignore. "I'm not sure," I toss back. "I'd have to shave the hair off to properly examine you."

Río's eyes go round. "No way are you shaving my manhood! Did you shave Bennett's pubes?"

Eww. I scrunch my face back.

Tristan jumps in, shaking his head. "Too much, Río. Too much."

"What?" the drummer asks, returning his foot to the floor. "I'm like Samson. You can't touch a strand of my hair."

Tristan smacks him upside the head. "On his head, dumbass."

The band continues their playful squabble while Bennett whispers into my ear. "I would let you shave me down there if you want. Would be hot."

Just like that, my attention is diverted from Río's disgusting—yet funny—theatrics to the promise contained in Bennett's eyes. "Not needed in your case, big boy." *Big boy?* Where is this woman coming from? "I can evaluate your progress fine with all your hair intact."

He adjusts himself. "Sure you don't want an up-close-and-personal look?"

Before I can respond, Tristan pipes up. "Hey, no hogging all Jenna's attention!"

Breaking Bennett's spell, I bring my gaze to the new keyboardist. "What did I miss, Mr. Polite?"

The guys around the table guffaw at my nickname for Tristan. They have to know I'm right.

"Luke asked if we want to go on a bourbon tour when we get to Louisville today," Tristan explains.

"Oh," I turn to face Bennett. While bourbon isn't my thing, it's his drink of choice. Before he can respond, I answer for both of us. "We're in."

"Cool!" Tristan's fist pumps the air. As does Río's and Coop's. Pierce doesn't react in the same way, but he's smiling, so there's that.

Luke captures our attention. "B, you don't usually join in our reindeer games. Are you okay with this?"

My brows close. He must stay away to protect himself. Well, not on my watch. My hand rests on his forearm.

"Seems like the little lady wants to do the tour, so sure. Why not. Count us in."

A couple of hours, plus the only therapy session of the day later, the buses pull into a bourbon distillery. "Are you excited to get the skinny on the alcohol?"

"I'm excited to spend more time with you," he corrects.

"Plus, fun time with the band. Which is as important," I add.

He pulls my back against his front. "I'd be happy to spend all this time in bed with you."

I relax against his hard chest for a moment. "No sex for two more days, remember?"

"Counting the minutes." I wait to see if he's going to say anything more, and am rewarded when he says, "This seems to be important to you, so I'll happily check out this bourbon trail."

I'll take this as a start.

Several hours later, we collapse onto the bed in his hotel room. "That was fun." I giggle. I down more than my share of sips of the brown water.

"Have to say, I had a blast." His head flops toward mine. "Thanks for forcing me to join the guys. I'd almost forgotten how enjoyable hanging out with them can be."

It's as if my limbs gain fifty pounds. Why does he block his road to happiness with the band? I'm going to make him see they have his back. I turn to my side. "They like you, Bennett. They treat you like their friend."

"I don't know about that. You were probably looking through bourbon goggles."

"I wasn't." I lift onto my elbow but can't keep my balance and wobble. "You need to see the band like I do. You're all in this together. Fighting against annoying media reports. Performing in front of thousands of fans. Let them in."

"What if I have everything I need without sharing my stupid shit with them? I have a great career, amazing venues to play music with my band, and you. I don't need anything else."

Ignoring the final part, I focus on how he described the band. My finger rubs against his stubbly chin. "That's the first time I've heard you call UC 'my band.'"

He bites the inside of his chin. "Well, I guess it is 'my' band. I'm the lead singer and all."

"That's not what you meant. The members of the band are your people. You are a group of friends getting together to play music, and not a bunch of individuals who perform onstage like you first described Untamed Coaster."

His eyes close. "I don't know, Jenna. I don't do friends."

I need to push him on this. I want him to understand he is amongst friends. "What am I?"

He sits up. "Jenna, what do you want me to say?"

My back hits the hotel's plush upholstered headboard. "Only what you feel. I can tell you what I see, but if you don't feel the same way, what good is it?"

He contemplates my question for a long while. "I don't know. There's always been a disconnect between me and the rest of the band. We enjoy performing together and have fun being on tour. However, I don't share my secrets with them."

"Not even with Luke?" Their manager is close with Bennett. He told me so.

"He knows more than most, but not everything." Bennett cups my cheek in his hand. "You're the closest one to knowing all of my secrets."

"I'll never betray your confidences. Ever." I reach over and kiss his nose. "I'd like for you to share more of your burdens with others. Maybe let Luke in. Tristan seems like a good guy, if you'd feel better with someone not original to the band."

"Have a crush on Tris, do you?"

"Oh, yeah." The back of my palm flies to my forehead. "I can't wait to get closer to him by spending all my time with you, like a good Black Widow would."

His hands cover my shoulders and pin me to the bed. "I better not be a way to pass the time."

A sarcastic retort is on the tip of my tongue, but it dies when I see the hurt look in his green eyes. "I was kidding." My honest reply fills the room. "I only want for you to open up to your bandmates a little more. Let them in. You might be surprised at their perspective on things."

"Why does this matter to you?"

I collect my thoughts and say, "Because you walk in a world few understand. *They* do. Let them help you wrestle all the pressures you're under."

He settles over my body, every part of his long frame warming me. "No one has ever cared about me the way you do, Jenna. You make it seem like I can share my life with the band, that my truths won't make them run away. They don't need to know my monsters; they have their own problems. To them, I'm the cocky lead singer, who handles all the minutiae and keeps UC running."

My gaze roves over his perfect face. "What if they saw a fraction of the truth? Maybe about how hard it was when your father passed and you decided to join the band?"

His cheek ripples. "They were there."

"I'm sure they knew your dad died and you dropped out of high school when Darren asked. But did you share your feelings back then?" I trace his eyebrows. "How hard this was for you?"

"They knew."

"Fine," I relent. "They didn't leave you all alone to study for the test, did they? I know for a fact Darren used to quiz you for the GED. The others helped you prepare, too. Does that sound like a group of guys who didn't care?"

He drops onto his side. "Well, no. I thought they didn't want a high school dropout representing the band."

"Oh, Bennett. Darren told me how proud he was of you for passing the test on the first try. All of you took the GED together, because you all studied for it."

He doesn't say a word, but I can see him processing. After a few minutes, he whispers, "I guess you're right." He smiles at me. "We all celebrated when I passed."

"Because you let them in to help you. Can you remember how that made you feel?"

"Good. Proud."

"As you *all* should. How about when you selected Tristan to join the band?"

"It was a grueling process. Applicants submitted videos, which our team screened, passing along only the top ones. We met with a few candidates, but Tristan vibed with us right away. It took some time for him to be a part of UC, but he's here now." His face swivels toward mine. "The rock climbing outing cemented it."

"See what happens when you come together as a unit to achieve a goal?"

"I'm not sure what goals we still have to achieve."

"How sad." I turn on my side. "Don't you—meaning UC as a band—have any milestones you still want to achieve?"

"We're selling out stadiums, have won a few awards." He waves his hand. "I guess it would be cool to win an Oscar for best song in a movie."

I latch onto this. "What an awesome goal! What do you have to do to make that happen?"

He shakes his head. "I have no idea."

"How about this. Why don't you research what it takes to win, and then talk with your band members about it?" I use the pronoun "your" on purpose, and consider it a win when he doesn't correct me.

"Or, I could ask Luke. It could be fun to work toward a goal again. See if we can reach it."

I nod, keeping the tears in check. This man is opening up to his band whether he realizes it or not. "The challenge will be worth it."

His hands skim down my body. "Thank you. I haven't felt this much excitement about UC in a long time."

"Glad to be of service."

His pupils dilate. "I know how else you can be of service."

"The doctor said two more days."

"Fuck the doctor."

My hand flies in front of my mouth but it doesn't prevent my giggle from escaping. "I'd rather not."

"Good thing, for his health." He covers my lips with his and our kiss escalates to off the charts in no time flat. Before I know it, I'm naked and his mouth has trailed between my legs. "I now have only one goal, and it's to hear you scream my name."

He slides two fingers into my body and pumps while his tongue encircles my clit. "Oh, Bennett. Right there." My hand clamps down on the top of his head.

"Got you, Sweetheart."

Boy, does he. Tingling begins at my toes and races throughout my body until I'm clenched around him. With one more flick of his tongue, I spiral into the stratosphere, shouting, "Bennett!"

When I return to earth, I loll my head to see him smirking. Guess he earned it.

"You're so responsive, Jenna. It's like you were created for me. You challenge me not for what *you* can get out of it, but to make *my* life better. You make me do PT so I'll heal faster, not letting me go off script and reinjure myself. You encourage me to be a better man." He brushes the hair away from my face. "How could I not fall in love with you?"

"You can't." The words escape my mouth without direction. My heart pounds.

# Chapter Fifteen

He settles himself over me. "I do love you, Jenna Westfield. I've told you before at Secluded Rest, and I'm repeating it now. You make me feel things no one else has ever made me feel. You're here not because I'm the lead singer of UC, but because of your desire to help me."

"Anyone could've gotten you to this point." Even as I say this, I know it's not true. So many others would've joined the tour for the excitement and access to either the band or fans, none of which hold any allure for me.

Still in his jeans, he leans against the headboard, pulling me like a naked ragdoll next to him. "Tell me, what if one of Michelle's referrals had gotten their hands on me?"

I flinch at her name. "She refers patients to my crosstown rival who has multiple therapists working for him in six locations."

"All right. Do you think he would've agreed to take me on as his patient?"

"In a heartbeat. He does anything for publicity."

"Tell me, how have you capitalized on my status to improve your business?"

His question stumps me. "I haven't."

"Exactly. How have you leveraged our relationship"—his finger-tips cover my now open lips—"however you define what's going on between us, for your own gain?"

"I'd never do that."

"See? This is how you stole my heart. What else could it be? All you do is make me want to be better, do better."

"We haven't even had sex yet."

He chuckles. "You think sex is my deciding factor?"

I tuck the blankets around my naked chest. "It always has been for me."

His finger taps my chin. "Are you saying you won't know if you reciprocate my feelings until we do the deed?"

My heart screams to admit how it's feeling. That sex plays no role in defining how deeply he's crawled under my skin. How I consider him before questioning my own feelings. Yet, my brain overshadows. While he's not as over-the-top as Darren was, he's the definition of chaos. I need time to sort through it all. Don't I?

"Sex surely will play into my equation."

"This orgasm didn't sway you?" His finger runs down my cheek. "Or the others I've given you?"

I know I'm being ridiculous, but I can't form the words to tell him how I feel. Darren and his death almost destroyed me—how can I allow myself to get into this same position again? "Bennett, you mean a lot to me, to everyone. You are so worthy of love despite the fact your father passed away, leaving you with a mother who isn't capable of showing her heart."

"This right here is how I know you're the woman for me." He hugs me against his body, his heart beating like one of Río's drum solos. "I can wait for you, Jenna. For the next couple of days until we meet the doctor's random threshold to have sex. For weeks afterward, if that's what you need. I want you to know I'll always be here for you. Protecting you from the media, smoothing things over with UC, and allowing your dreams of owning multiple physical therapy clinics to soar."

I'm overwhelmed. He's laying himself bare, saying the things I've only dreamed of hearing. Why can't I tell him he's everything—and more—I've ever wanted? Why can't I trust my feelings? Or his?

I lick my lips. "Bennett," I pause to study his earnest face. "You're important to me, and not only as my patient. I've broken every single rule there is with you." I glance down. "Even now, we're having this discussion while I'm naked and you're shirtless."

His nose nudges mine.

"I'm scared," I whisper.

"Me too," he replies.

"I can't go through what I went through with Darren ever again."

"I don't have any intention of dying anytime soon."

"Good." I rest my forehead against his shoulder. "The media is brutal. I'm not sure how to stay above the fray."

"Which is why UC has a PR team."

"Ma—" I don't finish this sentence. I don't want him to know her true opinion of him. For some reason, the need to protect him overrides everything else. No, not for *some* reason. I'm unable to cut him to the quick with another mother's less than glowing opinion of him.

"Don't worry. UC's marketing machine will be on it."

He completed my reference to "Ma" with "marketing." His world doesn't include any hint of a mother figure, while mine is my closest confidant. This makes my heart reach out to him.

When I don't reply, he continues, "I want to be the man you can rely on at all times. To help your dreams come true in any way I can, and to cheer your successes from the sidelines. You care about me not because I'm UC's lead singer or another rock star notch in your bedpost. In fact, these are demerits for you. I've never had anyone wiggle into this space in my heart." His palm covers his left pec. "What else could this feeling be but love?"

My response sticks in my throat. His heartfelt confession almost breaks me, but I can't bring myself to say what he wants to hear, what's weighing on my tongue. Instead, I entwine our fingers and squeeze. "I can't say what you want to hear."

"Yet." He kisses the back of my palm. "I know you love me, and I'll wait forever to hear you say the line."

---

Bennett's tender words about waiting for me reverberate through my mind as the day progresses. As if by tacit agreement, our interactions are more lighthearted, although we've yet to watch our *Godfather* marathon for me to be proven right about the better of the two movies.

As soon as we sit down in a Chinese restaurant, Río challenges Pierce to a wonton throwing contest. Luke rubs his hands on the tabletop. "Guys, really?"

Ignoring their manager, Río picks up a crispy noodle, takes aim at Pierce's open mouth, and tosses. It bounces off Pierce's chin and lands on an empty plate, resulting in Pierce's laughter—a sound I haven't heard in ages. He fishes into the bowl and picks up another noodle to throw at Río. For his part, Coop cheers for Pierce while Tristan joins in by encouraging Río. Luke's red cheeks give the impression he wants to crawl under the table. I glance at Bennett, who remains away from the game while more noodles are lobbed across the table.

He needs to participate, be part of their antics. Not keep himself so apart. Surprising myself, I shout, "You got this, Río!" The drummer points a noodle and tosses it at me, but it falls short.

Bennett's head swivels from me to the guys. Tristan and I clap as Río scores and Pierce chews. After a couple more unsuccessful rounds, Bennett leans on his sexy forearms. "C'mon 007, show 'em what you've got!"

Happiness bursts through my veins as he joins the band's harmless antics. For his part, Pierce does a double take at Bennett, sets his sights on the drummer, and gets the noodle directly into Río's mouth.

He, plus his UC supporters, cheer. Bennett actually lets go and laughs.

When the game finishes—Pierce beat Río by one point—Bennett punches the winner's arm. "Well played, 007."

"Helped having you in my corner." The two smile at each other. Warmth spreads through my limbs.

The server arrives and all mischief ends as the serious business of refueling begins. Banter around the table is light and easy. Bennett joins more conversations tonight than I've ever witnessed. He's receptive, and the guys seem excited for his participation.

When the last wonton is devoured, Luke clears his throat. "Guys, I wanted to talk with you about *Untamed Coaster Unleashed*." The table goes silent. "The movie's going to be number one in the world for the fourth straight week in a row."

Everyone claps. Bennett kisses me, hard, on the lips.

"I've tasked the PR team to hype the movie, so don't be too surprised if reporters want an interview or two."

"That's one interview I'll be happy to sit for," Bennett pronounces.

I consider his words—plus his desire to win a best original song award. Seems like the right time to poke the bear. "Hey Luke," the weight of a dozen eyes land on me. "What do you think it would take for 'Refocused Destiny' to win an Oscar for best song?"

Bennett's hand lands on top of my thigh. I don't turn my head, simply lean forward to hear the manager's answer. Luke says, "I'm sure it would take some campaigning, but if you'd all like, I can see what needs to be done."

Río leaps to his feet, his hips wiggling from side to side. "Hell, yes, I'm in!" Next to him, Coop joins in on his antics. Bennett's next to stand, followed by Tristan and Pierce. The room buzzes with their new, united goal.

The rest of the evening rushes by. Once we finish desserts and coffees—teas for Bennett and me—we're whisked to the stadium where the band shares an even more fantastic concert experience with their fans. After the meet and greet, Bennett tucks my hand in the crook of his elbow. "You're coming with me."

He doesn't allow me to ask any questions, simply keeps me pressed against his side as we travel through the bowels of the stadium. He opens a door and we're outside, an unseasonably warm breeze brushing my cheeks.

"Can I ask you now where we're going?"

"Nope." A black sports car pulls up in front of us and Jeb pops out. With a salute to Bennett, the roadie tosses a key fob to the mysterious man at my side, and disappears into the stadium.

Alone, Bennett leads me around the front of the car and opens the passenger door. He motions for me to enter. "After you." I slip into the car, marveling at the supple black leather seats and dashboard that looks like it belongs in an airplane.

A second later, Bennett slams the driver's door. "Are you ready for this?"

Excited yet confused, I ask, "What's this?"

"A good fucking time."

He presses a button and the car roars to life. He plugs an address into the GPS, and we take off down the side road blasting The Light Rail's latest. My sexy driver joins their lead singer on the vocals. A crossover between the two bands flits through my mind, but disappears when we take a turn on what feels like two wheels.

Knuckles white on the roll bar, I exclaim, "Whoa!"

"Checking the suspension." He makes a few more quick turns through empty streets. "Handling too."

When the color returns to my hand, I relax into the seat. I haven't seen Bennett this carefree in . . . forever. He knows the car's limitations—plus his own. He's babying his right thigh, probably even more than he needs to. My lips are sealed.

Following several more turns, during which I manage to remove my hand from the roll bar, the GPS announces we're here. Bennett parks in a secluded spot near a couple of picnic benches, which, given the late hour, aren't in use.

I blink into the dark woods in front of me. "Where are we?"

"You're going to love it." He unbuckles his seatbelt and presses the button to release mine. "Don't move."

He rushes around the front of the car and opens my door, offering me his hand to help me stand. All five of his rings kiss my fingers. Once I'm on my feet, he keeps my hand in his. With care, he guides me across the dark lot toward another set of picnic tables facing a ravine. "Have a seat."

I drop down onto the bench, waiting for an explanation. When none is forthcoming, I say, "They don't like streetlights around here, do they?"

"There's a reason for that," he chuckles. "They want to avoid light pollution."

"I've only heard of light pollution hurting microbes in phosphorescent waters." When his eyebrows raise, I clarify, "I saw a documentary about a bay in Puerto Rico that has an issue with light."

"Oh. La Parguera, I presume?"

I squint. "I think that was the name."

"Let me save you a trip. I enjoyed La Parguera, but the bioluminescent bay on the island of Vieques, off Puerto Rico, is truly enchanting."

"I've forgotten you're a world traveler."

"Hazards of being a rock star." He pulls me closer to his body. "Now, look up."

We both raise our chins to the inky sky. A minute later, something shoots across. "Oh my God!" I point. "Did you see that?"

"Yup. There's a meteor shower here tonight. I wanted to experience it with you." Quiet ensues, as we watch the celestial dance.

"This is beautiful." I kiss his cheek. "Thanks for bringing me here tonight."

"I wanted to share this special evening with you." He kisses my forehead.

I sit up. "The black sports car didn't hurt either, huh?"

"I asked Jeb to rent the Jaguar." He glances toward the car. "It's been a hot minute since I've been able to drive somewhere for fun, without being chased by the paps."

We lapse into silence, remembering my birthday dinner, which ended with a car chase. Back then, his injury was still fresh. "Whether avoiding the media or eating up the open road, if you ever need someone to vouch for your driving skills, I'm your girl."

He tugs me to his side. "I'd say you're my girl for all things. I deserve a medal for how patient I am in waiting for you to realize I mean the same to you."

"Cocky much?"

"You have no idea." We resume watching the meteor shower. He points to the sky. "Make a wish."

I close my eyes and wish I'm always able to make him feel as special as he's making me feel now.

When I blink them open, his green gaze is on me. "Want to know what I wished for?"

My mouth drops open. I issue a husky, "Yes."

"I wished for you to believe what I feel toward you is real. And it's never going to go away."

"Oh, Bennett." My hand strokes the stubble adorning his cheeks. I pull my body into his. Serenaded by crickets and illuminated by zipping meteors, we kiss.

"I don't want tonight to end," he confesses.

"This is pretty darn special," I admit. The breeze picks up slightly, causing a chill to race through me. I snuggle closer to his warm body.

"You already know my new goal for UC, which you so cleverly set into motion with Luke at dinner tonight. How about you? I know you want to open six more physical therapy clinics in three years. You're already working on number four. What else is on Jenna West-field's horizon?"

"I've been so focused on achieving this goal that there hasn't been room to add another."

"Are there any awards you could win? How about hobbies you want to start?" He kisses my lips. "A particular man you want to fu—"

My fingers stop his mouth from completing his dirty sentence. "I'd like to be recognized for my PT offices. Maybe win a local award for best PT in the Hamptons."

"I knew you were harboring some professional accolade ambitions in you somewhere." He plants his chin on top of my head. "Do you have any personal goals?"

I lean back, causing his head to realign. "Do you? Seems to me all of your goals have been UC-driven." Two can play his game.

He stares into my soul. "Get the woman of my dreams to fall in love with me."

How can I resist this man? "Well, what are you going to do to make that happen? Standing around and looking all sexy-like fuels lust, not love."

He smirks. "So you think I'm sexy?"

I shake my head. "That's what you took from what I said?"

He chuckles, then tips his head upward. "I thought taking her to see a celestial show was a good start."

My gaze raises to the stars. "Yeah, it might be."

Another meteor streaks across the sky as if to punctuate Bennett's last thought.

This man, who appears to the world to only be a cocky rock star, has the softest heart. His mother—by biology and nothing else—failed in her responsibilities to show him love and protection. His father might have been well-meaning, but enabled his mother, then died when Bennett was only a teen. His girlfriend dumped him for his best friend. As a result, Bennett's so closed off. Except with me. To everyone else, he may be the lead singer of UC. To me, he's . . . *everything*.

My acceptance of this truth brings me to my feet. I grab his hand and tug him upright. "Let's go back to the hotel."

His eyebrows raise and come together, but he doesn't question me. Instead, he kisses the top of my head and wraps his arm around me. Following another exhilarating ride, we're in his hotel room. A space that doesn't have wheels is more than welcome.

He tosses his shirt onto a nearby chair. "You're staying with me tonight."

Not a question. And why should it be? Still, I need to tease him. "Pretty sure of yourself, huh?"

He stalks toward me, stopping when our toes nearly touch. "Yes."

My breathing picks up at how he devours me with his gaze. He doesn't move, simply stands in front of me, his body heat warming me from the inside out. I never had any intention of using the key Luke got for me anyway.

I can't maintain my false bravado. "Alrighty then." With trembling hands, I lift my shirt over my head.

Bennett grabs my hips and slams our bodies together. His mouth kisses the side of my neck where it meets my shoulder. "Your scent of bourbon and vanilla, topped with Jenna perfection, has been driving me nuts all night." His lips capture mine.

His own woodsy cologne amps me up. I raise to my tiptoes, sliding my bra covered breasts against his hard chest and entangling my fingers in his silky hair. His hands drop around to my butt and I leap up to wrap my legs around his waist—before remembering why I'm on this tour in the first place.

"Let me down." I don't move my legs for fear of aggravating his injury.

He squeezes me. "Not a chance in hell." He walks across the living room area of the suite, toward the closed door to the bedroom.

I remain pliant in his strong arms, the only logical thing I can do. However, I can't stop myself from kissing across his square jaw.

When he stops moving, he bends his knees until my feet are flat on the floor. "Now let's take care of this, shall we?" Before I know what he's talking about, the sound of my bra unclipping echoes throughout the bedroom. His palms cover my bare breasts. "Perfection."

The next thing I know, we're both half naked and horizontal on the hotel's very luxurious and very large bed. I want to be united with Bennett more than any other person in my life, but the physical therapist in me makes one last gasp. "One more day."

He growls. "We've made it this far, twenty-four more hours won't kill us. I still have many more ways to make you come undone without being inside you." He slides my pants down my legs.

*God, I love this man.*

Everything comes to a screeching halt around me, even though Bennett's busy laving my nipple.

"Bennett." My entire body's wound tighter than one of Coop's guitar strings.

He lifts his head from my chest. "I'm all yours, Sweetheart."

This is it. The opening—as it were—I need. I open my mouth.

Someone knocks on the hotel room door.

# Chapter Sixteen

I blink at the noise, trying to understand what I'm hearing. Bennett doesn't acknowledge it, merely crawls on top of me. Our lips clash in an out-of-control dance.

The knocking morphs into banging. Even the doorbell—who knew hotel rooms have doorbells?—rings several times. Bennett's fingers skim down to the top of my thigh.

A voice wafts in from the hallway. "Bennett, open up. I know you're in there!"

My boyfriend collapses on top of me.

The assault on the door continues.

"Luke," Bennett sighs, then focuses on me. "Don't go anywhere. I'll be back as soon as I kick the dickwad's ass."

Luke bangs again.

"Fuck!" Bennett jumps away from me, adjusts his jeans, and exits the bedroom. The door remains slightly ajar.

On the comfy bed, a smile plays around my lips. Our interruption doesn't dim my light spirit. I love this man, and he loves me. Or is it the other way around? My hands stretch above my head, and I perform snow angels above the comforter as I hear the front door open and close.

Bennett grouses, "What the fuck do you want?"

"I'll let you get back to whomever—or whomevers—are in your bedroom in a sec. I need to ask you if you know where Jenna is. She's not in her room."

At the sound of my name, I sit straight up. Why is the band's manager looking for me?

Bennett shares my sentiment. "Why?"

"Look, something happened. Have you seen her?"

"Since you think I have a couple of groupies in my bedroom, why are you asking me?"

Bennett's sarcasm spurs me to my feet. I toss his T-shirt over my head. Since it drops to my knees, I don't bother with my pants and cross the threshold to the living room area.

"Luke?"

Two heads spin in my direction. They both mutter my name, Luke with relief and Bennett with possession.

The slightly shorter man with shoulder-length brown hair a couple of shades darker than my man's takes a few steps in my direction. "You're here."

Bennett growls, "Where else would she be? And why on earth could you think I was with groupies?"

Luke's shoulder bumps up and down. "I needed to be sure. Listen, we have to talk. All of us." He points toward the sofa and chairs.

My stomach plummets. What's going on? We settle on the sofa— me on Bennett's lap, even though I tried to sit like a lady—as much as I can wearing only a T-shirt. His T-shirt.

In a chair opposite us, Luke closes his eyes. "I'm not going to sugarcoat this. There's an article."

Of course there's an article. Or fifty. Or one hundred. All of them hating on me as UC's Black Widow. Claiming I've settled in on my next prey, namely the lead singer.

Luke doesn't stop talking simply because my mind is supplying its own narrative. "A Lissa Baker says she had a wild night in the Hamptons with you, Bennett, including drugs and alcohol. Says you two had uninhibited sex, although she described it in excruciating detail. Claims you were complaining about Jenna to her all night." His gaze bounces to me. "She said you were Darren's pusher, and you encouraged him to take his fatal overdose as a way to keep him under your thrall."

I lean back against Bennett, my palm preventing my gasp from ricocheting around the room. For his part, Bennett kisses my cheek.

"She claims Jenna's causing UC to implode," Luke finishes talking.

My ears ring. I shake my head. No, no, no. I never would've done anything to hurt Darren like that. Nor come between UC. *Was Bennett complaining to her about me when I was in the ladies' room?* My entire body goes cold.

Bennett's hands weigh down my shoulders. He snarls, "She's a freaking liar."

"I know," Luke replies. "Let's start at the beginning. Who the fuck is this Lissa chick?"

"She was Bennett's high school girlfriend." The words pass my lips by rote.

The manager sits taller. "She was, B?"

"Yes," Bennett hisses. I try to squirm off his lap, but strong hands on my shoulders press down, not allowing me to move. Providing me an unusual comfort.

I disengage from their conversation, swimming inside my own brain. Lissa told reporters a multipart lie, one which most people will believe. How could she do this, after the way she treated a teenaged Bennett? She and his ex-best friend messed him up back then, and she's doing it again to him. What kind of sadist is this woman?

The kind that has it out for me, clearly. Her venom is unbearable. I try to lean forward. Bennett draws me back against his chest.

"What are your thoughts, Jenna?"

"Jenna's innocent," Bennett growls.

"I need to hear her side of the story," Luke protests.

Bennett's fingers dig into my shoulders. "This is total bullshit."

Is this how my life is going to be? Women coming out of the woodwork to complain about Bennett being with me? Is he worth it? Am I?

I know the answer to the last question—no way. If I leave the tour now, I can slip under the radar again in Aroostook. UC will continue its tour without a blip—my still unprofessed love for the incredible man behind me notwithstanding.

"Jenna?"

When I'm out of here, these awful articles will stop. Everything will go back to normal for UC.

"Jenna?"

Protective walls around my heart start to reform. The ones I built when Darren died and somehow allowed Bennett to take down. Stupid. Stupid. Stupid.

Bennett kisses my cheek and whispers my name in my ear. "Jenna?"

My head swivels toward him. I don't try to look into his eyes, I don't want to. All I want to do is escape. From Bennett's arms. From this hotel room. From Louisville.

"Talk to me, Sweetheart."

His endearment zings straight to my soul. Catching my breath becomes more difficult. Why is this happening? The universe must not like it when I'm happy. Do I deserve happiness? First it took my grandmother. Then Darren. Now it's trying to take Bennett away even though, thank God, he's still very much alive.

The man's warm hands skim my frigid arms. Yes, he's very much alive. "You didn't spend any time with Lissa?" My voice ticks up at the end indicating I'm asking a question rather than stating a truth.

"You know I didn't. She's a lying bitch, among other things."

I stare at the beige carpet. "How could she do this to you?"

He chuckles. "This, I'm sure, gave her a nice payday. I'm surprised she didn't hand the paps some photos from back then."

"Actually," Luke pipes up. "She did." He passes his cell to us, which Bennett takes without disturbing me from his lap.

Despite not wanting to, I stare at the screen as Bennett bounces through several pages. Photos of a teen Bennett, still cute but nowhere near as sexy as today, with adoration in his eyes for the girl-next-door Lissa, with her long blond hair and blue eyes. Not the current plastic, extensioned, Botoxed version. The story paints quite the picture of young love.

Bennett flips through more screens, faster as the headlines change to focusing on me. Ruining UC. The Black Widow. Preparing to strike again.

I address Luke. "If I leave, do you think this will die down?"

Behind me, a tenor voice rumbles, "You're not going anywhere, except with me."

"Some of it would quiet down, yes," Luke answers. His gaze bounces between Bennett and me. "But remember why you're here in the first place—to give physical therapy to Bennett. Among other things, I'm sure you don't want to leave your patient before his therapy is complete?"

"He's almost healed." This is the truth. Hell, we were about to have sex, proving he doesn't need me. No one does. I can escape to Aroostook and hide in my anonymity. "He can keep up the exercises without me."

Bennett asks, "Did you forget about the ones we haven't done yet?"

I don't answer, just keep on trying to leave his lap, which he continues to resist. Going limp, I say, "I can leave instructions."

Luke pushes to do his job. "So I'll confirm to our PR team that this whole wild night with Lissa never happened."

"Yes," Bennett passes the cell phone back to his manager. "Even if my heart weren't otherwise occupied, I'd never touch that skank again with a twenty-foot pole."

His protest does nothing to soothe my aching conscience. He didn't tell Luke I'm the woman he loves. Why would he? Who needs a Black Widow in their life unless they also like playing Russian roulette?

Luke taps on his phone. "Great. We'll deny her sex, booze, and drugs claims." He swallows. "I'm hate to ask this, but we want to be perfectly clear in our response. What about your supposed complaining to her about Jenna?"

The encounter replays in my mind, even though I tried to deny it before. No way did anything remotely close to this happen. I guess she thought we were together and wanted to insert herself in the middle.

Bennett's hands go around my waist. "Lies."

The manager nods. "Jenna?"

Because he used my name, I stare at Luke. He continues, "I think we really need to address her allegations about your relationship with Darren, and the fact you weren't involved in his death in any way."

Without energy, I say, "That's not what his mother said in the recent article."

Bennett tugs at me, securing me against him. "When we visited her, we got her to see how wrong she was. Right?"

"We tried, B. I'm not convinced we persuaded her all the way." Coffee-colored eyes hold me immobile. "Although, thankfully, she isn't quoted in this article."

I state the truth. "I wasn't even in the same state when Darren passed."

"007 was the first to find him," Bennett says in a strained voice. "Why do we have to keep rehashing all this shit? Didn't I give an interview to Jeremy Davis recently, and address what happened?"

"We have to respond because the media refuses to stop." Luke's reply gets to the heart of the matter.

"I can't prescribe pills." I find some reserve deep within to stand up for myself. "I never encouraged Darren to take more pills than he needed."

"We know, Sweetheart."

"We do." Luke picks his words with care. "Perhaps we can put out a statement about how you tried to help Darren get his problem under control."

"Which means I'd have to admit to knowing he was addicted—which I didn't."

"None of us did," Bennett adds.

Luke queries, "Are you sure you didn't have an inkling, Jenna?" In rapid succession he piles on the questions. "Were you aware he was still taking pills at all? How much did you push to know? Was there anything more you could've done to get control over him? Why didn't you reach out to me or the band? Do you think—"

Each question is like a body blow, gaining more momentum with his unrelenting pounding. His accusations grow. Combined with Lissa's awful article and the recent terrible articles about me as UC's Black Widow, plus Ma's stern warning against Bennett before I left home, it's as if the three words I almost said to Bennett can never blossom.

My heart cracks.

I can never be happy. I don't deserve it.

My breath catches.

Around me, Bennett and Luke have dissolved into a battle over me.

Stop. This has to stop.

I can't control my emotions any longer. Tears cascading from my eyes, they pour down my cheeks and sobs drown out the building tension.

# Chapter Seventeen

"Shh, Sweetheart, stop." Bennett's arms pull me against his naked torso, with his lips on the back of my neck.

"Shit, Jenna. I didn't mean it the way that all came out."

My hands never waver from over my eyes. I don't want to see the destruction I've brought to UC. Hearing it was bad enough.

"I'm sorry for badgering you like that," Luke reaffirms.

Bennett lifts his lips from my neck to agree. "Damn straight you are."

"You know how I can get, B. I run things down without engaging my brain first sometimes."

I don't blame Luke for voicing the things already going on inside my head. Through hiccups, I get out, "I did know Darren was prescribed Oxy during his treatment and that he was able to return to UC faster because of the medication. I thought he was only taking one if he was feeling pain. Even though I reminded him if he'd taken one that day so he wouldn't take another, I had no idea he was addicted."

Bennett's hands rub up and down my arms. My gaze remains on my bare legs draped over his jean-covered ones. "Even if you knew he was an addict," he adds. "You had no way of knowing what was going on that night. You weren't there."

"I did talk with him on FaceTime."

"Could you see any pill bottles in the frame?"

I remember back to that night. "No. But I knew he took a pill before you all went out."

Luke asks, "Did you encourage him to take another during your call?"

"No, of course not. I told him not to take another until the next night, at the earliest."

"See?" Bennett jumps in. "That's all the truth we need."

I manage to staunch the flow of tears. "The truth doesn't matter. Whatever sells."

The room's silent. I use this time to even out my breathing and slip off Bennett's lap. My being a diversion has run its course. Thank God I kept my stupid feelings to myself.

Before I can repeat my decision to leave, Luke says, "You just gave me a great idea, Jenna. I need to get the band here for everyone's input." He picks up his phone and starts tapping. "They'll be here soon."

"It's like three in the morning." More proof this isn't my reality.

Bennett laughs. "You're with rock stars, Sweetheart. This is midday to us."

"Unless you want to meet with the band in only a T-shirt." Luke points to me. "Or half-dressed"—he points to Bennett—"you two should get cleaned up."

Bennett stands and shakes his manager's hand.

I must be in a delirium. A nightmare. I'll wake up and none of this will have happened. It's the only solution. I pinch the back of my palm. "Ouch."

"You're definitely in Kentucky." Bennett bends down, puts his hands under my legs, and lifts me up. "We'll be back soon."

"I've got this," Luke replies.

Bennett carries me into the bedroom. When my feet touch the carpet, I say, "I don't understand."

His green gaze spears me. "Here's what it boils down to. I love you. You said you need more time to reach the same conclusion about me. Which you will." He licks his lips. "We deserve space to figure out what this means for us and how we want to grow as a couple. All the rest is noise."

"But . . . what Lissa told the reporters. About you. The photos. About me and what I'm doing to UC."

"All lies. Well, except for the high school stuff. Listen, I'm used to this shit. The only difference here is that some of it is true. What it doesn't talk about is how she left me for Curtiss. Can't imagine why she didn't tell the reporters about that." His snaps his fingers. "Oh, let me guess. It's because it paints her in a bad light."

I meet his gaze. "But what about Darren and the . . ." I can't bring myself to say the words Black Widow aloud one more time.

"Also fake. Our PR team handles shit like this all the time. The only reason it's causing a bigger deal is because you're involved." He bends his knees to be level with my line of vision. "And because I hid the real reason why you're here on tour with us, out of my own stupid pride. It's not like I wanted to admit I don't know how to jump."

His wry tone brings a reluctant smile to my face. "That's not what happened. You jumped just fine."

"Alright. It's worse if I can't stick a landing."

A giggle bubbles up, yet I ask a serious question. "How can you want me to stick around?"

"How could I not?" His retort is immediate. "Don't let the media get inside your head. The only people on the planet who know what's going on between us is us." His hand bounces between our chests. "You and me."

"I don't want to come between the band."

"Which is exactly why you won't." He places his hands onto my shoulders. "If you were like the press is portraying you, you'd be relishing all the hype. Wanting to keep the spotlight on you." He pauses. "What are you doing right now?"

I swallow. Aiming at the hollow of his throat, I murmur, "Trying to figure out a way to disappear so you guys can go on without this awful glare."

"See?" I stare at his delicious skin, and a tingle creeps up my body before I shut it down. Mostly. "Wrong answer. We need to face this head on. Show the world how strong UC is and, more importantly, how much you mean to me."

I work through what he's told me. I need his expertise more than ever. "I'm a physical therapist, Bennett. When I was with Darren, there was little media attention, so this is far outside my wheelhouse. Are you sure?"

"Yes. Want to know what else?" His hands go to the hem of his T-shirt hanging on my body.

"What?"

"You're mine. All mine. I think the press is jealous of this fact."

"Don't be ridiculous. I have eyes. I've seen the women who hang around the band. Heck, I remember the girls you used to leave with before." I pause. "They were gorgeous."

Bennett's lips tighten. "Are you with me because of how I look?"

"No. Of course not."

"Would it matter to you if I were fugly?"

"So long as I find you attractive, that's all that matters."

"When I tell you I think you're the most beautiful woman I've ever met, inside and out, do you believe me?"

I shake my head. "No, I'm not. I'm not a double-D. My hair isn't an arresting shade of blonde. My lips aren't—"

"Want to know what I see when I look at you?" He interrupts me. "I see a capable woman who knows how to heal people, with a body that was created to fit mine unlike any other." With one step, he invades my personal space. "You're all that and more to me, Jenna. You challenge me, make me laugh, make me cry with your exercises sometimes." He grins. "How I see you is colored by who I know you are. Let others win Miss America titles, you've won the only title that matters—to my heart."

I look into his eyes and see only sincerity reflected back. He means every single word. How can I flee when the leader of the band has placed me at the center of his world, where I dream to place him in mine? The possibility of not being around Bennett is like cutting off a limb, where no amount of therapy would bring my life back to normal. Sure, there would be workarounds, but I'd never function the same way I do when he's with me.

He adds, "You have my heart, Sweetheart. Forever."

The dam bursts, and I pull his head to mine. Our lips explode in another kiss, more intense than ever before. A draft hits my butt as he pulls his T-shirt up and off my body.

The front door slams shut, and male voices penetrate our heated interlude. "Fuck," Bennett exclaims. "When will these people leave us alone?"

Despite the circumstances, I giggle. "We'll figure it out."

"Damn straight." He steps back, his heated gaze raking over my body. "Let's get you cleaned up so we can face this mess head-on. Then, I want you under me for hours."

I don't answer him, but my heart screams "Yes!" I allow him to bring me into the bathroom and turn on the water. In the meantime, he strips off his jeans.

"In you go." He nudges me toward the spray, but not before I catch a glimpse of my blotchy face in the mirror. I never was a good crier, as Kara used to chide me.

Under the showerhead, we wash each other. He takes special care around my eyes, while I focus on his tattooed arms. If I were to dive any lower, I'm not sure we'd ever get out of here.

"Here you go," he passes me an oversized white fluffy towel while tucking a similar one around his trim waist. "I'll be waiting in the bedroom."

For the first time, I'm happy not to have hair that requires any special work to make it presentable. I scrape my locks away from my face and put it into a ponytail before brushing on some blush and mascara. Satisfied, I join him in the bedroom where Bennett stands in a pair of workout shorts and a Cole Manchester tour tee. He looks good enough to eat.

"There she is. You've already got color back in your cheeks."

"It's called blush."

"No. It's called being a fighter. You've got this."

He kisses me again and tugs my towel off my body. Standing naked in front of him while he's fully dressed is an unexpected turn-on. What isn't with this man? My hands slide down his arms as his tongue invades my mouth. His growl precedes him pulling away. "No more of that, missy. Not if we don't want to keep the band waiting another hour. Or two. Make that five." He chuckles.

I join him, the laughter cathartic after the earlier meeting. Not to mention what we're about to face. I glance down, surprised to see my suitcase. "How did this get here?"

"One word: Jeb. I think he has a thing for you."

I picture the huge roadie with the bad back. "I helped him, you know?" Bennett raises an eyebrow at me as he places my suitcase on the bed. "He complained about soreness in his back, and I gave him some exercises to help ease the strain from moving all the equip-ment." I open the case.

Bennett's gaze focuses on my clothing, and he picks out a matching panty and bra set. Green. "I bet he appreciated your attention."

"Not in that way," I protest, swiping the lingerie from his hands. While I put them on, he pulls out a black tunic and matching leggings.

I shake my head. "Nah. Not going to wear funeral colors to discuss this latest mess." I swap the top for one with a floral pattern and slip into it. Barefoot, I pad to the mirror, happy with how I look even if it's only for the band.

"Damn, you're fucking hot. All the guys are going to want what I have."

I keep my opinion of his ridiculous statement to myself. Instead, I quip, "Yet you're the one who can't seem to close the deal."

His hands land on my butt. "Believe me when I tell you that you're not going to be able to walk for a week when I do." He kisses me, hard, leaving me breathless.

Stopping with his hand on the doorknob, he says, "Ready to hear Luke's idea?"

Just like that, all the positivity taking up space in my body ebbs. My shoulders sag and my chin tilts toward the same beige carpet that's been underfoot since our return from the meteor shower. I can't believe an evening that started on hopes and dreams has devolved into one fueled by turmoil and insults.

"Hey," Bennett strides over to me. "This is going to work out, I promise. You're way too important to me for it not to. I've got you."

"And the rest of the band has you," I remind him.

"Hmmm." He pecks my cheek. "Let's go."

This time, Bennett doesn't allow for any wiggle room, as his arm goes around my shoulders and, together, we enter the living room area. Luke, Coop, Río, Pierce, and Tristan sit around the dining room table, drinks in front of them.

"Glad to see you've helped yourselves to the bar," Bennett notes.

"You snooze, you lose," Coop retorts.

"Besides," Río adds, "Food hasn't arrived yet." He dons an evil grin, causing me to giggle.

Bennett's head jerks toward me, and his body relaxes. He kisses my temple and whispers, "I'd do anything for endless giggles from you tonight." We walk over to the bar area, where he points to a bottle of red wine and I shrug. He pours me a glass, gets himself a bourbon, and we take empty seats next to the band's manager.

"I'm going to dive right in, since we all know about the latest article about B and this Lissa Baker chick. I think it would be best if you guys address it head on during your next concert tomorrow, er tonight. B, you can point out the only truth in it about you two dating in high school. Then share how it ended and how the rest is lies."

Next to me, Bennett nods. "I can do that."

Luke continues, "Then, I think it's time you all address the stupid Black Widow rumors."

I flinch, and Bennett puts his arm around me. Claiming me in front of his bandmates who are, without a doubt, his best friends.

Río says, "We got you, Jenna. You're no more a killer arachnid than Coop's a smiley elephant." He punches the guitarist on the shoulder.

Giving his shoulder a rub, Coop says, "We can talk up how you're here giving therapy so Bennett's injury can heal faster."

"No." My voice is much steadier than I could've hoped. "Bennett hasn't addressed his injury publicly, so I don't want to out him now to save my hide."

Pierce's head pops up, and he stares at me. Clearly, he's not a fan. He tolerates my being on tour because he doesn't have any other choice. His eyebrows raise, but he remains silent.

Tristan is the one to break the quiet. "I get it. How about we say Jenna's here because we needed to add a physical therapist to the crew due to some recent injuries. Keep it broad."

I lean in toward the table. "That's not a lie, either. Jeb needed some pointers about how to strengthen his back muscles and I helped him out."

In my ear, Bennett whispers, "I'm sure he'd prefer a rub down." I smack his stomach, causing him to grunt.

Unaware—or more likely ignoring our antics—Luke says, "Great idea. We decided to add a physical therapist to the tour and chose Jenna due to her previous connection with the band. Keep it as close to the truth as possible."

Río adds, "We can say we chose her because of the movie. Reminded us how great a girl she is to have around." He grins at me.

Seems like most of the band agrees with his assessment. I chance a glance at Pierce and can see he's not on board. At. All. The entire band has to make this announcement from the stage, though, or it won't work.

Luke barrels forward. "This is great, guys. We should write this down so you can all talk onstage."

"Awesome! You guys never let me talk when we're performing," Río exclaims.

"That's because we never know what shit will come out of your mouth," Bennett replies.

Coop notes, "It'll be more powerful because Bennett's the one who always talks for the band." Tristan agrees.

Pierce looks like he was forced to eat raw egg whites, his face having taken on a green pallor. While the guys continue to hash out the statement, he pushes away from the table. Without a word, he spins on his heel and stalks out of the room.

Around me, all talking and good humor plummets. If he isn't on board, this won't work. And I'll be the person who broke up the band for real.

Bennett jumps to his feet. "I'll go knock some sense into him," he vows.

*No, don't do it.* This has to be his decision, not one forced on him. I can't be the one to voice these thoughts, however.

Tristan stops Bennett. "No. You'll only exacerbate the situation. I'll go." He slams back whatever's in his glass and follows Pierce out the door.

"He'll come around," Coop declares.

I don't think so. He looked ready to explode and puke at the same time.

"He will," Luke agrees. "In the meantime, let's finish the statement." He looks at me. "Don't worry. This will work out, I promise. Now, B, what are you going to say about Lissa?"

Still standing, Bennett begins his story about his ex leaving him for his best friend Curtiss back in high school. All the while, he walks behind his band members, touching their backs as if to thank them for being there with him. For him—and me. This is the most touchy-feely I've ever seen him with his bandmates. I need to make him see how they're coalescing around him.

"She told me she was 'saving it'"—he uses air quotes together with his tongue sticking out—"for marriage. I was a freaking horny teenager, and her declaration was like showing red to a bull, but I was a stupid fool and agreed to hold off. So, we didn't have sex back then, and now she's claiming I never got over her." His eyes roll.

"This Lissa is a bitch," Río says when Bennett finishes sharing their sordid history. "I wonder what Curtiss"—he hisses the last syllable like a snake—"does now? He's probably some balding dud who sells used cars."

His description makes my cheeks half inflate. Having his support means a lot. Having all their support does, with the glaring exception of Pierce.

"So that's Lissa," Coop concludes. "We've also got Jenna figured out. The only missing link is UC apparently being broken up by this slip of a woman with truly amazing hands." He manages to get it out before laughing, which sets off the rest of the table.

"Yeah," Río holds his sides. "She's like our blonde Yoko Ono. Who, by the way, got a bad rap."

Luke agrees. "No argument here. But I don't think you should share your opinion with the world. Why don't you stick to the fact that you guys aren't going anywhere?"

The two remaining band members agree.

While I appreciate all they're doing, without Pierce, it's going to be for naught. The only other cherry on the top that's missing is Darren's family. At least they're "unavailable for comment."

Yet another knock sounds on the front door. Assuming it's Tristan, I rush to answer it only to see a server from the hotel wheeling in food. "Guys," I announce, "your third dinner is here."

"All right!" Río stalks toward the trolley as if he hasn't eaten in years. Addressing the beautiful woman unloading the tray, he says, "Let me help you."

I find Bennett and nod toward the gorgeous server. He shrugs, then blows me a kiss. After sampling the number of women he has, I need to trust he's ready to settle down. With me. It's the latter point that blows my mind.

Río escorts the server to the front door while I take in the buffet of amazing foods awaiting us. Coop and Luke don't hesitate to pick up plates and start piling them high. I take another small sip of my wine and check the time. Four o'clock. *In the morning.* How is this my life?

Around the table, Darren's overdose is discussed in brief terms. I'm dismissed as a possible accomplice without any thought. Then, conversation turns toward the upcoming leg of the US tour, ticket sales, possible new merch to add to the store, Darren's scholarship program. Even new material.

The band operates differently from most others I've heard about, since they write their songs as a group. No one is the designated chief lyricist, nobody takes the lead on music. They bounce ideas off each other in between scrambled eggs, French toast, and paninis.

For the life of me, I can't help but think of them as a family. Coming together to fight off a threat. Supporting each other . . . including me.

Except Pierce. He doesn't want anything to do with the intruder —the black sheep of the family. If he can't agree to make the statement, it'll fall flat.

I'll be back to square one.

I need to brace myself for this possibility. No matter how much I love Bennett and he loves me, without the approval from the entire band, it won't work.

I'll have to leave.

I pray it doesn't end this way.

# Chapter Eighteen

Tristan and Pierce never returned to the band meeting. Coop and Río ended up leaving around five, while Luke stuck around another half hour before almost crashing and Bennett forced him to go to bed. In his own room.

When the door closes behind him, Bennett notes, "Alone at last. But I'm more tired than Luke looked. Let's go to bed and sleep, Sweetheart. Things will look better in the morning."

I don't remind him that it's already morning. My chest swells with hope he's right, but I doubt it.

Together, we walk into the bedroom, shedding our clothes along the way. I'm too tired to brush my teeth or take off any remaining makeup, and I just crash next to Bennett. With a kiss goodnight, I escape into anxiety dreams.

On a gasp, I jolt up in bed after bobbing and weaving away from a man with a machete. When the phantom attacker recedes, my gaze lands on a sleeping Bennett. He looks much younger in repose. All the weight of his world is off his shoulders—and apparently transferred to mine.

The bedside clock says it's now ten, meaning I've gotten a little more than four hours of sleep. But I know my body. Once awake, I'll never get back to sleep.

I slip out of bed, careful not to wake the hot rock star. Making a trip to the bathroom, I put on my leggings and another tunic, and escape to the kitchen to heat water for tea. It's time to calm down and face reality.

On the sofa, I call Ma. It rings straight through. Where the heck can she be at this time of the morning? Well, I guess it is almost midday. I leave her a message and call Court.

She doesn't say hello or anything, simply dives in with "How are you holding up?"

"Better than I thought possible," I reply. "Bennett's been wonderful, as has the band. Well, all except Pierce."

"He's still not your biggest cheerleader, huh?"

"Not by a long shot. The guys are going to make a statement at tonight's concert about Lissa and all the media surrounding my return. It'll mainly be accurate, with a couple of omissions to protect Bennett and me." I dunk my tea bag. "Well, Pierce is the wildcard."

"That's all you can hope for, right?"

"Yeah. If Pierce doesn't join in, it'll fall flat. I can't imagine he'll say anything to support me." I sigh. "He still blames me for what happened to Darren."

"That's bullshit."

I love how she always defends me. Needing to get out of my own head, I say, "Okay, enough about me. What's going on with you?"

She fills me in about her love life, which is as full as always. Court's never lacked for male attention, lucky her. But she's also never had anyone special. "Then there's the clinic."

Her change of subject seems ominous. "What's happening?"

"Well, aside from the media circus surrounding you running off with a rock star." Her laugh sounds forced. "Things were dying down lately. No more reporters were camping out, since they've all come to realize you're with UC. Most of the patients rescheduled their appointments, and the pace of new ones was returning to normal.

However, we have had a couple of incidents." She takes a breath. "Nothing major at all. I've been able to handle everything."

"Incidents?" I repeat the word that's been rattling around my brain since she dropped it. "What's going on?"

"First of all, I've asked Felipe, and he said nothing's happening at his clinic, so they're centered around this one."

Abandoning my teacup, I yank on my ponytail. I repeat, "What's going on?"

"There have been some threats."

Threats? "To the clinic?"

"Yes. Someone's been leaving messages on our machine that we shouldn't be able to keep our license since the owner is off gallivanting with a rock band. However, it was the graffiti on the clinic wall that raised more alarms."

"Graffiti?" The timbre of my voice raises on each syllable. I glance toward the bedroom and lower it. "Was anyone hurt?"

"This is why I love you, Jenna. You don't care about your physical property, only about your patients and employees."

"Court, skip the niceties. Is everyone all right?"

"Yes. Whoever it was did it after hours, so there was only property damage. I didn't bother with insurance, so as soon as the police give their go-ahead, I'll have the wall repainted."

My eyes close, absorbing everything. "Thanks. This is how I know you're the absolute best person to be in charge." I squeeze the teabag and, needing to get out some of this nervous energy, I walk across the room and throw it away. "Tell me about the graffiti."

"Oh, you know what graffiti's like."

Her vague answer sets off even more alarm bells. I try a different tact. "Do you have photos? You must—text one to me."

"It's nothing really."

Abandoning my tea, her evasiveness is what makes me pace around the room. "I'm sure. But it is my building, so I'd like to see what we're dealing with. Do you think it's kids or something more serious?"

"The police didn't say it was gang related, if that's what you're getting at."

"So, it's more directed?" As in specifically aimed at me.

"No. I mean yes. That is to say, it's nothing. Really."

My stomach churns at how she's failing at being evasive. "Court, send me a picture."

"I never could keep things from you. Fine." Tapping tones reach my ears. "Sent. Just keep it together when you see it."

"When am I ever off-kilter?" *All the time since Bennett.* I'm not even "with" Bennett. I mean, I haven't been with him yet. But he's given me how many orgasms already? *Great, now you're arguing with yourself.*

My fingers open the text she sent and I collapse into a chair. "This can't be happening."

On the side of my building is a massive black spider with the words, "Don't leave your health 2 a Black Widow." I drop my phone into my lap, screen facing upward.

This is more than graffiti. Graffiti is some random letters and symbols. This is a message. God, I hate the Black Widow nickname. I didn't cause Darren's overdose. I'm not hurting UC now, either. Well, they do have this mess to deal with because I'm here. But it's the media's fault, not mine.

From far away, I hear, "Jenna. Jenna. Are you still with me?"

Swiping tears off my cheek, I retrieve my cell and press the speaker. I don't even have the energy to hold the phone to my ear. "Sorry, yes. I'm here."

"Painters will be here tomorrow, or as soon as the police give me the go-ahead."

Wonderful. Aroostook gets days to take in this "graffiti." "Which wall is this?"

Please don't say the one facing the road. With any luck, they put this on the side—or better still, the back.

"It's next to the front door."

"Of course it is."

"Of course what is?" A sleepy, sexy Bennett enters the living room area, wearing only a pair of shorts hanging low around his hips.

I can't. I just can't. First the band has to deal with the article and now my business does too. It's too much. My head shakes with all the pent-up rage.

His expression morphs into concern. "Jenna," he slides on the couch next to me. "Talk to me. We can handle whatever this is. Together."

From the speaker, Court yells, "Take care of my girl!"

His eyebrows pull together. He reaches over and plucks my cell out of my hand. His distinctive tenor voice rings out through the suite. "Hello?"

"Bennett?"

"Yes. And you are?"

"Courtney. Remember me, from the clinic? I'm taking care of things here while Jenna's working with you."

My gaze doesn't stray from his as I remember their scant interactions. "Right. You're her manager at the clinic I got my PT from in Aroostook."

"You got it. I was catching our girl up on what's been happening out here."

Without lifting my head, I instruct, "Tell him the rest."

Court continues, "Well, I had to send her a photo of graffiti that was drawn on our wall. The police already are involved. No one was hurt and this will be painted over as soon as I get the go-ahead from the police."

"You said you sent a photo to Jenna?"

Even as she responds in the affirmative, he's in my texts and opening the most recent one from "Court." I don't move as he takes in the spider and words. "Fuck."

"I'm handling this. It's just one stupid prank."

I finally find my voice. "It's not a prank and you know it, Court."

"Okay, fine. It isn't. But there's nothing you can do from Kentucky or wherever you are right now. I'm handling it."

"You shouldn't have to do this. It's my fault. If I hadn't gone with UC on their tour, this wouldn't have happened."

Bennett's head snaps toward me. "This isn't your fault. If anything, it's mine. If I didn't need physical therapy, you wouldn't be here."

"Well, things have taken on a life of their own. The media's dubbed me the Black Widow, and now some freak in Aroostook is running with it." I stand. "I should leave."

From the phone, Court yells, "No. Stay!"

Bennett gets to his feet as well. "If you go now, the media will have won. That you actually are a black widow. Do you really want that?"

I whisper, "No."

Court questions, "What would you do if you came back here anyway?"

"I would deal with the cops and get the wall repainted."

"Done and done. Next?"

Sliding down onto the chair, I come up empty. Me, the person who's always in control, is subject to the whims of the media and now, apparently, a graffiti artist. "What about our patients?"

"Like I told you before, we're almost back to the levels we were at before the whole Bennett thing happened."

Next to me, Bennett sucks in a breath. "I'm sorry," he says to me as well as Court. "I didn't mean to ruin your business." He sits and rubs his right thigh. "I only wanted to get help, stay under the radar."

"Which you did," Court says. "Speaking of which, how's your therapy coming along?"

"Good. I'm about eighty-five percent now." His posture straightens. "Jenna's moving me on to the most advanced exercises and I'm down to one session a day."

"Great to hear. Keep up with those exercises, and you'll be better than normal by the time she's done with you."

"I will," Bennett promises.

Something about the graffiti's been bothering me, though, so I grab the phone from Bennett and stare at the photo again. The graffiti wall mocks me. "Hey, Court. Does anything about this graffiti strike you as odd?"

"Odd? No, not really. Other than how much time they took in drawing all the details of the spider."

There's something about the spider. I just can't put my finger on it.

Bennett jokes, "Maybe the artist has a pet spider?"

Or maybe the artist is an actual artist. Or someone who tried, and failed, to become one. "I think I know who did it!" On my feet again, I speedwalk from the television to the fridge. Years of growing up together, watching her draw everything from rabbits to tractors to men. Thaine. My high school boyfriend who she stole with a drawing. Well, and by opening her legs.

Her name expels from my body with venom. "Michelle."

From the phone, Court asks, "Who?"

For his part, Bennett's mouth drops open as he watches me from the chair

"Michelle did the graffiti. I'm sure of it." I resume pacing. "She always was great at art, even went to college for it. I remember her trying to make a splash in the New York City art scene when we were in school. Her failure brought her back to Aroostook—"

Court completes my sentence. "Where she's the receptionist for a doctor."

"Your mother mentioned something about this to me." Bennett runs his hand through his hair. "Shit. She's crazier than I had pegged her."

Nerves inside my body chase each other. How can we leverage this truth against her? "Too bad we can't do the same against her."

"She's not the owner of her business," Court reminds me.

"I know." Think, Jenna, there has to be a way to trap her . . . I have to get her back somehow. "Hey, Court, do the police have any leads?"

"No. I handed over our alarm footage, but whoever did this—I mean, Michelle—was careful to stay out of the camera's range."

Bennett asks, "How about the graffiti itself?"

His question forces me to bring up the ugly photo again. Sitting next to him, we both examine every square inch. "It would've been too easy," he chuckles, "If she put her initials by the spider, huh?"

Both Court and I laugh. Bennett managed to break the tense standoff from a few minutes ago. Grin still across my cheeks, I face the man in front of me. I mouth, "Thank you."

He blows me a kiss.

"Oh rats," Court says. "The police are coming up the walk. I better run. I'll keep you posted."

"You better." The line goes dead.

Green eyes bore into me. "I don't want you doing that again."

"What? Talking with Court?"

He waves his hand. "No, of course you have to keep on top of your business. I mean, don't ever leave me alone in my bed. I turned over to find your side cold and empty." He crosses his arms.

"I woke up and couldn't fall back asleep." Honestly, I didn't try. "I didn't want to disturb you. You looked so peaceful."

"You know what didn't look peaceful?" His finger circles his face. "Waking up solo."

My head tilts. "So you'd want me to stay in bed, while fully awake mind you, so that you don't wake up alone? You know that makes you sound like a child. Or a serial killer."

"Or someone desperately in love with a woman who seems to be slipping through my fingers."

"Oh."

He hooks his fingers into my waistband and drags me against his bare chest. My heart screams at me to admit how I'm feeling, but I can't quiet my thoughts about how Lissa's trying to torpedo Bennett's career. And Michelle's putting a wrecking ball to my business.

Into my neck, Bennett says, "I have to do my PT before meeting with the band to hammer out the details about our speech to tonight's audience."

"During your meeting, I need to work up a press release for At Your Service PT." My fingers run down his back. "I'm ready to start when you are."

"Sweetheart, I'm always ready to start."

I giggle. "I meant your physical therapy, Rock Star."

"Can't blame a guy for trying!"

I smack his chest, enjoying the banter. Still, my worries about Michelle and Lissa are never far from my mind.

# Chapter Nineteen

After we finished our therapy session, Bennett took a shower and headed to sound check. I stayed behind to work on a press release about the graffiti. In my heart, I know Michelle did it—but how to prove it?

Sitting back from my tablet, I reread my work. I'm no marketing expert, but I think this will do the trick. It addresses the situation head-on as well as makes an oblique reference to my nemesis. She'll get the subtle references, even if no one else does. Yes. Gets my point across without stating it for all to see. I email it to Court.

My phone rings ten minutes later. "Hey, Court. What did you think?"

"That you missed your calling. You should be in PR! I love it."

Her words put a smile on my face. "Think it will do the trick?"

"I can't go that far, Jenna. She'll definitely know you're on to her. I hope this ends now, but we shouldn't be too certain of ourselves."

I sigh. "I know you're right. Do you think I should come home? Call it a day with UC and chalk this whole experience up to wild days?" Even as the words fall from my mouth, I know—in my heart—I don't want to play into Bennett's insecurities. Nor do I want to leave him.

"Don't go jumping to conclusions here. I didn't say that. Excuse me." She obviously pulls the phone away as I overhear her talking with someone, I think another therapist, about a course of treatment. "Sorry about that. Austin asked me a question."

Austin. A person I haven't thought about since I left. Time for me to get my head back into the business. "How's he doing?"

"Austin? Oh, he's doing well. Still needs some guidance with his patients, but he's a go-getter. Sometimes a bit too much for his own good."

"Yeah. I hear you." I giggle. "Bennett can't stand him."

"Can't imagine why not." Court full on laughs. I bet she and Nese would be good buds. "It's not like he's trying to get in your panties or anything."

"Hey! He might be into cougars, you never know." Despite what I told Bennett, I suspect he may be onto something.

"More like he's trying to seduce you into giving him his own clinic."

Court's probably on the money about him. I tap the table. "You're definitely right there. He told me flat out he wants to manage a new clinic. I keep putting him off."

"He'll get there. Just not today. Or tomorrow."

"So," I bring us back to the issue at hand. "Think I should come home now that Bennett's down to one therapy session a day?"

"No, I don't. You're handling most of the fallout from the tour. This press release is brilliant. Twisting it around and starting a contest for slogans for T-shirts involving our eight-legged friends is next level."

I blow on my fingers. "I wanted to turn this nightmare into something positive." My positivity deflates. "Still, it feels wrong to be gallivanting with UC while everything's spinning out of control."

"I know Michelle's not the only piece of this puzzle. Lissa's article sparked a lot of media attention."

"Yeah. I guess I should be happy it pulled attention away from the graffiti incident. That didn't even make the national media." I glance around the empty hotel suite and my heart rate spikes. "Court, Bennett's been gone for hours. The band had a sound check, and he was going to talk with them. About the speech tonight about Lissa. And me."

"Everything will work out. I believe that."

"I wish I had your confidence. You know I never meant to put any strain between the band members, but I am. Pierce can barely stand to look at me."

"He was Darren's best friend, right?"

"Yes."

"Give him more time to come around. Bennett has. Tristan, Darren's replacement has. Seems to me the others, Coop and Río, have as well. Pierce will too."

"That's what Bennett said. It's so hard for me. I want to press a button and have everything normal, you know?"

"You mean, you want to control the situation? Nah. I wouldn't have imagined!" She adds a snort-laugh to punctuate her sentence.

"What's so bad about liking control?"

"Nothing, in small doses. Not the oversized helpings that you thrive on." She pulls the phone away to talk with someone else. "Listen, I have to run. Send out the press release as is. I've got it from here."

Before I can reply, she clicks off. Fine. After one final read-through, I email it to the list I've curated entitled "Press Release Contacts." I can only hope a couple of reporters call me to ask for additional color. I'd love to *color* outside the lines on Michelle's face.

After checking in with Felipe about my other clinic, and my contractor about the third one under renovation, I sit in silence. Better get ready for tonight's concert. I go to my suitcase and check out my clothes. Leggings, jeans, and the dress Court gave me won't do. Especially tonight. I need something that says I'm not the Black Widow.

I strum my fingers on the table. What can I wear?

Nese.

The stylist might be able to help a girl out. I text her:

> Concert clothes SOS

STOP BY MY OFFICE!

I should try to channel her lightness and sunshine. Lord knows, I could use some of that. In spades. More importantly than anything, though, I want to be this woman for Bennett. After the Lissa article and everything he's had to deal with—on his own—he deserves this treat.

Clad in jeans and sneakers, I make my way to the conference room she took over as The Closet for the concerts in Kentucky. While not as spacious as the one in Madison Square Garden, it overflows with options. Five racks of male clothing are the centerpiece, one for each of the guys in the band. I gravitate to the one with a few pairs of black leather pants and run my palm over one of them. Bennett's going to fill these out tonight, making every woman drool. Heck, I need to swallow my own saliva thinking about him in them.

"You're here! Great." Nese floats toward me, obviously in her element. "The band's not expected for a while, so we have plenty of girl time. What look are you going for tonight?"

"Anything not related to spiders."

Her head tilts as her eyebrow raises. "Alright. We'll stay away from all my outfits with more than two arms."

I emit a giggle. Her crazy humor gets me out of my own head for the first time in a while. I need to trust things will work out for the best—Court has the fort well in hand at home, Luke's wrangling the band here. The least I can do is not look anything like a bug needing to be squashed.

"How about I go for rocker chick?"

Her nose scrunches up. "Nah. Not your vibe. I'm thinking sexy schoolgirl. A short plaid miniskirt, white button-down. Yes, I think that will make all the guys cream their pants."

"Nese, I've never been a private school student in my life."

"All the more reason to walk the walk now." She physically turns my body toward some more racks near the back part of the room. I thank the gods for this trove of women's clothing. She flips through several pieces, pulling a few into her hands, while I check out a different spot.

I hold up a black vest. "What do you think of this?"

She purses her lips, then nods. "It might work. I'll have to see it on you." Moving at light speed toward a shelving unit, she asks my bra size and throws a black bra and panty set at me. Next, she asks, "You're a size seven shoe, right?"

"Yes."

"Great." She pulls out some shoes, from ballerina flats to stilettos and even another pair of sneakers. "Now, go try everything on." She shoos me toward a curtained area.

I stand in front of it. "I'm surprised you even have this here. The guys strip out in the open."

"Hey, a girl's gotta get some eye candy somehow." She motions for me to try on her treasures. She winks. "This is special reserve."

I shuck my clothes and try on the panty set, which does enhance my average attributes. The skirt goes on next, then the button-down. I try it on tucked in but think it looks better untucked. The last thing I put on is the black vest. Do I look like some overaged wannabe?

"Let me see you!"

Nese spurs me to slide open the curtain. I blurt, "I don't think this really is me. I'm like a grandma pretending to be in nursery school."

Her face rises to the ceiling and she laughs. "It's absolutely fab

that you're hooking up with Bennett, Mr. Leather Pants himself.
How can't you see how positively gorgeous you are? Come here."

I close the distance between us in bare feet. She walks around
me, ties the bottom of the shirt. Tilting her head, she asks me to tuck
it in.

"Better. Now take off the vest." I do. "Nah, put it back on." Her
finger taps her lips. "Unbutton the top three buttons of your shirt."
When I comply, she nods. "Two more."

"Two," I yelp. "My bra will be hanging out."

"Not hanging out, but I want to give it more airtime. Humor me."

I do, then resist the urge to keep my hands in front of my chest.

"Perfect. Now, which shoes?" I don't answer her, simply let her
circle the options I left on the floor. "None of these will do. Wait
here." She scampers away.

I stand in front of the full-length mirror. The black bra, which
was barely visible before all the unbuttoning, is now on full display.
Not in a raunchy way. It actually makes me feel sort of hot. In a
Jenna way, of course.

"Here. Try these on."

A clunky pair of combat boots bang on the floor, and my gaze flies
up to hers. "You do see what I'm wearing, right?"

"Oh yes. I do, and so will everyone else when I'm done with you.
Now put them on."

Putting on a pair of socklets, I walk over to a chair and slide my
feet into the boots. Wiggling my ankles, I'm shocked at how comfortable they feel.

"Stand up. I need the full effect."

I get to my feet, then do a slow twirl at her direction. Nese claps.
"Girl, no one's going to call you anything other than motherfucking
hot when they see you tonight."

My cheeks flush. Guess you don't get to be the stylist for a group
of guys without having their foul expressions rub off on you.

I glance down. "Are you sure this all works together?"

"Only two things are out of place now—your hair and makeup.

Lucky for you, we've got that covered too, and they'll be excited to have a new head to work on. Go see the artists in the back and come back when you're done. I think you're my favorite masterpiece." I turn to head out when she stops me. "I need a photo!" She takes like a million pictures of me and us. "Now go. I can't wait to see the band's reaction when you're done. Make sure you let me introduce you to them, got it?"

"You deserve one hundred percent of the credit for this outfit." When I realize I haven't given one thought to Michelle or Lissa or the speech that may or may not happen tonight, I give her a fierce hug. "Thank you for this, Nese. It means the world to me."

"You're amazing. Don't let anyone try to make you feel otherwise." She sends me to hair and makeup.

After I've been powdered and eyelined and curled and primped and prodded more than I thought imaginable, I'm ready to go back to The Closet and present myself to Nese. All the women back here have complimented my outfit, yet I still can't help but feel out of my element.

I stand in the hallway, out of sight of the crew and roadies hustling to prepare for tonight's concert. From inside The Closet, I hear the band laughing. Even Pierce. It has to be a good sign, right?

On this hopeful thought, I text Nese that I'm ready and waiting. A couple of minutes later, she bursts through the door, stopping on a dime. "Holy. Shit."

My cheeks half inflate. "Is that a good holy shit or a bad one?"

"A fucking great one. Turn around." I comply. "You're perfection. I can't wait until Bennett gets his eyes on you. All of UC, for that matter." She tugs on my arm. "Walk behind me. I get to do the grand reveal."

I'm swept up in her element. Inside The Closet, I remain behind her, holding her hand. All around us, the guys keep going about their business. "Hey guys," Nese says.

They keep talking.

She clears her throat and tries again, to no avail. I squeeze her hand, but she shakes her head. A second later, she brings her right hand to her mouth and whistles loud enough to alert the concertgoers on the other side of the stadium.

At least she gets her wish. All eyes are on her.

"That's better. I want to show off my latest work of genius."

She moves to the side, leaving me alone in front of the band. I force my hands to remain at my sides and not to shift my weight between my feet. It's not easy.

"Take me to school with you, Jenna!" Río's the first out of the gate.

Coop quips, "I can be your teacher."

"Looking fine, Miss Westfield," Tristan adds, ever the gentleman.

Bennett steps forward, cutting off the peanut gallery's comments. He doesn't say a word, merely advances toward me in his body-hugging leather pants. I need to thank Nese for this gift—as does all womankind.

He licks his lips, his gaze eating me up like I was an ice cream cone. When I think he's about to say something, he motions for me to twirl around like Nese did before. Only her gesture didn't have his lascivious overtone.

Keenly aware I'm in front of the entire band and crew, I refrain from shaking my hips. Instead, I take my time in blinking at every wall before returning to stare at him. I want to ask his opinion of my outfit, or at least give Nese credit for it. But I'm immobile and mute until Bennett releases me from his overheated stare.

"Nese," he bellows.

From off to the side, she replies, "You can't fuck her in front of all of us!" Snickers follow her outburst. Of course, my cheeks become hot.

"Not going to give you all the satisfaction that's mine alone," Bennett says. "I *was* going to give you a huge bonus, but not with such a potty mouth."

"I take it back," Nese backpedals.

He rubs his hands together. "Check your next paycheck," he

quips to Nese. Under his breath, for my ears only, he says, "I can't believe you're more sexy now wearing those boots and miniskirt. Are you trying to kill me before I take the stage?" He crowds my space.

The rest of the room disappears. All my focus is on Bennett. "You like?"

"Sweetheart, if I liked the way you looked any more, I'd be in cardiac arrest. Which wouldn't be good for performing purposes."

I nod. "You're right. Although, I'd have to do mouth-to-mouth to bring you back."

With a reverent touch, he plays with my current curly locks. "All you'd have to do is kiss me once and I'd be a goner." His gaze skims me from head to toe once more. "I have no words."

"For a frontman, that could be a problem."

"Yeah." His ring-adorned fingers slowly, finally, *finally*, reach out and grab my hips. Tugging me toward his leather pants, he whispers, "I love you."

Can I do this? Should I? How can I not? I wrap my arms around his neck and draw his head to mine. Inhaling, I admit, "I love you."

Bennett's eyes widen, his only tell that he heard me. The tip of his tongue extends beyond his kissable lips. "Are you sure? After all, we haven't had sex yet."

This man. *My* man. Who just threw my words back in my face. I mimic his retort to me when I said the same thing to him. "You think sex is my deciding factor?"

His eyes crinkle at the corners as he chuckles. "With you, I'm not sure."

It's beyond time for me to lay my heart bare. "It's never been that for me. I fall in love with a man's soul. Even if the sex is bad, if I love him, it wouldn't bother me."

"Sweetheart, it won't be bad between us. Believe me."

"I do." The need to come clean drives me to share. "You've been through so much in your life. You've overcome and succeeded based on your raw talent and ambition. Lots of men have good voices but never get near a small stage, let alone the massive stadiums you pack regularly."

He licks his lips but doesn't say anything.

"Your internal drive has kept UC on track to reach the amazing milestones you've hit. More than your drive, though, it's how you've reacted to all those hurts that calls out to me. You're loved by more than me, Bennett. Your band members and Luke, all love you too. And you could love them as well, if you let yourself. They're not Curtiss about to steal your girl and break your heart. UC performs like an amazing group, but can you imagine how everything would gel even more if you were out there with your closest friends?"

"I don't know about that."

"And this, right here, is why I love you." I kiss him, but he doesn't reciprocate.

"I don't get it," he admits when I pull away.

"Your vulnerability calls out to me. I love everything about you, including your potential. I want to be standing at your side when you embrace their love and reflect it back at them. I love how cocky you can be onstage, how you treat your fans with respect." I line up my body against his again. "Above all, I love how you love me."

"On this last thing, we both agree." He brings our lips together for what feels like our first kiss. "I love your purity, how you cheer me on with my physical therapy, how when you simply enter a room, the air lightens and my heart sings a more beautiful song than anything in our repertoire." He takes a breath. "I love how you see me. I hope one day to be worthy of such a vision." On a groan, he pulls me closer. "Say it again."

Drunk on the look in his eyes, I repeat, "I love you." I kiss his nose. "I love you." My lips land on first one, then his other, cheek. "I love you."

He kisses me as if his entire band wasn't surrounding us. As if he wasn't getting ready to sing in front of thousands of people. As if I'm the only woman in the world. I return his passionate kisses without thought of these facts either.

A male cough from behind us causes us to break apart. Bennett keeps his forehead glued to mine. "What?"

Luke says, "Five minutes."

Bennett's entire being rises and falls. "Never enough time." We remain locked together for a couple more minutes, until he steps back. "Make sure you're backstage in my line of sight. I need your spirit with me. Oh, and 007 has agreed to join us on stage tonight when we talk with the audience."

My body sags in relief. "I want to thank him." Bennett bows his head, and I leave my man to approach the bassist. "Pierce."

He turns to me, his light blue gaze a chilling winter blast. "Hey."

I swallow. He's not going to make this easy for me. "I, uh, wanted to thank you for agreeing to address the audience tonight. I'm not self-centered enough to think you're doing it for me, but it means the world to Bennett that you're standing up for him."

"Yeah, well, no matter what, he's my brother."

I'm not going to push him anymore. I lean forward and give him in a hug—which he doesn't reciprocate. I'm fine with that. "Thank you."

Our awkward moment ends when the band's called to huddle in The Closet. Without looking at me, Pierce joins the rest of them for their pre-show ritual, which ends with a collective whoop. Then they bound toward the stage.

I use this time to gather my scattered wits. I walk over to the curtained area to gather my discarded clothes. My cell shows one missed call from Ma. Not going to return it since I have a concert to attend, so I shoot her off a text that we'll talk tomorrow. Leaving everything, including my phone together with all of the bands' stuff in a pile on a chair, I enter backstage and am rewarded when UC plays their first song to the crowd.

I inhale the buzz. The speech tonight will clear the air, it has to. The press release will take care of Michelle at home. I should listen to Court and Nese and trust the system. Everything will be all right from this point forward.

It has to.

# Chapter Twenty

The guys are more amped up for this concert than I've ever seen them. Bennett's still careful with how he stalks on the stage—because there's no other way to describe his sexy prowling movements—yet he continues to interact with his fans. The women in the front rows, in particular, seem to appreciate his spending a bit more time with them than in the past.

He turns around, giving the audience the delightful view of his leather-clad butt while beaming at me. In this moment, we're connected. United. It's us against the world . . . and I feel sorry for the world.

Nudging my chin toward the crowd behind him, I break our connection. He blows me a kiss and spins toward the front of the stage—with care, of course.

Jeb strolls up to my side, his tatted arms on full display given he's wearing an Untamed Coaster tank top. "They're looking great out there."

I face the mountain of a man. "They are."

One of his arms disappears behind his back. "I wanted to thank you for your suggestions. My back isn't hurting as much as it was. The other crewmembers also appreciate them."

My heart warms. This is why I became a physical therapist from the beginning. To help people. "I'm glad."

"Do you have any more suggestions? I know you're not my doctor or anything, but your tips help so much."

Remembering how embarrassed he was at our first meeting, his asking for more help seems to come easier. "I may have a couple of more exercises for you to try." I touch the middle of his back. "Does it hurt here?"

"No, it's lower. To the side."

I touch where he indicates and nod. "I definitely can help you out." My hand drops. "Remember, though, the exercises I'm giving you are only for you. If any of your friends need help, please ask them to see me. Especially if they're not hurt exactly where you are." I know I'm supposed to stay focused on my singular, sexy patient, but how can I not help someone in need?

After giving him a few more strengthening exercises, we watch as the band finishes up their set. At least working with Jeb helped pass the time so I didn't obsess over what's coming up next. Namely, me.

"Thanks so much, Jenna. I don't care what those rags publish about you, you're A-OK in my book."

On impulse, I give him a hug, stretching to my tip toes.

"Uh, oh. Boss Man's giving us all sorts of evil eye. Better skedaddle."

Before I can protest, Jeb's disappeared into the darkness. I cross my arms over my chest and glare at Bennett. For his part, he sets his jaw. He doesn't get to dictate who I speak with—or even hug.

The rest of the band surrounds him and they wave to the crowd. Knowing what's about to happen, I need to lighten the air between us, even if we're the only two people aware of what went down. When our gazes meet again, I lift my miniskirt to show off the black panties Nese provided, rocking my hips back and forth. From the smile gracing his face, I'd say that did the trick.

Good thing because the guys stay on the stage rather than race back here to change for the encore. My brain stutters seeing all five men standing there.

Bennett wipes his face with this forearm. "How are you doing, Louisville?"

Screams echo throughout the stadium.

He jokes, "That good, huh?"

More clapping ensues.

"Well, the whole band is up here not because we want to sing for you, but because we have something we want to discuss, if that's all right?" Bennett's statement is met with more positive energy.

Río leaps in front of Bennett. "We don't know how many of you read gossip sites, but there's a new article about our boy Bennett that we simply can't let slide." He places his hand on the lead singer's shoulder. "Asshole journalists got it all wrong."

"Maybe not *all* wrong," Bennett says. "Just like ninety-nine percent. I did date a girl named Lissa Baker in high school." He shakes his head. "No accounting for teenage taste."

Coop walks to the front. "Want to share with the class what happened back then?"

"Not really," Bennett replies. "But I guess I have to." He smirks, and several people—women—whistle. "The short story is she dumped me to go to the senior prom—mind you, I was only a junior at the time—with my best friend."

The crowd boos.

"That's rough," Pierce pipes up. I appreciate his participation.

"Yeah, well I got over her when you brought me onboard Untamed Coaster!"

As if on cue, the audience yells their approval.

Bennett continues, "I hadn't seen this girl since high school, until a few weeks ago when she showed up at a restaurant where I was eating dinner in the Hamptons, New York. We talked, briefly, and she slithered away. Where she belongs."

Hisses emanate from the crowd.

"And then she sold a fake story to the tabloids that you two hooked up," Pierce finishes. "She sucks."

Coop repeats, "They're all lies!"

Yells rise up from the masses before them.

"Let that be a lesson to you all," Río proclaims. "Lying to reporters is a dangerous business."

The audience screams.

Man, they have these people eating out of the palms of their hands. Amazing. If only they didn't need to go on to the next part. When Tristan takes the mic, my stomach clenches.

"But that's not where the story ends, folks. Our guy here," he places his hand on Bennett's shoulder. "Has been seen out with Jenna Westfield, Darren's girlfriend at the time of his death. The media has unfairly dubbed her a Black Widow, insinuating all kinds of crazy shit against her and UC. They're wrong."

My weight shifts from foot to foot. At my side, Nese tugs on my elbow. "They're doing great," she whispers.

I can't move my head from the stage. "I hope so."

"Tell us, ladies and gentlemen," Río asks the crowd. "Does it look like we're going anywhere?"

A roaring, "NO!" resounds throughout the stadium. Río flicks his arms up in the air to egg them on, and they amp up their denials.

"Anyone who's met Jenna knows she wouldn't hurt a fly." Coop's support buoys me.

Pierce stands at the forefront, causing me to hold my breath. He lifts his mic. "She wasn't responsible for Darren's overdose, no matter how the media spins it."

All the air whooshes out of my body and I collapse forward. Nese strokes my back as tears freefall down my cheeks. Pierce stood up for me. In front of thousands of people, many of whom probably are recording the band's performance.

I'm still bent over when Coop adds, "We don't normally address stupid stories like this one, but we felt it was important to put an end to it tonight."

From my position near the floor, more clapping reverberates through my body.

Tristan joins in, "The moral of the story is this—old girlfriend bad, Jenna good, story over."

"This is why we're Untamed Coaster," Bennett's tenor rings throughout the venue. "'Cause we're wild and free, but always look out for our own!'"

I glance up to see all five guys with their fists in the air, like they do before they take the stage. A story everyone knows is rooted in their beginnings at the amusement park, thanks to the movie.

The crowd raises their fists into the air, reflecting love back at them.

"I need to get their change of clothes ready. Can you stand?"

Nese's kind words force me to take stock of my body. I nod and she helps me return upright, steadying me. She hands me something, then leaves to help the band change for the encore.

I only have a few seconds to register I'm holding a new shirt for Bennett before the band enters backstage. In a daze, I roll over the features of the man I love as he approaches me. "How'd we do?"

"Great."

He grins, opening his arms wide. "In that case, give me some sugar!"

I don't hesitate. I leap up, wrapping my legs around his trim waist clad in leather. My arms go around his neck. "You all were amazing out there. How did you get Pierce to say what he did?"

"My hands are on your ass and you're asking me about another guy? First Jeb and now 007—a man could get a complex."

"As if."

He studies my face. "You were crying."

"Happy tears."

"Those are the only sort allowed from now on." He gives me a quick kiss. "Seems like I have a gorgeous woman in my arms and thousands of people out there waiting for an encore. Whatever shall I do?"

I giggle as I kiss him. "Give them what they want before giving us what we need."

"Hell yes."

He's kissing me again as Luke yells, "Two minutes!"

"Put me down. I have a new shirt for you."

"Only for now. I'm not letting you go afterwards." He lowers me to the floor and strips. I check out his ripped torso, my tongue licking my lower lip. "Stop it now. My leather pants don't have that much room."

I step back and hand him the shirt and steal one of his lines. "See you on the flip side."

I'm rewarded with another quick kiss before he bounds over to meet up with the band, ignoring my yelling at him to walk.

Nese nudges me in the ribs. "Guess things went well?"

"You could say that." I turn to her. "Thank you for being with me earlier. It meant more than you know."

"Us girls have to stick together."

I hug her and whisper, "We sure do!"

After the encore ends, the band returns backstage and is ushered into The Closet to change into street clothes since we're traveling tonight. I follow them, sad I'm going to have to put my leggings back on.

"Keep the outfit," Nese tells me. "It looks hot on you. All the band would agree."

"Are you sure? Doesn't it belong to the band?"

"Girl, if any guy here wants to wear this outfit, I'd pay them money!" She laughs.

"Guess you have a point."

I leave to retrieve my clothes when Luke approaches me. His coffee-colored eyes skewer me. "I think they did great out there. Got our side out better than any PR article could."

He sounds so confident. "I hope you're right."

He taps my back. "There always will be detractors, but I believe we put Lissa and the Black Widow to rest."

"Hey, you've had your time." Río bullies his way over. Damn. Shirtless, the man's as ripped as Bennett, if not more so. "We always have Bennett's back. Tonight, we were happy to have yours as well."

"Thank you so much." I give him a hug before I'm spun around to Coop. "We've got you, girl."

Not to be outdone, Tristan comes over to us. "I bet after tonight, the media will think twice about attacking you." Because he didn't make a move to me, I wrap my arms around the new keyboardist.

I step back and thank the men who stood up for me onstage. Everyone's here except Bennett and Pierce. The former I'm sure I'll see soon, not so sure about the latter. "What you said about me out there means so much. Thank you from the bottom of my heart."

I'm shocked to see the missing bassist approaching the outskirts of our little group, but he steers clear. I can't expect any more out of Pierce than what he offered from the stage. Which meant so much.

Bennett joins us, wearing a darker pair of ripped jeans and a Backdoor Clouds T-shirt. "Have you been keeping my girl occupied while I was changing?"

"Don't you know it?" Río laughs. "Remember, Jenna, when you get tired of this one, I'll be ready for you."

"Don't plan on that anytime soon," Bennett growls at his drummer, who only laughs harder.

"Come on," Coop taps Río. "Let's stop giving them a hard time."

Tristan joins the duo. "Yeah, I'm ready to hit the bus and rest up for the next show." The three of them, plus Pierce, join Luke and leave The Closet.

"Looks like we're the only two left. Well, except for Nese and her team, who clearly want us to disappear so they can break this place down."

Bennett puts his arm around my shoulders. "By all means. Let's go to the bus." We take a few steps. "My bus," he clarifies.

"I think that's a foregone conclusion."

"Better be." He kisses my cheek. "I have big plans for this ride."

"Me too, Rock Star. Me too."

# Chapter Twenty-One

When I climb the steps to enter the bus, a mixture of excitement and nervousness takes residence throughout my body. I've been on Bennett's bus countless times, but usually with the excuse of physical therapy. Of course we've done much more than that, but tonight's the first time we have an agenda—actual, full-blown, never-going-back sex. It feels weird, as if we put it down on our calendar.

Questions swirl:

What if he doesn't like it?

What if I forget how it all works?

What if he gets me out of his system tonight?

"I can hear you thinking from across the bus." Bennett hands me a glass of champagne. "We don't have to do anything tonight if you don't want to."

Am I that transparent? "No, I want to. The doctor's restriction is over. You're good to go." I pause. "So long as you take it easy."

He pushes my still curly locks away from my face. "Oh, I plan on taking it slow. Very slow. I want to savor every single moan that comes out of your delicious mouth." He kisses me as if to punctuate his last sentence.

I sip my champagne and sit on the sofa, facing the blank screen of the television. Might as well come clean. "I'm nervous."

"Believe it or not, so am I."

I rear back. "Pu-lease."

"I am, Sweetheart. Sure, I've had sex with women who didn't matter to me. You, on the other hand, mean more to me than anyone ever before. I want to make a good impression on you, so you'll keep coming back for more."

"I sincerely doubt that will be an issue. You've already made a good impression." I guzzle my champagne and flip the now-empty glass. How did that happen?

"Have you enjoyed all the other stuff we've done?"

How can he even have the smallest question about it? "You know I have."

"Good. Because we're going to do all that, and then some. Tonight's a big night for both of us, Jenna. I'm ready if you are."

This is it. My last chance to turn around and return to Aroostook. Deal with the fallout Court's handling on her own. My gaze takes in the man next to me, and I know none of that will happen. I belong here. With Bennett. Possibly forever. My breath hitches.

He asks again, "Are you ready?"

I sit up taller. "Yes."

He doesn't say anything, simply places my empty flute on the table. For the first time, I realize he doesn't have a glass. Before I can say anything about it, he clasps my cold hand and brings it up to his mouth. Staring directly into my eyes, he kisses the back of my palm. "I love you, Sweetheart."

"I love you back, Bennett."

It's as if speaking these words shot me with the strength I was missing. I want to be with this man. It's time to prove it.

I lean forward, and rain tiny kisses all over his face. When I reach his lips, it's like one of those meteors we watched the other night exploding across the sky. The next thing I know, our shirts sail across the tiny room and my new black bra ends up on the floor.

"Wait," I admonish. "Nese gave me that. Don't you want to pay proper homage to her work?"

"It looks beautiful on the floor." He pauses. "Wherever it is."

Smiling, I shake my head. I'll model it for him later. Not wanting to give the bus driver a show, I say, "Let's take this to the bedroom."

Bennett complains, "Hey, that's my line." He stands and helps me to my feet, kissing every square inch his lips can reach.

By the time we enter the back room, my fingers have managed to unbutton his jeans, yet my miniskirt is still firmly in place. "Nese is a flipping genius. You're the sexiest schoolgirl I've ever seen."

"Then you got her vision. Your black leather pants onstage rock too. Not that these jeans don't as well." I roll the jeans down his muscular thighs. They come off, together with his shoes and socks. I suck in my breath. "If your fans could see you now."

"Nope. For your eyes only."

Plus the others who have been in my position before. Why am I thinking about them now? The ghost of his former bandmate tries to join our party, but he's not allowed. Like his prior groupies. There's no room for anyone else in this bedroom. Only us.

I break the silence by noting, "I like the sound of that."

He seems comfortable in only his black boxer briefs. So relaxed, in fact, that he strips them off his body. If I looked like him, I'd be naked all the time. "You're gorgeous." My fingers work their way down his musculature, delighting at how his muscles jump in response.

His fingers skim the top of my skirt. "Can I take this off?"

"I don't know, can you?" Sassy girl is back, but Bennett doesn't seem to mind.

"Oh, I most certainly can." His lips cover mine in a kiss unlike any other. Like a homing pigeon, his fingers unzip the skirt and it falls to the floor. He holds out his hand. "I need those panties."

"I don't think they'd look good on you." Where is this fresh mouth coming from?

"No, but they'd look fabulous in my pocket as I play for thousands."

"You'd do that?" I squeak.

"You have no idea, Sweetheart. Now hand them over." He opens and closes his hand several times.

I take a deep breath and slide them down my still-booted feet. "Here you go."

His response is to sniff, then rub his face around them. "Damn. So sweet." He tosses them on top of his own underwear. He stares at my boots. "I like those too, but they'll be in the way when your legs are around my waist."

I bend down and unlace them, taking my time to remove one boot, then the other, and tossing the socklets on the floor. When I stand, I'm as bare as he is. I lick my lips.

"Come here, beautiful." His arms encircle my body, and our kiss is so hot it could scorch the walls. Bennett steals my breath, as well as all rational thoughts. I'm reduced to a quivering mass of feelings, all of which are being directed by him. As if on stage leading the band, he's running this interlude like a master conductor.

"I want this to last," he murmurs against my ear.

"Sounds good, so long as you don't reinjure yourself."

He pulls back. "I don't know. If I get hurt again, you'd have to stay with us on tour longer. It might be incentive for me to be reckless."

I tap the center of his chest, capturing his necklace for a moment. "Not so fast. Who knows what injury you could do to yourself? You'd have more doctors involved. Maybe I couldn't give you therapy for whatever you hurt."

"I love it when you talk PT to me. You make me sweat."

I curl my arms around his broad shoulders, loving the way the muscles beneath his tatted arms dance. "Message received."

"Good. And here's another message for you—I'm going to give you five orgasms tonight."

Five? "Don't set such a high bar. I'll be thrilled with one so long as it's from you."

"Believe me, we're both going to remember this night for years. Now, get on that bed and open your legs. I want to see the goods."

"The goods?"

In response, he growls.

Deciding to let it go—for now—I get on top of the bed and lie on my back. My legs are yanked apart by the impatient lead singer.

"There. Not so hard, was it?"

My gaze flicks down his torso to his cock pointing at his belly button. "Looks hard to me."

"Damn, woman." He flings himself onto the bed and crawls up to me on his hands and knees. He sucks his index finger. Then, gaze locked with mine, he inserts it into my body causing me to arch my back. A second finger joins the first, plunging in and out.

"Oh," I cry out, my head thrashing on the pillow.

He chuckles. "Like that?"

In response, I bite my bottom lip. I've never been this turned on so quickly, yet he has me squirming in no time flat. When his thumb rubs my clit, an orgasm detonates in my body.

I don't have time to recover at all when his tongue laps at my still-throbbing pussy. "You're so sweet. The reason I call you Sweetheart," he admits.

I can't comprehend what he's saying, since his tongue is doing magical things to me. It's as if my first orgasm rolled into another. And another.

Covered in sweat, the back of my hand pushes my hair off my face. I'm sure the curls are a mess now, but I can't summon any energy to care. "Bennett," I begin. All of my bones have sunk into the bed, taking my two remaining brain cells with them.

He sits on his haunches, wearing only a delicious smirk. "I like it when I can reduce you to only saying my name."

"Bennett," I try again.

He laughs. "Yeah, just like that."

My arm extends toward his body, but he's too far away. "I want to touch you." *Five words in a row. A new record.*

"Like this?" He gives himself a long stroke, causing me to moan. He repeats the motion again.

When he goes for a third downward stroke, I find the strength to sit up in the bed. "No. Let me."

Still sitting on his heels, his hands drop to the bed. His gaze bounces between his hardness to me and down again.

Sliding my knees forward until they touch his, I bend and kiss his tip. A salty bit that had leaked coats my tongue—I sit up and stick my tongue out to him before swallowing his essence.

"I was going to take this slow, but not now." He pushes me onto my back, then turns me onto my stomach. He shoves a pillow under my hips, and my legs are spread open again. "You are too sexy for your own good," he rumbles as his fingers enter me from behind.

"Trying to keep up with you."

"Then hold on."

With this warning, I hear a foil packet open and a second later he pulls me up to my hands and knees. His cock prods at my entrance, then slides in an inch. Pulls back. In. Out. Over and over until he's buried deep inside.

"I love how you hold me so tight." He kisses the ear he was whispering his praise. "It's like you were made for me."

"You," I pant. "Feel." He pushes in and out, harder this time. "So." His hands slide down to my hips. "Good." He squeezes my butt cheeks.

"You're perfect." He kisses between my shoulder blades.

His hips change direction, swiveling in a circular motion, igniting all sorts of explosions behind my eyes. All I can do is push backward to meet his thrusts. For once I'm happy I don't have big boobs, as what I do have are swinging with the force of him. Another orgasm sparkles on the horizon. "Again?"

"Definitely."

Everything around me fades to black as pleasure overtakes me. I shout, "Yes!"

Again, not waiting for me to recover, Bennett pulls out and flips me onto my back, securing my legs around his hips. I lock my ankles, holding on as he pounds into me. His lips find mine. "Once more. For me, one more time." Sweat races down his chest while he continues to thrust into me, harder and harder.

"I can't." At this point, I only want him to share some of the ecstasy I've already received. I lick some of the wetness off his defined chest.

Above me, he pronounces, "You're wrong." His hand reaches behind his back and he grabs onto my ankles. Leaning away from me, he plows even harder.

The new angle shifts something deep within me. A soul-crushing orgasm threatens for a second, then recedes. Bennett continues pounding hard, his mouth contorted in a mix of pain and pleasure. He orders, "Now!"

I don't know from where, but the orgasm from a second ago races up from my toes to explode out of the top of my head. As I scream my completion, I see white except for Bennett's face, which is bathed in light. He ceases all movement, then roars his own climax.

With a series of kisses over my cheeks, he lays on top of me. Welcoming his weight, I wrap my boneless arms around him. The only noises are panted breaths and wet flesh sliding against the other.

He slips onto his side, his fingers securing the spent condom. "I'll take care of this. Then you." He kisses me one last time as he disappears out of the room toward the bathroom.

I stretch. This man rocked my world on its axis. What preceded tonight's activities pale in comparison. If there was any doubt, Bennett owns my world.

He stalks through the open door, a washcloth in his hand. "How are you feeling, Sweetheart?"

Why lie? "Amazing."

"I like the sound of that. Now open for me."

What? Again? "Bennett, I don't think I have it in me—"

"Not so soon." He bends down and kisses me. "I want to make sure you're all right."

I muse aloud, "No one has ever done this before."

"Then another point in my favor." He presses the wet cloth against my core, taking the sting out of his previous amazing use of it. I moan at his ministrations, causing a self-satisfied smile to overtake his face.

He tosses the washcloth onto the floor and crawls into bed behind me. My body curls around him as he entwines our limbs. We remain locked together.

I giggle.

I feel him smile. "What's that for?"

Tracing his tattoos, I reply, "You lived up to your hype."

"You more than surpassed yours." He rubs his nose against my cheek. "I did get five orgasms out of you."

Can't deny the truth. "You did. Not sure how."

Behind me, his body swells. "It was us."

His statement hangs in the air, then alights in my heart. I twist so we're facing each other. "We're blessed."

He pushes the hair away from my face. "I've never thought of that word as applying to my life. Ever." With a gentle touch, he kisses my lips. "But with you—us—I think you may be right."

I clasp his hand. "Oh, Bennett, you're blessed in so many ways. Maybe not with your family, but with your band of brothers. With Luke. And Jeb and Nese and Danny the bus driver and everyone associated with UC. You're surrounded by so many blessings. Even the fact that you were able to hire Kieron as a new guitar tech on such short notice. Believe me, you are blessed."

His cheek goes in and out as he contemplates what I've told him. I reach out and smooth his eyebrows, but remain silent. He needs to understand what I've told him is true.

"They're all contracted to do what they're doing for me. You're not."

My heart hurts at how he's processing this. I'm about to argue with him, when he adds, "Well, you sort of are."

# Chapter Twenty-Two

I freeze. He can't believe I'm only here—naked—because I'm contracted to do a job? My *job* is to give him physical therapy, not get him off! My mouth drops open to tell him off when I stare at his face and my teeth click as they shut. Reflected back at me is sheer anguish.

No, no, no. This is not the way things were supposed to go, not with the man I love. His deep-rooted trust issues cannot be brushed aside. He has to *believe* in the reason I'm here, with him, now. More than that, he needs to embrace this conclusion for himself.

He pushes away from me. In a tone overlaid with love, I say, "Bennett." He stops moving, which I take as a good sign. I continue, "Do you remember when we met again at the movie premiere?"

His eyebrows come together. "Yes."

"You'd pulled your groin muscle and were in pain. You didn't want anything to do with me, right?"

My hand drops to his injured muscle. His gaze snaps to the only place we're connected.

"Right."

I cover his upper thigh with my palm. "Your doctor said you

needed physical therapy if you wanted to be able to perform at UC's scheduled concert tour dates. Luke told me he had to talk you into agreeing to any sort of therapy."

"He did," is pulled from somewhere deep inside him.

His whole world is imploding. I remove my hand. "Luke was adamant you come to At Your Service PT. Well, actually, he was more determined that I be your therapist."

He nods.

"I wasn't convinced. I was an administrator, not seeing patients anymore. Want to know what changed my mind?"

"The money?"

A small huff escapes. "Fine, yes, it played a part. I saw taking this job as a way to get another clinic up and running fast, so I'd be closer to my goal of ten. But it wasn't the main motivating factor for me."

"That's not what Luke told me."

"Because it *was* what I told him." I suck in a breath. "What prompted me to take you on as a patient was"—dare I admit this? I straighten my shoulders. "Darren."

The ghost I had banished reappears.

Bennett runs his hand through his sexy hair.

Without waiting for him to respond, I rush forward. "Darren always had wonderful things to say about you. He told me about your early days with the band and how you struggled. He used to play pranks on you to get you out of your head. He helped you study for the GED because he knew how important finishing your education was to your self-worth."

Bennett blinks several times.

"He loved you like a brother. I don't know if he ever told you—or if you were able to hear him if he did. I figured, if he loved you so much, there had to be something more to you than a cocky lead singer. Quinn's movie showed me glimpses into the man you are underneath." My hand now moves up his chest to cover his heart.

Although he doesn't respond, his heartbeat increases. Faster. Faster. Faster still. "Do you know what this *job* has done for me? It reminded me how much joy I get in working with patients and seeing their progress. So thank you for that."

He grabs my wrist and drops it onto the bed. At least he's still here with me. I have to take my wins where I can.

"Can you see a difference between merely doing a job and enjoying interactions with the people on the job who give it meaning?"

He swallows. "Like doing all the promo shit, but feeling pride when Luke says we did a good job?"

Not a perfect example, but I'll take it. "Exactly. Like how you bonded with Luke over it."

"I wouldn't say we bonded."

"Fine. But you accomplished something that you received praise for from him. Tell me, what would happen if you did a poor job at one of the promo events?"

He jerks his head backward. "Luke would hand me my ass."

My gaze drifts behind him for a second. I want to tap his amazing butt, but refrain. "So you do a good job in order not to disappoint Luke."

He ponders what I said for a moment. "In a way."

"Great. So you see, you can be contracted to do a job, like a promo appearance, but your behavior is guided by how you want to please your manager because he means more to you than the single appearance."

"I guess."

I push forward. "You see how the one informs the other? You must do your job because you're a professional. You do it well not to disappoint your"—I almost say "friend" but search for a more appropriate descriptor, in his world—"manager. The fact you met Luke because of UC doesn't play into the fact that he's your frien-acquaintance."

Bennett settles on his back. "If he disappeared from UC tomorrow, I guess I would miss him," he allows.

Score! "You'd miss his not being around and razzing you?"

His cheeks inflate. "Yeah. He's annoying as hell, but a good guy. I think we'd all be adrift without him steering the ship."

Finally! We're making progress. It's time to press my luck. "So, you can understand why even if I quit doing your physical therapy, I would stay with you." I turn onto my side and stroke his hair. On a whisper, I say, "Because I love you."

Given the rigid set to his jaw and how tight his limbs are, I take the fact he hasn't moved from the bed as a positive. A small one, but still.

"We met—again—because I agreed to be your therapist. I'm here right now, in your bed, because I want to be." *Please let him agree.*

"You're not with me because of the money?"

"No."

"Your contract isn't forcing you to stay?"

I contemplate my response. "Well, the contract makes me want to finish your therapy and see you back to one hundred percent. It'll end when you're healed. Professional ethics say I'm not supposed to enter into a relationship with any current client—I made Darren wait until our therapy was over." My face relaxes. "You, however, blew my mind from the beginning."

He turns again onto his side, facing me. "Please tell me you're not saying all this stuff because of the contract."

What his mother and bitch of a high school girlfriend did to this amazing man! "I'm your physical therapist because Luke twisted both of our arms. I'm a very satisfied woman because you took my arm"—I hold it out straight—"pulled me against your very sexy body and said you wanted to do all types of naughty things to me. You fulfilled each and every promise more than I expected was possible." I screw up my courage and kiss his lips. "Because I love you."

His eyes squeeze shut. I allow his internal battle to go on as long as he needs, praying he'll realize his assumption about me is unfounded. As is his crazy notion that UC are a bunch of colleagues who play music together.

Green eyes open and stare at me. "I have no option but to believe you. Because I love you, too, Sweetheart."

"Oh, Bennett."

I lunge at him. Our lips lock together, trying to erase all the self-doubt he has surrounding a lasting love. Our lasting love. Our kiss starts tentative but soon transforms into passion. One thing leads to another and soon we're panting and sweaty and writhing in pure bliss.

After we take a shower, we retreat into the bus's bedroom cocoon once again. Under the covers, we get wrapped up in each other. "I'm glad you're in my life."

His confession brings a smile to my face. "Me too."

"Thanks for not letting me push you away."

"Never going to happen." My thumb flits over his luscious lips. "You know who else you can't push away? Your band."

"I'm not sure about them."

"You've known them longer than me."

"Well, true. They're a great bunch of guys and I have a blast hanging out with them." His forearm crosses his forehead.

"How about trying to open up a little to them?"

Pained eyes turn toward me. "All of them?"

"No," I backtrack. "How about we start with one?" I consider each of his bandmates. "What about Luke? He's not in the band, but you admitted you all wouldn't survive a day without his guidance."

Bennett wiggles his eyebrows. "You're not wrong there."

Not wanting to push him too far outside of his comfort zone, and considering it's approaching daybreak, I decide to leave this topic for another day. It's good enough he agreed to try with Luke. He'll be counting all the guys as friends soon. I know it.

A huge yawn overtakes my entire being. A second later, Bennett's yawn rivals mine. We both laugh.

He drags me closer to him and embraces me. "It's been a big day. Let's get some sleep—I need some time before I can go another round with you anyway. You tuckered me all out."

226 Arell Rivers

Giggling at his outlandish quip, I kiss him while laughing, another experience I've only had with him. "I'll hold you to it in the morning."

"You do that, Sweetheart."

---

Several hours and a few more orgasms later, the bus stops in the parking lot of another hotel. Dragging my overnight suitcase behind me, I approach our driver. "What town are we in, Danny?"

He has the decency not to smirk at us, no doubt knowing exactly what we've been up to. I could kiss him for his discretion. "We're in Memphis, ma'am."

My eyes widen. "Awesome!" I turn around and face Bennett. "I've always wanted to go to Graceland!"

Bennett chuckles at my exuberance. "I'll reach out to Luke to see if he can arrange a tour."

I skip off the bus and almost barrel into the man who can make this happen for us. "Luke," I yell, not allowing Bennett to say anything. "We're in Memphis. Think you can get us into Graceland?"

Bennett shakes his head. With a shrug, he adds, "As you can see, she's sort of excited."

Luke passes Bennett the room key. "I wouldn't want to disappoint your physical therapist. By the way, this hotel has a great gym you might want to try for your exercises today." He gives Bennett the rundown of the schedule, which is filled tomorrow but free for the rest of today. I rub my hands together.

We drop our luggage in the room and change. Which takes twice as long as usual because, well, Bennett. Once I'm finally in my leggings and tunic top and he's in his workout gear, we leave to check out the gym. He stops in the middle of the fully equipped room.

"Shit. I wish I could do more than physical therapy. This gym is stocked."

"You could do some upper body things," I suggest. "Not that you need it."

Aforementioned muscular arms pull me into a tight embrace. "How could I ever think the only reason you're here is because of the contract?" He kisses the top of my head. "It's for my body."

I punch his taut abs, and he emits the obligatory grunt. "If that's what you believe, then you better keep working out so my eyes don't stray." As if.

"Guess I always have my voice to fall back on." He winks. "And my huge cock."

"Oh yes, that's your number one selling point." At his triumphant grin, I add, "Asshat."

He rears back. "Hey! I was simply stating a fact. No need to get all personal on me." He advances. "Besides, I didn't hear any complaining last night. Or this morning." His hands land on my butt and he pulls me to him. In my ear, he whispers, "I could take you right here to remind you of how big it is. Give everyone a show."

I can't help but burst out laughing. "Add tremendous ego to your list." Reality rears her ugly head, and I step back from my patient. "This is inappropriate behavior between a therapist and her patient, Mr. Hardy." Several sets of eyes enjoy our antics. I shake my head and instruct him to begin his exercises.

The hour passes quickly. He's mastered most of the exercises with the exception of the skater leaps, at which he's still tentative. Given how far he's come, I've added a couple new items to his routine. After all, he thrives on challenge.

In and out of the bedroom.

I wonder how I can use this fact to get him to warm up to the rest of the band?

When we're finished with therapy, he walks over to a decked-out complicated machine with weights and cables. At my prompting, he sits and works out his upper body, wearing a happy expression. Which is mirrored by my own—and those of the females in the gym—especially after he tosses his shirt onto the floor.

*He's all mine, ladies.*

I decide to do some research into Graceland so we can get the most out of our experience, even though Luke's arranging for us to have a private tour tonight, after the mansion's "closed." Being a rock star has its perks.

Bennett stands and slings his shirt over his glistening shoulder. All eyes track him moving to the water cooler. Before I can get there, however, three gym bunnies surround him. I decide to hang back and watch their interaction.

The brazen women touch his body as if they have a right to do so. My man ducks and weaves like a pro boxer, all the while giving them the proper fan attention.

A lady in a body-hugging, bright blue jumpsuit exclaims, "I loved your movie!"

"I think you stole the show," a blonde-headed, big-boobed one in black says, trying to rub against his chest.

"So happy UC is back," another adds—this one in pink. "We have tickets for your show tomorrow."

An unfamiliar emotion swells. Jealousy. Guess I better get used to Bennett's receiving this sort of treatment. Darren had women coming on to him a lot, but I wasn't around much to see it. When I was, he made it obvious we were together. Should I go up to him now? I glance down at my attire and then over to the gym bodies on display around him, and decide to hang back. How is he going to handle this?

"I'm excited you'll be at the show," Bennett replies. "I'll make sure to reference meeting you at the gym today." The girls swoon. "Stop by the 'Will Call' desk, and I'll make sure you get something special."

The one with the big boobs purrs, "Thanks so much!" She glances at her friend. "We'd love to go back with you to your room to show how appreciative we are."

My eyebrows fly to my hairline.

Bennett chuckles. *My man.* "Ladies, thanks for the offer, but I'm in a relationship and I don't think she'd approve." He pauses. "Neither would I."

I slink into the hallway, watching through the window as he tosses back his plastic cup of water to the sound of their grumbling. "Hope you enjoy the show." He ambles toward me and it takes everything inside of me not to jump him.

In the hallway, he stands in front of me, arms wide open. "You're the only woman I want to show me how appreciative you are."

When he says stuff like this, there's no stopping me despite the fact he just finished a workout. Without hesitation, I wrap my arms around his pumped body. "Let's get you in the shower."

"Alone?"

"No."

# Chapter Twenty-Three

The next thing I know, he's picked me up and starts walking down the hallway. "Bennett, your pulled muscle."

"Consider this another exercise."

I don't move for fear of disturbing his balance. While romantic and fun, I worry about the damage he could do. When we arrive at the elevators, I say, "Point proven, in a dramatic way, Rock Star. Please put me down." When he doesn't shift my weight in his arms, I add, "If you do, I'll give you a blowjob in the shower." My feet can't hit the floor fast enough.

Fifteen minutes later, I make good on the incentive. After all, he did turn down a *quadsome*—is that a thing?—to be with me. Water pelting us, I use my hand to bring him to his full erection while kissing down his ripped chest until I reach my goal. My tongue swirls around the tip as his stance widens.

"You're driving me out of my mind," his gruff voice sails above me.

He pops out of my mouth. "Then I must be doing it right."

I return to teasing him for a moment until he growls and puts his hand on the back of my head. He doesn't push, yet simply adds a bit of pressure and encourages me to take him deeper. Which I do. His hips buck, and the expected guidance from his hand plays in tandem. My own fingers gently play with his balls, eliciting a deep groan from him.

"I know you said you'd give me a blowjob, and you're doing amazing. But I want to be inside you." He steps back. "Now."

Who am I to deny him this wish? With a final lick, I let his dick fall from my mouth and rise to my full height.

"Don't move." In a flash, he's out of the shower, opens a couple of drawers and holds up a condom, putting it on before he's back with me. "Now, let's see how wet you are for me." I have only a second to open my legs when his fingers enter my core. An approving smirk graces his face. "Very."

He turns me toward the tile and the next thing I know he's thrusting into my body. The combination of the shower water plus his pounding into me, not to mention the way his hands squeeze my boobs, proves to be too much. My toes curl into the tile floor as my orgasm overtakes me, clenching around him. Not a second later, he roars above me as he climaxes.

The water sluices over our bodies, nearly steaming on contact. I shake my head. "How can this keep getting better?"

He kisses the center of my back. "Because it's us."

After we use the shower for its intended purpose, we eat a snack from room service. A couple of hours later, UC's head of security, Elias, ushers us into our private stretch limo, complete with tinted windows, to take us to Graceland. Elvis's music plays while we cuddle in the backseat, Bennett's arm around my shoulder. I've never felt so protected. And adored.

I fidget with my skirt, playing with the hem that falls over my knees. For some reason, it seemed appropriate to wear it to "meet" the King. "Did I ever tell you my grandmother was Elvis's biggest fan? She watched all of his movies and had all of his records. Vinyl."

"The good old days." He stretches his long legs, then places mine over his. "Was this your grandmother who had breast cancer?"

I swallow. "Yes."

He pulls my upper body closer, resting my head against his chest. "It's wonderful you have so many happy memories with her."

When he doesn't continue, I force myself to ask, hoping for a positive response. "Do you remember any of your grandparents?"

"Both of them from my mother's side passed before I was born. I have a few recollections about my Dad's side. His father always had a twinkle in his eye and was a big radio guy, as in CBs and HAM stuff. He died when I was eight. Dad's mother liked to bake, but not cook. So when we went to their house, we'd get homemade cookies and cakes with takeout."

"They sound fun."

"They were." He goes silent for a bit. "She died when I was thirteen. Luckily, she never knew her son got sick a couple of years later."

My hand covers his heart next to my ear. "Thank you for sharing these happy memories."

"Thanks for reminding me of them." He kisses my forehead, and I snuggle closer to this man, who's fancied himself a loner, yet is surrounded by so much love. To be fair, he has let my love into his heart. It's time for more.

We pass a sign saying Graceland is ten miles away. I squeeze Bennett's hand. "Is this really happening?"

He squeezes back. "Stick with me, kid. I promise to take you everywhere you want to go." He chuckles "And places you didn't know were on your list."

Shortly, the limo slows as brake lights surround us. Even Bennett's sway can't make traffic disappear. I sigh, "Guess it'll take us longer than ten minutes to get there."

He repositions me on his lap, so my back is to his front. He teases, "Whatever shall we do to pass the time?"

"Rock Star," I lean my head back onto his shoulder. "Behave."

He kisses my neck, and I angle my head to give him better access. Into my ear, he breathes, "I promise to be as good as you deserve." He punctuates his vow by biting my earlobe.

Since I'm sitting forward, I see the divider is up between us and the driver. The hard pounding beat of Hunte plays on the stereo. The windows are tinted. No one can see us—dare we? My breathing picks up.

One of Bennett's hands skims across my chest and squishes my left breast. I've never had sex in a car before—never mind a moving one—yet my moan bounces off the walls. My legs fall open. *Who is this woman?* I consider this question for a split second and answer: a woman in love with her man.

Bennett doesn't hesitate. His hand slides up my leg to the juncture of my thighs. A finger rubs over the lace covering my core, which already is weeping for him. "What do you want, Sweetheart?"

My torso rolls.

His finger slips under the lace and touches me, sending sparks shooting in all directions.

"Ah!"

Bennett's hand withdraws. Before I can mourn its loss, his finger makes its way into my mouth and I suck my juices. He repeats, "What do you want, Sweetheart?"

All my brain cells have scattered. I say the only word I can. "You."

"Thank fuck."

Beneath me, his torso tenses as he pulls his wallet out of his back pocket. He takes out a condom, hands it to me, then tosses the wallet onto the seat. He tenses again and the unmistakable zip of his jeans fills the air. "Commando was the right choice."

"Seems like it." I busy myself by opening the packet.

He plucks the condom from my fingers and tenses a third time while he rolls it on. With a deep, lusty tone, he says, "Are you ready?"

"My underwear . . ."

"Not a problem." In one smooth move, my panties move to the side and he fills me to the brim.

"Oh. Oh!"

The fact we're in a semi-moving vehicle is of no import. With the music on and the divider up, the driver can't know what we're doing. My head swivels and I don't care people are in cars next to us, given the tinted windows. All that matters is I'm with the man I love.

His lips trail up my neck. Using his hand, he turns my face toward his and we kiss, tongues clashing. When we break apart, his hands go around my waist and he lifts me as if I weighed less than a feather.

Up.

Down.

My hands clamp around his wrists as my body moves. Around us, Hunte's music builds. My nipples pebble inside my bra.

"I love how you respond to me."

"I." I pant. "Love." I try to catch my breath, but fail. "You."

The traffic snarl opens and the limo picks up speed. One of Bennett's hands slips under my shirt and moves to my bra, then inside it. He kisses my neck at the same time he pinches my distended nipple. Excitement zings through my body. I clench around him.

"That's it, Sweetheart. Let go."

At his words, I fly free. "Bennett!"

The next second, he growls my name as he comes undone beneath me.

The limo passes through the famed musical gates.

I collapse onto his chest, which rises and falls in rapid succession. Like mine.

Bennett's hands return to my waist, and he deposits me onto the seat next to him. He removes the spent condom and ties it closed while I will my fingers to right my skirt.

The driver stops in front of a stately, stone-faced mansion.

Bennett pulls his zipper up.

I peer out the window, my mouth forming the perfect "O," even while my body feels boneless.

The vehicle's door opens.

Smirking, Bennett motions for me to precede him. I take the

driver's hand and step out of the limo, leaning on him a bit until I'm sure I can stand upright. Behind me, Bennett steps onto the street. Damn man looks as cool as if he were receiving an award. Until I look closer and realize his cheeks are flushed. My hand goes to my own cheeks, then bounce away from the heat. Guess that makes two of us.

A young woman, about twenty, wearing an Elvis T-shirt greets us. "Mr. Hardy, Miss Westfield, welcome to Graceland. I'm Elise, and I'll be taking you around the estate."

"Thank you," I reply. Bennett merely bows his head in her direction.

With his arm around my shoulders, we follow her into the house and through the foyer. She asks us not to touch anything and leads us past the ropes to walk through the living room with its oversized furniture. Bennett whispers, "Imagine what we could do on this sofa."

"Couldn't be better than the limo."

"Guess we'll have to try it and decide."

I giggle at his outrageous behavior. "I think we'll have to try a different sofa, Rock Star." I walk to the threshold of the music room, where two stained glass peacocks encourage creativity.

I study one. "This is so cool."

Bennett gives me a cursory glance as his gaze fixates on the piano in the center of the room. The first piano Elvis ever bought. He walks up to it as if to suck in inspiration from the King himself.

We're led through the seventies' style kitchen and past the stairway that goes up to the second floor. Elise explains that the upper floor has remained closed off to visitors following Elvis's death there in 1977. We are brought to the famous Jungle Room next, which more than makes up for the skipped floor. The room was renovated to resemble the look and feel of Hawaii, and boy did it do its job! The *pièce de résistance*, however, is the Recording Studio downstairs with its six old-fashioned television sets. Bennett spends time examining every piece of equipment and soaking in the atmosphere in here, Elise hard on his heels answering his many questions.

As I don't want to intrude on his special moment, I hang off to the side and pull out my neglected phone. I delete a ton of spam messages. Ma left me a voicemail sometime last night when Bennett and I were doing our "Love Me Tender" imitation, to borrow an Elvis title. In our case, it should be renamed "Love Me Hard and Long." I rub my red cheeks and shoot off a text to Ma that I'll call her in a little bit—I'm at Graceland! I include a photo.

Court's text reaches me next. Damn. Holding my breath, I open it. Seems like our local paper ran the press release I wrote about the graffiti, which has now been repainted. Good. She says things are flowing smoothly at the clinics, so I don't have to worry. I text her back, telling her I'll try my best. The fact Michelle hasn't retaliated means she's thinking about her next move, I know it.

I'm about to open Court's next text—sent two hours later—when Bennett and Elise reappear at my side. To Elise, he says, "Thanks so much for staying late to show us around."

Without my prompting.

My boyfriend is wonderful.

Elise's ears tip red. Even working in these famed walls can't prevent her from fangirling over a current-day rock star. Amazing. "When my boss told me who our special guest was going to be tonight, I jumped at the opportunity to take the tour. I love Untamed Coaster."

*Here we go again.*

"Why thank you." Bennett smiles. "Thank you very much."

I shake my head. At least he didn't try to layer in a Southern drawl.

Elise produces a Graceland program and a pen. "Do you think you could autograph this for me?"

"Of course." Bennett signs the program. It seems to take him longer than usual. "I added a note for the box office. Show it to them and you and a friend will be VIPs at our show tomorrow night. I look forward to seeing you backstage, when I can return the favor and be your tour guide."

"Oh wow," the poor girl melts under his green-eyed appraisal. With shaking hands, she retrieves her treasure. "Thank you!"

"Elise, could you tell us which restaurant we should try around here? Speaking for myself, I'm famished." The hotel room snack has long since been burned off—thanks in part to our extracurricular activities on our way here.

"Oh." Her head swivels toward me. "Of course. A couple of blocks away is a great little place." She stops. "It's nothing fancy, but it has good food."

"Sounds wonderful," I reply to her. "Who needs to waste money on hoity-toity food that leaves you hungry?"

"Right?"

She gives us the restaurant's name, which I plug into my phone's GPS. "See you tomorrow night."

Together, Bennett and I walk out of the famed home. Since the map shows the place she mentioned is only a ten minute walk, we decide to go on foot. He tugs an Elvis hat low on his forehead—a gift from Elise—and keeps his head down as we exit through the gates one final time and turn right.

We manage to get to the restaurant without any hassle and are seated in the back of the bustling eatery. The place is clean, flowers adorn every quartz-topped table, and televisions hang from the rafters playing a variety of shows from local news to a baseball game to a talk show. Bennett tosses his disguise onto the chair next to him. "This has been a damn great day."

"I loved touring Elvis's home. Have to say, though, it makes me happy not to live with the styles of the seventies anymore."

"I don't know. Seemed like you were into those peacocks."

"Well, they were fascinating. They had a purpose—to bring creativity. The rest," I shudder. "The rug in the kitchen would be the first thing to go."

He leans back in the chair, studying the menu. "Yeah, not your aesthetic. I remember the kitchen at your house. Not a scrap of rug to be seen," he teases.

"Nor at Secluded Rest," I remind him.

"Speaking of which, King emailed me the paperwork for the purchase." He smiles, his green eyes lighting up. "Looks like we're going to be neighbors. Although, I think it would be more practical if we shacked up together. Think about all the gas we'd save driving between our homes."

Inside, my center of gravity tenses, then falls. "This is moving fast."

"Sweetheart, I love you. You love me." His gaze flicks to me for confirmation, which I can't help but give to him. "Why keep it a secret?"

"I don't want to hide, if that's what you think. It's just, all the media—"

"Fuck them."

Our server appears. I'm the one who's embarrassed for his cursing, even if I agree with his sentiment. We give him our orders and he retreats to the kitchen.

I return to our conversation. "Not to mention Michelle. I'm not sure what her next move will be, but I doubt she'll back down now."

His hand covers mine. "All the more reason to stay with me. Together. We'll make a statement." When he reads the uncertainty across my face, he adds, "Your mother could have her own wing."

After what he's gone through with his own mother, I'm shocked he'd suggest such a thing. "Are you serious?"

"Absolutely. I want the woman I love to be surrounded with those who love her back. Your mother fills the bill, hands down."

Ma's not his biggest fan, but perhaps if I share this option with her, it would soften her opinion of him. "You're not playing fair."

"Never said I would."

Hashtag true. "I still don't know."

He nods toward my cell phone, resting on the tabletop. "Call her and ask."

"We've been missing each other. The last time she called, you were having your wicked way with me in the shower."

He grins wolfishly. "If I remember right, you were the one who suggested the blowjob." One eyebrow lifts.

I shrug. The television catches my attention as it's showing photos of UC performing on the stage in Louisville. I recognize the staging. Leaning across the table, I say, "They're going to play the speech from last night."

His gaze flicks up and locks on the show. It's set to silent, but the closed captioning does the trick. "Yup, they're replaying what we announced." We read the replay of last night. Was it less than twenty-four hours ago?

The camera pans to the show's hosts, sitting next to . . . Lissa. My breath falters. Bennett's, however does not. He leaps to his feet. I try to coax, "Be careful."

Ignoring me, he stalks to the television set. I join him and read the lies she's spewing. About how Bennett was the one who dumped her right before prom. Then ran off and joined UC, never to come back for her. He abandoned his best friend Curtiss as well.

Bennett's hands form fists.

Lissa spins tales about how she reached out to Bennett, but the rock star refused to acknowledge her once he signed with the band. The camera pans back to her. Big, fake tears streaming down her face, she claims Bennett knew she was pregnant with his baby when he left.

"No fucking way," Bennett snarls. He pulls out his phone. "What freaking show are they on? What station?"

How can I defuse this situation? Do I want to? I'm about to say something—anything—when the hosts invite people to call in with their comments, the telephone number flashing on the screen. Without hesitation, Bennett's fingers dance over the keys.

The show hosts do a double take at each other. Grinning into the camera, the woman with long, brown hair—Francis—beams, "Is this *the* Bennett Hardy, lead singer of Untamed Coaster?"

Bennett adjusts his stance. "Yes."

The male host, Logan, challenges, "Prove it. Let's hear you sing some lines from 'Upside Down.'"

Bennett's face contorts in disgust. While not a fan of what he's doing, I understand my man's need to clear the air. I grab his forearm and whisper, "How can they take any old caller at his word? They need proof." His face relaxes.

Into the phone, he says, "Only because you can't see me." Then he sings a few bars of UC's first number one hit. Someone in the restaurant adjusts the televisions so the show is playing over all of them. The volume is turned up.

Logan plays with his suit jacket. "Well, I can safely say that I'm a believer. It's a pleasure to have Bennett Hardy on the line."

His co-host gushes, "How can we get this hotter-than-any-other, uhm, singer, to come into our studio?"

My eyes roll. I want to grab the phone and tell her he's much more than window dressing. However, given the circumstances, I remain silent.

Ever the consummate professional, Bennett doesn't take the bait. "I'm calling in to rebut what your *guest* told the public. Everything she's said—with the exception of our dating in high school—is a lie."

His bombshell rings throughout the studio. And the restaurant, given how all the diners have stopped eating and are watching this train wreck.

Lissa's blue eyes fill with more fake tears. "We meant the world to each other in high school. You never stopped telling me you loved me." Fat crocodile tears roll down her cheeks. The only thing fat on her body.

"For fuck's sake, we were seventeen years old, Lissa. A lifetime ago."

I hope the show is on delay, otherwise the censors will be having a field day.

Lissa places her hand over her ample chest. "We meant the world to each other. You gave me the best gift of a new life." She bends forward and sobs, her arms stealing around her waist.

"Then it must have been immaculate conception, because we never had sex."

Bennett's truth echoes throughout the restaurant and the television studio. But it doesn't stop the show. His childhood girlfriend now sports black mascara running down her cheeks. "How can you say that, baby?"

"Because it's the truth."

The hairs on my arms raise at his tone. If he was in the same room as her, I would fear he might not stop himself from strangling her.

Francis consoles Lissa, passing her a box of tissues. Speaking directly to the camera, the host says, "Lots of teenagers get pregnant."

"Only if they have sex. Which. We. Did. Not."

Lissa waves a tissue in the air. Not in surrender, more like encouraging the hosts to continue her defense.

Logan's head swivels between his guests and the camera. "What happened to the child, Lissa?"

She hiccups. "Bennett ran off to join the band and refused to pick up my calls. I was so young, I knew I couldn't tell my parents." She raises the tissue to her nose. "I turned to his best friend, Curtiss, for help in reaching Bennett, but nothing worked." She blows her nose.

"For fuck's sake." At least Bennett said this for the benefit of the diners, and not into his phone.

Wary at how her story is going to conclude, I touch his chest.

Lissa lifts her head and pronounces. "I had a miscarriage."

# Chapter Twenty-Four

The murmurs among the restaurant patrons rise. On camera, the hosts look at each other, their mouths gaping.

Next to me, Bennett growls. He doesn't form words, just paces around the restaurant. Other patrons' heads swivel to follow him.

I need to do something to help. Without thinking, I grab the phone from his hand. "You're a liar. You never were pregnant with his baby."

Francis blinks. "Who's this?"

"Jenna Westfield." Crap. *What have I done?* Have I made this even worse for Bennett?

"As in Darren Hilliard's former girlfriend?" Logan pipes up. "Seems like the rumors that you're with Bennett are true."

Bennett steals the phone from me and refocuses the conversation. "Everything Lissa told you is a lie. Well, she might have had a miscarriage, I don't know, but the kid wasn't mine."

My phone chimes as Lissa bursts into tears again. Luke's name is displayed.

Get him off that show!

He wants to defend himself

Make the PR team do their damn job

I don't reply, simply tug on Bennett's arm during a brief lull on his end. When he glances at me, I hold up the text messages.

"We were together last month in Aroostook," Lissa whimpers. "*She* tried to come between us, but he rebuffed the Black Widow. He told me he didn't want to get caught up in her web, which he knew would end UC."

Francis stares into the camera. "Is that true, Jenna? Have you marked Bennett as your next victim?"

Anger propels me to reach for the phone again, but Bennett holds it above his head. He swivels on his heel, and presents his back to me while he says, "I called in to correct Lissa's lies. Have you watched any of the videos from UC's concert in Louisville? The whole band agrees with me. Did you even fact-check her story? Do your job." He disconnects.

My body vibrates. "How were you ever with such a vile creature?"

"It was high school. She had blonde hair and blue eyes, and I was horny."

"She didn't even help you out on that score."

"Lucky me." His arms encircle my body, allowing some of my ire to seep out. Given his loosening posture, he's probably feeling the same.

"Thank you." I drop my head backwards. "For defending me. I'm impressed with how you combated her ridiculous claims."

"Truth is an absolute defense."

I smile. "'I respect those who tell me the truth no matter how hard it is.'"

His eyes light up. "You're quoting the *first Godfather*. See, I told you it was the best of the series!"

Just like that, the tension between us breaks.

I become aware of the stares we're receiving in the restaurant. "Let's sit down."

Bennett's hand lowers to the middle of my back and directs me toward my abandoned chair. Once I'm settled, he sits across from me. "Well, that was unexpected."

"You can say that again." I rearrange the silverware at my place setting. "What's up with her?"

His fist bangs on the table. "I have no fucking clue." He pushes against the chair. "I wish I never met the bitch."

I drop my hand on top of his fist. "I thought your talk with the fans last night would have stemmed this."

"Yeah. I hoped so too. Looks like we're going to have to do more damage control." His gaze locks on mine. "We need to get the truth out there. How *dare* she say I got her pregnant and left her high and dry! Damn girl refused to have sex with me."

Frustration rolls off him in waves. "We'll break through. Your fans will know what happened, and who cares about the rest of the population? Like you've told me before, all that matters is we know the reality of a situation."

For the first time, his face relaxes. "How did you get so smart?"

"Sort of had to grow up when they started calling me Black Widow."

"Hey, we need to fix that too. You didn't kill Darren, and you're not breaking up UC. If anything, you're bringing us closer."

His words settle over me. "This means a lot to me." I lean across the table and kiss him.

Someone near us clears his throat, causing us to break apart. "Hi." A young man in his early twenties stands at the end of our table. Must be a fan.

Bennett stands and extends his hand. "Hello. I'm Bennett Hardy."

"I know." With his head, he gestures toward the back of the restaurant. "I'm here with my family. We couldn't help but watch the talk show."

Bennett spews, "Lies."

"Well, from where we were sitting, Lissa looks like the wronged one. Here you are kissing the Black Widow while the mother of your dead child is forced to cry on national TV. You should be ashamed of yourself."

Not a fan, then. Bennett starts to defend himself, but I toss a bunch of money on the table for food we didn't touch and put my arm around his bicep. In my *not to be crossed* voice, as Court dubbed it during school, I say, "You have your so-called facts wrong, but we're not going to convince you. Good day." I yank on Bennett's arm and, after several tries, he leaves with me.

As soon as we reach the sidewalk, I pre-empt his tirade. "Call the limo. We'll regroup in the hotel."

We walk around the corner and duck into an alley so as not to attract any more attention while we wait. A couple of minutes later, the limo arrives and we scramble inside.

"That guy! How could he believe her?"

"Lissa painted you in a pretty awful light."

"She made it all up! Maybe all the plastic surgery went to her brain."

"Luke and the PR team will sort this out."

My phone rings.

"Don't answer it."

I glance at the caller. "It's Ma."

He crosses his arms across his chest. "Unless she's been accused of breaking up the governor's marriage and having his love child, I think she can wait."

He needs my attention more than Ma. I dismiss her call. "There. I'll make you explain this to her later."

"Fine." He rakes his fingers through his hair. "I don't know what makes me madder. The fact I never touched her in high school and no one believes me, or her saying she lost my nonexistent baby." After a second he adds, "Or her spewing about you ruining UC."

There's no way around any of it. "It all sucks."

"It does."

We pass by Graceland, all the excitement from earlier in the day a distant memory. His phone rings this time. "It's Luke."

"Put the call on speakerphone." If the allegations against me are going to be included in this conversation, I need to be made privy.

Bennett does and Luke launches directly into his speech. "What the hell were you thinking, B? By calling in, you gave her story more legs. The PR team now has to work twice as hard to make her disappear."

"I had to defend myself. Almost everything she said was lies, except I was a stupid kid who told her I loved her." He seethes, "I never got any from her though—not for not trying—but the frigid bitch wouldn't let me."

"I don't care if she became a nun. What was the first rule I ever told you guys?"

Bennett stares at the carpet covering the limo's floor. "Never engage," he mumbles.

"What was that? Speak up."

His head levels. "You said never to engage. That was *your* job."

"What did you do?"

Although I understand the situation, I can't take the way he's berating Bennett. I interject, "He didn't mean to make things worse, Luke. He thought he could correct the record."

"Look how well it went for him. And as for you, Miss Black Widow. Your nickname is now stuck like glue."

I wince, shoving guilt downward.

"Hey," Bennett sticks up for me. "She's innocent in all of this. If you hadn't meddled in the first place and made me go to her for physical therapy, she would be back in Aroostook living her life."

*Boring life* I amend. Because life with Bennett is anything but dull. Filled with angst, true, but not dull. Not to mention passion. And love. So much love.

"We're getting nowhere," Luke's resigned voice fills the air. "Meet me at the hotel." The call disconnects.

I join Bennett in resting my head on the headrest, staring at the limo's ceiling. Without moving, I say, "Kinda like one of those reality shows on television."

"Yeah," he replies, equally keeping his head unmoved. In a fake broadcaster voice, he says, "Join us for another season of *Fucked Up Island*. Where lies lure you in and paternity tests await at every corner."

Despite everything going on, I giggle. "Sounds like you have a big hit on your hands."

His face swings toward mine. "I only want to play music and see the world through your eyes."

A buzz tingles through my body at his earnest declaration. I turn my face to him. "We'll get there."

"When?"

"Soon." I hope.

Without the traffic from earlier in the day, the limo soon arrives outside our hotel. Bennett thanks the driver while I scoot out and onto the sidewalk. Behind me, he hops out of the car and stops stock-still, his face a mask of pain.

His groin pull. I race to his side, not wanting to draw any attention to his upper thigh, especially in a public area. Lowering my voice, I instruct, "Wrap your arm around my shoulders and let me take the brunt of your weight. As soon as we get to the room, I'll ice it and help you work this out."

A second later, his arm snakes over my shoulder. To the outside, we appear to be a couple in love. Which, I guess we are. However, I'm the only person on earth who knows his muscle throbs with each shuffle he takes. I keep as upright as I can, considering I'm assuming a large portion of his weight.

The doorman opens the door for us and we maneuver inside, not noticing the ornate foyer or clerks standing at the ready along the wall. "Let's get you to the elevators."

"I can do this."

"Of course you can," I babble. "You can do anything. You're the lead singer for one of the hottest bands in the world."

He stops. "One?"

I almost collapse, knowing his sense of humor—and trademark cockiness—is returning. "There's Hunte. The Light Rail. Backdoor Clouds. Plus solo artists like Cole Manchester and Ozzy Martinez. So, yes, one."

"You know how to wound a guy."

"Keeping it real."

We continue down the hallway toward the elevator, with Bennett holding more of his own weight. He even shakes out his right leg, not too hard, another good sign. Keeping our heads down, we get on the elevator with a few other people, none of which seem to notice us. We're the last to disembark.

A grim-faced Luke lurks in the hallway.

# Chapter Twenty-Five

"You look like shit." Where's the affable Luke I've come to know?

Bennett's responds, "Fuck you."

"He aggravated his injury," I supply.

The manager sighs. "Great. As if we didn't have enough to handle. Let's talk in your room so you can get checked out."

The three of us make our way to our room—no more pretenses that I'm sleeping anywhere else. Once Bennett's changed into shorts and I've evaluated him, he sits on the sofa with an ice pack. True to his word, only then does Luke begin. "I've been in contact with our PR team. They liked the presentation you guys gave during the Louisville show, but it obviously isn't enough to counter the shitstorm from today."

Clearly.

He focuses on me. "Your clinic is also in the news. I assume you know about the graffiti incident?"

Bennett squeezes his own left thigh. "The spider?"

"Court and I have everything under control. She had the wall repainted and we put out a press release."

Luke adds, "Which didn't contain the fallout."

I remember being too distracted to open Court's second text—the one she sent after reporting about the local paper picking up our press release. "What do you mean?"

"Black Widow spiders now are painted on the sidewalks outside both of your At Your Service PT clinics. This time with sayings beneath them."

My hand flies in front of my face. "Michelle. I guess we were too clever in our press release." My shoulders slump. "We should have outed her as the culprit."

"Perhaps." Luke reads something on his cell. "Have to hand it to you, though. Creating a contest for T-shirt slogans about spiders was an excellent idea. However, Michelle"—he glances at me for confirmation of her name—"only took it as an added challenge."

I'm speechless. I have to get back there and deal with my business while I still have one to handle.

Bennett shifts forward in his seat, addressing his manager. "How serious is this?"

"Not going to lie, it's more than annoying but less than a fatal crash."

Well, there's that. I find my voice. "We'll fix it." No other choice.

Luke returns his attention to the lead singer. "Your collective problems are now the band's problems. This is a UC crisis."

Bennett's hand fists on top of the ice pack. "How many times do I have to tell you that I wasn't the father?"

"Do you have anyone to back you up?"

"What? That I wasn't sleeping with Lissa back then?"

"That's exactly what I mean."

The room goes still.

"It was high school. It's not like I'm still in touch with any of those people. I wasn't even close with them when we were in class together." His green eyes search the ceiling for answers.

"Fine. If not them, how about your mother? Would she be able to vouch for you?"

A humorless laugh falls from his lips. He opens and closes them several times, causing empathy to rise up in me. I answer for him. "Every mother believes the sun rises and sets on her child. No one would believe her."

Bennett and I share a glance. Luke exhales loudly. "You're right. C'mon, B, you must have had friends back then."

"My best friend back then was Curtiss. The jerk Lissa referenced on the show today."

Luke cracks his knuckles. "All right. We'll think of something. Maybe do research into the hospital she must've gone to with the miscarriage. Perhaps we can get the records."

"Not with medical privacy laws." My physical therapy training comes in handy sometimes. "You might be able to get something out of the staff. Off the record, of course."

Luke's coffee-colored gaze impales me, before moving to Bennett. "Keep thinking about witnesses."

"What about the bullshit that Jenna's breaking up the band? I hate that she's being portrayed as the enemy." Bennett reaches over and squeezes my hand.

The manager semi-smiles at our joined hands. "I can handle it."

"You shouldn't have to," I reply.

The fact Bennett's standing up for me, even in the face of all the crap Lissa dumped on his lap, makes my heart flip. Despite the whirl-wind swirling, I have faith that nothing will come between us.

Luke gets to his feet and paces around the room like a cornered tiger. "Coop, Río, and Tris are on your side. Have to give it to you straight, though, 007 and the Hilliards are less likely to come to your defense."

Bennett moves the ice pack on his thigh. "007 participated last night."

Was that only last night? My shoulders lower. "Has Darren's mother said anything else to the press?"

"No," the manager assures me. Then takes it away. "I have almost zero faith she'll stay quiet in the face of Lissa's interview." He checks his phone. "Right on time, Francis and Logan reached out to her for her opinion."

No need to read it.

Luke's pacing accelerates.

Bennett's phone blares an Eminem song. He picks it up, silences it, and tosses it onto the coffee table. In response to my angled head, he says, "Mom."

Could this day get any worse?

"I'm going to call the PR team to strategize. Maybe reach out to Jeremy Davis again. He's written good articles about UC in the past. For the love of God, do not leave this room." He takes a step toward the door. "And don't call in to any shows, podcasts, or reporter friends. Got it, B?"

"Not going anywhere," he grumbles.

When Luke focuses on me, I raise my hands and nod. Satisfied, he stalks out of the room.

Bennett opens his arms wide. I can't resist his invitation and crawl into his embrace, careful not to disturb the ice pack or reinjure his pulled muscle. With my head on his upper pecs and his chin on top of my head, he says, "We'll figure this out."

I don't want to say this, but I feel the need to offer. "I should go home. The clinics are suffering because I'm not there."

"No. They're being targeted because you're mine." He tugs me tight. "Doesn't matter where you are, no one can change this fact."

I let his confidence buoy my flagging spirits. "I'm causing you problems with the band. Pierce won't talk with you."

"He was talking last night. He'll get over it." He shrugs. "Or we'll hire a new bassist. You're the most important person in my life."

His first admission causes warmth to spread throughout my chest. The last one, though, not so much. "That's not right. The band needs its bassist. You need him," Pierce seemed to be getting over my imaginary role in his best friend's death last night. Then there's Darren's mother, who equally hates me—although that's nothing new. And

Michelle's vendetta against me back home. Add Lissa to the toxic brew, and we're sinking fast.

"I need you more."

Not wanting to continue this endless cycle without an off-ramp, I remove the ice from this thigh and suggest he check out the muscle pull. He gets to his feet and begins to do an abbreviated version of our exercises.

I follow him. "Does anything hurt?"

"No." He even tries full-blown skater leaps. "Okay, these hurt."

"They're more advanced. So long as the others don't bother you, I think you'll be fine. Why don't you take a shower?"

"Join me?" He holds out his hand.

"As inviting as that sounds, I better reach out to Court. I need to make sure the clinics are all right."

He frowns. "Why don't you turn it over to UC's PR team? They're professionals—I bet they can fix things for you without breaking a sweat."

My hands fist on my hips. "It's my business, Bennett. I can handle this."

"All I'm saying is why bother? Take advantage of the team around me. That's what they're here for."

"I'm not in the band," I remind him, emphasizing my point by poking his chest. "UC retains them—of which I'm not a part. If no one else, Pierce will tell you that."

He steps backward. "Sheesh, I'm only trying to help you."

"I've been handling my business all by myself for years now. I think I know what I'm doing."

"I'm sure you can, Sweetheart, but wouldn't you prefer to pass all the work over to someone else? That way, we can enjoy our time together."

His mansplaining rubs me the wrong way. I stab him with my evil eye. "I am perfectly capable of running my business."

"I wasn't saying you're not. Only that you should let the professionals do their job."

"Professionals?" My voice rises. "Like how you defer to Luke's every suggestion?" *Low blow*, but I'm mad.

Anger suffuses his body. "You do you." He storms out of the room, muttering "Lissa," and "Curtiss," and "mother" as he makes his way to the bathroom. Before he slams the door, I hear my own name added to the list.

The cocky lead singer of Untamed Coaster can shove it. I'm the reason At Your Service PT exists, and I'll keep it afloat, dammit. I punch the button for Court.

"Hey, you," she answers. "I got the sidewalks repainted."

Of course she could troubleshoot this, but it's my mess to clean up. "I appreciate it. Guess my press release didn't work as well as we hoped it would. I think it's time for me to stop gallivanting with a rock band and come home to deal with all of this."

"I have it handled from here. What more could you have done? Repainting makes it go away."

"For what? A day? I'm thinking about installing security cameras. Even though Michelle's been good at avoiding being caught on video from the street, I'm sure to catch her red-handed with more strategically-placed cameras."

"Well, that's not a bad idea. But you can contact companies online and I can oversee the installation."

"At both locations? What about the new one that's just getting renovated?"

"Right now, there are only two places. Felipe and I got this."

"What if—"

"Jenna. What is this call really about? Did you get into a fight with Bennett?"

I shout, "No!" A second later, I take a deep breath. "No, we're not in a fight. Not a big one, anyway. He's just being . . . a privileged rock star."

"Well, he sort of is one, right?"

"Totally." I plop onto the sofa. "It's my responsibility to make this issue at the clinics go away."

"I hear you." A pen taps on a desk. "There is something I've been keeping from you. Cancellations are on the rise again. I triple checked, and patient numbers are definitely lower."

My stomach knots. "You shouldn't have to take on all of this. The business is my responsibility."

"You deserve this time away. With a super-hot, talented singer who makes your world shatter."

My knees knock together. "I never said that."

"Didn't have to. How about this? I promise to keep you in the loop about numbers and graffiti outside if you send me a picture of Coop that I can't find on the internet."

The object of her interest catches me off guard. "Coop?"

"Come to think of it, a photo of Río would be fine, too. Both of them are not bad on the eyes."

"None of the band is," I agree. "You know all this is rubbing me the wrong way. I really should be home."

"How about this. If cancellations increase by ten percent, I'll give you a shout."

"Ten percent?" I tuck my hair behind my ear, and it immediately pops out. "Five." I shove it back again. "If anymore graffiti appears, I'm there."

"Seven and I'll handle the paint."

My guess is the actual number is pretty high if she started off this negotiation at ten percent. I'll give her another week but if anything else happens, I need to be there. It doesn't matter what's going on with UC. Our conversation ends with me promising to send her a previously unseen photo of the guitarist. And drummer.

On the table, Bennett's phone rings again and the name "Ma" appears. The shower's running. She's probably worried after seeing Lissa's interview. I sit straighter. No way could she be as bad as he says. I swipe his phone. "Hello?"

An older woman's voice asks, "Who's this?"

"Mrs. Hardy, this is Jenna Westfield. I'm, ah, friends with your son." Not sure he'd want me to classify our relationship differently with his mother.

"Oh you are, are you? Westfield. You're the one people call the Black Widow?"

Thinking this wasn't my best idea, I deflect. "Bennett's taking a shower." Crap. That sounded bad. I plow ahead, "Can I take a message?"

"Now you're his secretary too?" When I remain silent, she continues, "Well, tell my *son* that I saw the interview with Lissa. Let him know I remember when he was in high school and fawning all over the girl like a lovesick puppy. I also recall his father dying on me." She huffs into the telephone. "Just a few moments later, my *son* left me behind to join that damn band of his, and never looked back. If his sister were here, she never would've abandoned me like he did. Got all that?"

Her venom is palpable, and it spikes my own simmering anger. In as even a tone as I can muster, I reply, "I'll let him know you won't be any help in rebutting Lissa's claims."

"Damn straight."

She starts to say something else, but I'm done. I don't want to hear it, so I pretend to have a bad connection and disconnect the call. The man never stood a chance with such a loathsome woman in his house.

Next, my phone chirps with an incoming text. Seriously? Who else wants to bother me today? My sister's name appears.

> I know you're busy, but I'm having a hard time juggling kids, work, and hospital runs.

Hospital runs? I thought she and her husband had this all figured out. Between her schedule as an anesthesiologist and her husband's cosmetic surgery practice, things always seemed to be organized chaos in their home.

> What are you talking about?

How don't you know?

She can be so dramatic!

> Tell me

Ma's been diagnosed with stage 4 pancreatic cancer. She has weeks to months to live

My phone falls to the floor, my sister's texts bouncing off the walls of my mind. Especially "How don't you know?"

How *don't* I know?

Because I've been playing physical therapist with a cocky rock star, who swept me off my feet and away from all my ethics.

Because I delved into the fantasy life of touring, with everything I needed provided at the crook of a finger.

Because Ma called me several times and Bennett distracted me from answering, causing me to treat her almost the same way his awful mother treats him.

On a sob, I rush to my suitcase, tossing my clothes into it without caution.

The bathroom door opens and Bennett comes out, wearing a

towel around his waist, UC pendant hanging off his necklace, and wet hair framing his face. "Where are you going?"

"Home! I never should have left!"

---

Next up is the last book in the Passionate Beats trilogy, MIC DROP ~ *this time with dual pov's* ~ releaseing next month. Please pre-order it on Amazon, https://geni.us/UntamedCoaster4, and add it to your GoodReads TBR list, https://geni.us/UC4GR!

Stay up-to-date with me by joining my newsletter, https://geni.us/UCNewsletter!

# A Note from Arell

*Dear Fabulous Reader,*

Thank you so much for reading EXTENDED BRIDGE, the second installment in the Passionate Beats trilogy, part of the Untamed Coaster series!

This story is told entirely from the point-of-view of physical therapist Jenna Westfield, who is fighting her own demons - including the death of her former patient/boyfriend and UC's original keyboardist Darren Hilliard. Lead signer Bennett Hardy is a powerful pull, but obstacles continually are thrown between the pair.

Jenna struggles to come to grips with her feelings toward Bennett, who has professed his feelings early on. You can't help be be swept up into this emotional tale, and root for this couple to find their happy ending! The trilogy comes to a rollercoaster of an ending in the last book, MIC DROP, up next!

As usual, some of my own life experiences appear in EXTENDED BRIDGE ∼

- I'm lucky to live close enough to New York City, and I've attended many concerts at the famed Madison Square Garden. It's such an electric place! While I haven't performed on the stage (believe me, you wouldn't want that!), it was fun letting my imagination run wild with all the possibilities.
- How fun would it be to have your own personal stylist? I really enjoyed writing the scenes between Jenna and Ness - and getting those awesome reactions from Bennett!
- While I never have been to Graceland (it's on my bucket list), I wrote this scene with the help of videos on YouTube. Then I asked my friend Gwyn, who had just visited, to review what I had written and she said it was like I had been! Such a compliment!

**Please stay in touch! Subscribe to my newsletter** at https://geni.us/UCNewsletter **or join Arell's Angels, my reader group on Facebook**, http://www.facebook.-com/groups/arellsangels ∼ **or both!!**

If you have any questions, feel free to email me at http://Arell@ArellRivers.com. I love chatting with readers!

Thanks for devoting your precious time to EXTENDED BRIDGE. I hope you better understand Jenna now, and are buckled up and ready for the final book in the Passionate Beats trilogy, coming next!

All my love,
Arell

# Gratitude

Extended Bridge couldn't have happened without so many awesome people!

This book is dedicated to my college bestie, Gwyn Novak, who generously agreed to proof the section about Graceland since she just visited. She gave it her seal of approval! Hope this part sings straight to your heart!

Big thanks to my at-home support system ∼ my husband, Big Mike (plus our two cats Luna and Loki, with their unique brand of support!), and my Mom. They're small in number but off-the-charts in cheerleading abilities!

Extended Bridge wouldn't be what it is without the fantastic group of editors I've assembled on my team. My plot coach, Theresa Leigh of The Fairy Plot Mother, developmental editor Trenda Lundin of It's Your Story Content Editing, editor Nancy Smay of Evident Ink, and proofreader Roxanne Blouin, all really helped bring this story to life. In addition, Dar Albert of Wicked Smart Designs sealed the deal with this truly delicious cover! Yum!!

I would like to give a shout out to Shauna and Becca of The

Author Agency. They have provided so much guidance in how to best package this trilogy ∼ I couldn't have done this without them!

To my fantastic alpha reader Taylor Delong - you rock! Thanks for all your comments that truly helped Jenna and Bennett soar.

Big love to my ARC Team!! Each one of you warms my heart with how much enthusiasm you have for all of my projects, including this new band, Untamed Coaster. Thank you for taking the time to read, review, and share EXTENDED BRIDGE!!!

My Facebook reader's group, Arell's Angels, is my go-to place to hang out, check out hot photos, and simply just vent! Shout out to "Arell's Insiders" who post daily and keep the group rockin' with your wit and devotion. To all the Angels who participate in our Hotties of the Month, daily games, my crazy Facebook Lives, sneak peeks, collaborative stories, and author takeover Sundays ∼ you make this journey so worthwhile! And there's always room for more angels!

I'm so lucky to have met, in person and virtually, so many wonderful authors who are so giving of their advice, support, and friendship. To my fellow Kissed by Romance Authors, Taylor Delong, Libby Waterford, Mary E. Montgomery, and Nicole Locke, you are the reason! 💜 Thanks, too, for all the support from Claire Marti, Darby Fox, Sophia Henry, Anne Lange, and Lilly Wilde!

To everyone who picks up this book, I hope you're "Strapped, locked, and loaded!" If you enjoyed EXTENDED BRIDGE, please share it with your friends and write a review on Amazon, https://geni.us/UntamedCoaster3, and/or GoodReads, https://geni.us/UC3GR. I can't wait for you to read the rollercoaster conclusion of Passionate Beats in MIC DROP!

Blessings,
Arell

# About the Author

For as long as Arell Rivers can remember, she has been lost in a book. During her senior year in college, she picked up a romance novel ... and instantly was hooked!

Arell started writing her first book because the characters were screaming at her to do so. The story came out in her dreams and attacked her in the shower, so she took to the computer to shut them up. But they kept talking.

Born and raised in New Jersey, Arell has what some may call a "checkered past." Prior to discovering her passion for writing romance, she practiced law, was a wedding and event planner and even dabbled in marketing. Arell lives with two adorable cats and a very supportive husband who doesn't care that the bed isn't made or dinner isn't on the table. When not in her writing cave, Arell is found cooking in the InstantPot, working out with Shaun T, or hitting the beach.

Want to keep up to date with Arell? Sign up for her newsletter at https://geni.us/SinsNewsletter. All new subscribers receive a special gift!

# Also by Arell Rivers

**Untamed Coaster**

*A found family/he falls first series following the rock band of the same name*

SINFUL BEATS, http://geni.us/UntamedCoaster1 (Quinn and Callum) (crossover from Sins of the Fathers)

Opening Strains, https://geni.us/UntamedCoaster2, Passionate Beats trilogy (Bennett and Jenna, book 1)

Extended Bridge, Passionate Beats trilogy (Bennett and Jenna, book 2)

Mic Drop, http://geni.us/UntamedCoaster4, Passionate Beats trilogy (Bennett and Jenna, book 3)

Animal Beats (Río and Hayden) - up next!

**Sins of the Fathers**

*A billionaire series about the children of 3 notorious businessmen*

VICE, http://geni.us/Sins1 (short story, originally published as "Tinsel Bomb" in the 2021 anthology TINSEL AND TATAS)

ANGER, http://geni.us/Sins2 (Theo and Amelia)

PRIDE, http://geni.us/Sins3 (Xander and Madison)

IDLE, https://geni.us//Sins4 (Paige and Jesse)

**The Hunte Family Series**

*An enemies-to-lovers series about the dynasty created by rocker Braxon Hunte*

Out of the Red, https://geni.us/OOTR (Brax and Sara, set in the mid 90s)

Out of the Shadow, https://geni.us/hunte2 (King and Angie)

Out of the Gold, https://geni.us/OOTR (Melody and Chase)

Out of the Blue, http://geni.us/Hunte4 (Trent and Cordelia)

Out of the Box, http://geni.us/OutoftheBox (box set of books 1-4 plus a bonus novella)

### *The Hold Series*

*A second chances series about rock star Cole Manchester, his publicist Rose Morgan, and their friends*

Hold On, https://geni.us/HoldOn (prequel novella for Cole and Rose)

No One to Hold, https://geni.us/NOTH (Cole and Rose trilogy, book 1)

Hard to Hold, https://geni.us/HtoH (Cole and Rose trilogy, book 2)

To Have and to Hold, https://geni.us/THTH (Cole and Rose trilogy, book 3)

Take Hold of Me, https://geni.us/THOM (Wills and Emilie)

Hold Still, https://geni.us/GDwdlls (Ozzy and McKenna)

Hold Me, http://geni.us/HoldMeBoxSet (box set of books 1-3, 6, plus a bonus novella)

### Kissed by Romance collections

*Anthologies written by the Kissed by Romance authors: Taylor Delong, Nicole Locke, M.E. Montgomery, Libby Waterford ~ and me!*

Steamy Shorts, https://books2read.com/SteamyShorts (4 quick reads guaranteed to bring the heat / my story is OUT OF THE SAND in the Hunte Family series world)

A Kiss at Midnight, https://books2read.com/AKAM (5 interconnected novellas about New Year's Eve at the Grandview Lodge / my story is OUT OF THE JADE in the Hunte Family series world)

# Connect with Arell

- Subscribe to Arell's newsletter at https://geni.us/UCNewsletter
- Join Arell's Facebook Group, "Arell's Angels" at http://www.facebook.com/groups/ArellsAngels
- Like Arell's Facebook Page, http://www.Facebook.com/ArellRivers
- Follow Arell on Instagram, http://www.Instagram.com/AuthorArell
- Hang out with Arell on Amazon at https://geni.us/ArellRivers
- Check out Arell on Goodreads, https://geni.us/ARGoodReads
- Follow Arell on BookBub, https://geni.us/BookBubFollow
- Head over to Arell's website at http://www.ArellRivers.com
- Email Arell at http://Arell@ArellRivers.com

# No One to Hold

ant to go on another tour with my first rockstar hero, Cole Manchester? Read the trilogy that set the standard for Passionate Beats!

*Enjoy the first chapter of* No One to Hold, *Book #1 in The Hold series!*

**Succumb to Cole Manchester—talented, witty, charming, sexy and oh-so flawed—a womanizing rock star whose shallow life is transformed when he experiences love for the first time.**

From the outside, Cole Manchester seems to have it all: looks, fame, money, awards and women. When tragedy strikes, he realizes how hollow his life is, and opens the door to the one thing he's never considered ... finding love. He's inexplicably drawn to the quiet wall-flower who works on his team, a line he knows he shouldn't cross.

After devastating heartbreaks, all Rose Morgan wants is to blend into the background. Working at her dream job as a publicist, she's safely hiding in plain sight. Until her client, the irresistible Cole Manchester, notices her. Rose must ignore her desires in order to protect her bruised heart ... and keep her prized career.

Cole needs Rose to teach him how to love. Rose needs Cole to teach her how to trust. Together, they form a bond ignited by passion but fueled by insecurities. When her mother's interference collides with his fan's twisted plot, Cole and Rose may find themselves with No One To Hold.

Somehow I endure the first hour of the party.

No. Not party. Wake.

Two hours ago I placed a blood-red rose atop my mother's casket on this freezing February day. Now, I'm trapped in my parents' house, choked by a tie, listening to stories about her while pretending everything is okay. It's *not* fucking okay.

When I can't take it anymore, I collapse onto the step at the foot of the stairs, looking at all the people milling around the family room. They are eating catered food off Mom's good china. Swilling drinks from her favorite wine glasses. Photos of her are displayed every-where, some in frames and others in the scrapbooks she spent hours creating.

Reaching between the spindles of the banister, I pick up a frame off the closest table. It's a photo of Mom and me at the Grammy

Awards a couple of years ago. She's beaming, clearly enjoying herself. I trace her beautiful smile with a calloused fingertip.

A bunch of Mom's high school students surround me like yipping hyenas, giving me little choice but to put down the photo, stand up and join them. They're on the cheerleading squad Mom coached. They all seem to be talking at once, making it impossible for me to follow their conversation, and a few of the girls seem star struck to be near me. Some even cast what they obviously think are flirty, seductive glances in my direction. Seriously?

One girl points her cell phone at me while the others titter. My hand flies to block my face in a gesture I've perfected after years of protecting myself from the paparazzi.

Rose Morgan, my ponytailed and bespectacled account rep with the Greta VonStein PR Agency, appears at my right. I take my first deep breath since being surrounded, knowing Rose will take care of the girls.

"Ladies, a word," she says. She's wearing what she always wears— a skirt and blazer—this time in black. Ushering the group deeper into the family room, Rose says something I can't hear and then takes the would-be photographer's cell phone. After pushing a few buttons, she returns it to the girl, who mouths the word *sorry* to me. Quickly, the cheerleaders disperse. Rose to the rescue. Again.

Returning to my side, Rose places her hands on my cheeks. My breath catches at the contact.

In a low voice, she says, "It's all taken care of, Cole."

Behind her glasses, her blue eyes are filled with compassion and some other emotion I can't identify. They seem like they belong to someone much older and wiser than me, not to a woman who's a few years younger than me.

I close my eyes to block out everything except the feeling of her hands on my skin and the comfort they're pouring into me. The intensity of the sensation startles me back to the present, causing my eyes to pop open. Clearing my throat, I say, "Thanks for the save. It's kinda weird being fangirled here."

Rose drops her hands and I immediately crave her soft warmth. "I'm so sorry for your loss," she finally says. "Your mom is—was—a wonderful lady. I remember the first time I spoke with her, right after you'd signed with Greta. She couldn't believe you had a publicist." She shakes her head. "Her exact words were, 'I can't believe other people will really follow what my Cole does.'"

I laugh. It's a rusty sound. "I can hear Mom saying that."

Smiling, Rose says, "After you took her to your first Grammys, she sent me a lovely thank you note and gift basket. She was so proud of you."

"Mom never got tired of talking about when she met Adam Baret there." Mom's teenage heartthrob sent a very nice arrangement to the funeral. I'm sure she's looking down on us from above, blushing.

"Take some time and stay here with your father and brother."

My gaze follows hers to the kitchen, where Jayson and Dad are hugging. It's just us now. And Jayson's boyfriend, Carl. "I plan to."

"Family is so very important. Lean on each other." Her tone leads me to believe she's speaking from experience, although I wouldn't know. Up until now, all of our conversations have been strictly business.

I nod. Swallowing past the lump in my throat, I say, "Thanks for making the trip from Los Angeles." I pause at my use of the city's formal name. Everything's taken on an odd sense of formality over the past days. "And I appreciate how much you've kept the paparazzi away from us."

"I wanted to be here for you." She reaches out like she's going to touch me again, which sends a flicker of anticipation through me, but her hand stops and returns to her side. My disappointment shocks me.

She continues, "And don't worry about all the cards and gifts your fans are sending to the office. We'll make sure everything receives a response, and the stuffed animals and other presents will be distributed to children's hospitals."

I shake my head at her use of "we." That idea has Rose's signature, not Greta's, all over it. "My fans are really sending stuff?"

"You mean a lot to them." Her lips quirk into a small smile, and I feel my mouth move upward in response.

"I left a card from Josh with the others over there." She motions toward the front hallway table. "Thought you'd want to see it."

"Thanks." I first met Josh four years ago at a meet-and-greet. His love of music reminded me of myself at his age, so passionate. His single mother was unable to pay for a violin coach, so I arranged for him to have private music lessons. He must be fourteen by now.

She nods, sending her ponytail swinging. For the second time today, I find myself ensnared by her blue eyes. They're an icy blue, yet they're bright with emotion behind the thick lenses of her glasses. How have I never noticed their remarkable color before?

After a beat, she says, "Let me know when you're planning on returning to LA, and we'll set up some appearances for you. In the meantime, Greta wants me to issue a release on your behalf, thanking your fans for their support and letting them know you'll be spending some personal time with your family." She gives me a quick hug and walks off in Dad's direction.

Business never stops for long.

My agent, Russell Waldock, and his wife fill the void left by Rose. At fifty-five, he's one of the most powerful men in LA, yet he's also very down-to-earth, which drew me to him. "I appreciate your coming all the way to New Jersey for Mom's"—my voice breaks—"funeral."

Russell claps me on the back. "Julie was a great lady, Cole. Always looking out for you. And she was fierce. The way she scolded me about your music video for 'Prowling' made me feel like I got caught rifling through my father's *Playboy* collection." His wife smiles at him.

I chuckle. "She always called it my 'racy' video."

"Well, she wasn't wrong there," Russell agrees. No, she wasn't.

His wife picks up a photo of Mom and Dad holding hands on a

beach in Hawaii and then returns it to the side table. She asks, "How's your father holding up? This has to be hard on him."

I glance over at Dad. "He's okay. It's been . . . rough."

How *is* Dad going to handle this? Mom's touch is everywhere in this house, in his life. They were married for so long they used to complete each other's sentences. "I'm trying to do whatever I can. Of course, Jayson and Carl live nearby."

"Let me know if you need anything, okay?" Russell says.

"Thanks. I'm grateful you arranged for the label to give me an extension on recording my next album."

Russell nods. "Call me when you're ready to go back to LA. No rush."

They each give me a hug. "Thanks again for coming," I say. "Will do."

I circulate around the room, numbly making small talk with acquaintances I haven't seen in years. I'm standing in the dining room with some family friends the next time Rose crosses my line of vision. She's in the front hall, running her fingers over the framed photo of Mom holding me when I was a baby. She wipes a tear from her cheek and looks up.

Our eyes meet.

We both freeze.

After a long pause, she retrieves her coat and walks out the front door. I catch a breath as if my heart just restarted.

I continue circulating and reminiscing about Mom. Around nine, Jayson and Carl leave to take care of their new puppy. Only Aunt Doreen and her family remain. "How are you doing, Cole?"

"I'm okay," I lie. Yanking off my tie, I ask, "How about you, Aunt Doreen?"

"About as well as I can be. I want you to know you can always count on me, whatever you need."

"Thanks."

We discuss mundane things, like how beautiful the funeral was and our amazement at how many people came to the wake. After a pause, she says, "You know, I swore to my sister that I would keep an eye out for you. She really wanted you to settle down." She picks invisible lint off of my blazer.

Can't she give this a rest? Even today? I sigh. "There's no one in my life at the moment. Frankly, I'm not interested."

"I understand. But getting through tough times is easier when you have someone by your side. And celebrating the good times is better, too. I intend to hold you to the promise you made to your mother and me before your career took off." She looks deep into my eyes. Her green gaze mirrors mine. And Mom's.

Trying not to squirm, I say, "I've kept my promise, Aunt Doreen. I don't have a bad boy reputation."

"That's true, thanks to your publicist, but we both know that running through women like tissues is not exactly living up to the spirit of your pledge." I stifle the urge to roll my eyes. "Just think about what I said. And let me know if I can help you in any way, honey. I love you." She gives me a peck on the cheek, and after another round of goodbyes, leaves the house with her family.

Aunt Doreen's comments remind me of my last conversation with Mom—how can it be I won't have another one with her? I try to swallow over the lump in my throat, but end up coughing. Mom made me promise I would settle down. And I can't deny that Aunt Doreen's words have struck a chord. At the cemetery, everyone had a hand to hold. Even my younger brother. I had Dad's, and he needed me. But it's not the same.

Taking off my blazer, I walk into the kitchen and roll up my sleeves. Grateful for something productive to do, I join Dad in packaging up all the leftover food and arranging it in the refrigerator. It looks like casseroles mated in there.

I'm exhausted, but suspect neither one of us is quite ready to face going upstairs. As has become our nightly custom since I flew back home, he pours two fingers of scotch for each of us. Tonight, I bring the stack of sympathy cards from the hallway to the dining room table before sitting down.

"Want to look at these?" I ask.

He shrugs. "Sure."

I hold up the first card and glance at the scribbled signature. "This one's from Josh."

Dad smiles at the card with the violin on the front. "You still paying for his private violin lessons?"

"Yeah." I squint, trying to read his chicken scratch. "He sends his 'condulances.'" We both smile at his attempt and clink our scotches.

Jessie Anderson's distinctive handwriting catches my eye. "Jessie and Amanda sent a card."

"Another one in the long line of ladies you've dated." He uses air quotes around "dated."

"Yeah, well that didn't end up how I expected." Jessie is gorgeous, and when Rose set us up on a publicity date, I thought we'd be in bed within hours. Shaking my head, I trace her girlfriend's name on the card. The two of them are great together. Like Mom and Dad are. Were.

Clearing my throat, I say, "Jessie's filming her TV show, so they couldn't be here. They send their love."

"Jules—Julie—your mother," his voice catches. I reach over and pat him on the shoulder while he collects himself. "She never missed one episode of Jessie's show. She had a group of friends over every Thursday night for a viewing party." He smiles. "I made myself scarce those nights. To be honest, they scared me a little."

We both laugh, then stop short as if we did something wrong. Maybe it's too soon for laughter. Dad knocks back his scotch, then stares blankly into his empty glass.

I reach out for another card, but drop my hand. I can't concentrate any longer. "Let's call it a night, Dad."

Sad brown eyes meet mine. He looks so tired. "I'll put the glasses in the dishwasher and you get the lights."

Our chores completed, he slowly leads the way upstairs. On the landing, Mom's perfume lingers. Dad pulls me in for a long hug and whispers, "Goodnight, son. I love you."

"Love you, too."

Walking to the doorway farthest from my parents' room, I enter my childhood bedroom. The room is as I left it ages ago, filled with all the stuff I once considered important. Posters of musicians—some of whom I'm privileged to call friends now. The thought makes me smile. Posters of models, generally glistening wet. Seems like my tastes haven't changed much over the years. Just my access.

I sit down on my old twin bed, feeling horribly alone, wishing a woman were here to put her arms around me and tell me everything will be okay. I'm thirty-two fucking years old. Shouldn't I have someone special in my life by now?

Images of Rose from today replay in my mind. The connection I felt when she touched me was . . . What am I thinking? She works for me. Besides, she's all business, all the time.

Shit, I'm living the life most guys only dream about. I have money, fame, millions of fans across the globe, houses on both coasts, people to do my bidding at the snap of my fingers and a very steady diet of gorgeous women. There can be nothing wrong with my life-style if it's the American dream. Right?

Looking up to the ceiling, lyrics start to form. Grabbing my trusty notebook, I scribble down the words that are tripping over themselves to come out.

---

Read the rest of Cole and Rose's story on Amazon,
https://geni.us/NOTH!

www.ingramcontent.com/pod-product-compliance
Lightning Source LLC
Chambersburg PA
CBHW031606240626
47153CB00002B/651